Suck It Up

Suck It Up

Brian Meehl

Delacorte Press

Published by Delacorte Press
an imprint of Random House Children's Books
a division of Random House, Inc.
New York

This is a work of fiction. Names, characters, places, and incidents either are the product of the author's imagination or are used fictitiously. Any resemblance to actual persons, living or dead, events, or locales is entirely coincidental.

Delacorte Press and colophon are registered trademarks of Random House, Inc.

Visit us on the Web! www.randomhouse.com/teens

Educators and librarians, for a variety of teaching tools, visit us at
www.randomhouse.com/teachers

Library of Congress Cataloging-in-Publication Data

Meehl, Brian.
Suck it up / Brian Meehl. — 1st ed.
p.   cm.
Summary: After graduating from the International Vampire League, a scrawny, teenaged vampire named Morning is given the chance to fulfill his childhood dream of becoming a superhero when he embarks on a League mission to become the first vampire to reveal his identity to humans and to demonstrate how peacefully-evolved, blood-substitute-drinking vampires can use their powers to help humanity.
ISBN 978-0-385-73300-7 (trade) ISBN 978-0-385-90321-9 (lib. bdg.)
[1. Vampires—Fiction. 2. Heroes—Fiction. 3. Identity—Fiction.] I. Title.
PZ7.M512817Su 2008
[Fic]—dc22
2007027995

The text of this book is set in 11-point Sabon.
Book design by Trish P. Watts
Printed in the United States of America

10 9 8 7 6 5

First Edition

Random House Children's Books
supports the First Amendment and celebrates the right to read.

For my ladies: Cindy, Holly, and Kendall

IVLEAGUE

IVLEAGUE.US

Website under construction.
Launch date to be announced.

1

Commencement

"In the end is beginning." Luther Birnam's deep voice rained down from the high platform, charging the air above a wide semicircle of cadets. "In the beginning is end." Standing in white graduation gowns, the handsome young men and beautiful young women blazed with pride. "Today, you end your life as a Loner, and begin your new life as a Leaguer!"

The cadets erupted in cheering applause.

The last student in the arcing line clapped with just enough enthusiasm not to be noticed. For the ten months Morning McCobb had attended Leaguer Academy, being invisible had been mission number one. It wasn't easy. It never is when you're the class freak.

At sixteen, Morning was younger and skinnier than his cookie-cutter classmates. While their gowns swelled over the bodies of hunks and hotties in their late teens and twenties, Morning's robe hung from his bony shoulders like it was still on the hanger. Even his hair was different. The male cadets had coifs that never moved from their last mirror check. The women had wavy manes that bounced to perfection. Morning's hair resembled a patch of wheatgrass small animals had recently bedded down in.

As the cadets continued to whistle and fist-pump, Morning's dark eyes scanned the line. They reminded him of dogs straining at their leashes. He wished he had the X-Men superpowers of Banshee. He would strafe the cadets with a sonic blast, stunning them into a hypnotic trance so Mr. Birnam could finish his speech.

Unfortunately, Birnam tossed them another bone. "Today ends your long night as prisoners of darkness, and begins your day as masters of light!"

The roar of approval was doubled by the throng of teachers and visitors jamming the grandstand. The sound bounced around the great cavern inside Leaguer Mountain like bottled thunder.

Adding his token applause, Morning realized the powers of Banshee weren't enough. He needed the skills of the supervillain Dr. Chronos. Wielding his powers of time-compression, he could fast-forward the commencement to over. It wasn't that Morning wasn't excited about graduating. He was. The sooner he got out of Leaguer Mountain, the sooner his classmates would stop rubbing his face in the dismal truth. While they looked like perfectly chiseled Abercrombie models, no amount of pumping iron would ever make Morning buff. No surge of hormones would ever change his face from boyish to manly. He was stuck with peach fuzz and a body that was more stick-of-gum than stud. And there was nothing he could do about it. Ever.

That's how it was with vampires. Shape-shifting allowed, aging not.

Of course, Leaguer vampires didn't call it "shape-shifting" anymore. In Vampire Vocabulary and Leaguer Lexicon class, Morning had learned that "shape-shifting" belonged to the dark ages of the twentieth century. All vampires who belonged to the IVL—the International Vampire League—had word-shifted to the more scientifically accurate "cell differentiation." CD, for short.

The crowd hushed as Birnam raised his hands. "To commemorate your journey from darkness to light, I will now present your diplomas. When you hear your name, demonstrate the mastery of your powers by ascending the platform in one of the Six Forms. After receiving your diploma, you will then descend in the only incarnation you will ever need again: a Leaguer among Leaguers."

Morning's stomach flopped like a landed fish. He dreaded this part of the ceremony. Yes, in CD 101, he had stumbled through the Six Forms of cell differentiation and managed to pass, but it was like being the worst kid in gym. He never knew how he was going to screw up; he only knew it would probably end in humiliation.

For Morning, this wasn't the worst part of being a vampire. The worst part was the irony of it all. As a kid, he had dreamed of an accident transforming him into a superhero. Like the spider bite that turned Peter Parker into Spider-Man. Or the lab accident that mutated Jon Osterman into Dr. Manhattan. Unfortunately, Morning's little snafu involved a *vampire* bite. And yeah, being a vampire came with a few superpowers, but it wasn't exactly a skill set you used for saving people.

Mr. Birnam called the first name. "Dieter Auerbach." A brawny young man jogged forward. After a few strides, his white gown billowed, and a sleek gray wolf darted from under the falling robe. The wolf trotted toward the tower.

"Our first graduate has chosen the Fifth Form: the Runner," Birnam announced.

The wolf broke into a lope, surged forward, and leaped onto the lowest platform protruding from the spiraling tower. With flawless grace, the animal sprang from platform to platform. When Dieter's wolf landed at the top next to Birnam, the crowd rewarded him with applause.

Birnam held up a long, rolled diploma. The wolf spun and CDed back into human form. Dieter was now sheathed in skintight, black underarmor. The glistening material accented every muscle in his flawless body.

The sight of underarmor gripped Morning in panic. He pulled at his gown, peeked underneath, and sighed with relief. Yes, he'd remembered to put on his black Epidex.

One of the things Morning was thankful for was that he had become a vampire *after* Leaguer scientists invented Epidex. Before Epidex, when a vampire CDed there was no way he, or she, could take their clothes with them. When they CDed back to human form they came back butt naked. Of course, there were still some vampires, known as Loners, who practiced all the old ways, and could care less if they ran around naked. Loner vampires streaked, Leaguers didn't.

In Leaguer Science, Morning had remembered enough about the history of Epidex to manage a C on his final. Epidex was invented when a vampire scientist asked, "If human skin is an external organ, could an artificial skin be invented that became both an external and *internal* organ?" After many failures, a Leaguer egghead invented Epidex. Somehow, Epidex combined a carbon-polymer blend with nanotechnology into a living tissue that fed off the electrical current that flowed through all bodies. And somehow, when vampires CDed, the big electrical surge it created transformed the Epidex into an internal organ. It stayed that way until the vampire switched back to human form and the Epidex re-externalized. While Morning knew his less-than stunning summary of Epidex wouldn't earn him an A, he thought he at least deserved a B because of his clever conclusion: "Epidex is the underwear of under-wears."

Birnam called the next name. "Rachel Capilarus." As a raven-haired beauty stepped out from the arc of students, Morning's chest tightened. Birnam had jumped from an A name to a C name. He wasn't going in alphabetical order. Anybody could be next. Morning ignored the knot-tying convention in his stomach and focused on Rachel. She broke into a run. As distractions go, you couldn't do better than Rachel. Of all the gorgeous women at Leaguer Academy, every one of them wished they could CD back to human form, just once, as Rachel Capilarus.

Rachel raced across the parade grounds toward Leaguer Lake. Its still water held a perfect reflection of Birnam's tower. She ripped open the top of her gown, sprang off the ground, and missiled out of her robe in a rac-ing dive.

As Morning's eyes clung to her contours, he remem-bered the downside of Epidex. While it saved him from streaking, it denied him the ecstasy of seeing dozens of beauties do the same. It wasn't a total loss. Seeing them in Epidex was like a vampire version of the *Sports Illustrated Swimsuit Issue.*

Rachel's body slapped the lake's surface and disap-peared. A small wave tracked her position as she torpedoed underwater. The wave swelled, signaling she had CDed into something bigger. A dorsal fin punctured the surface, knifing through the water.

"Ms. Capilarus has chosen the Third Form," Birnam proclaimed. "The Swimmer."

The fin submerged. The water settled to an ominous calm.

Even though Morning thought performing a final CD for graduation was about as bogus as football players dancing in the end zone, he found himself holding his breath.

The water near the base of Birnam's platform bulged upward, then erupted. A great white shark shot toward the top of the tower. Birnam thrust a diploma over the edge. At the peak of the shark's leap, its jaws snapped open and snagged the diploma. The second before gravity planted its gaff and pulled the shark down, the creature CDed back into Rachel. She grabbed a pipe protruding from the platform, spun on it like a high bar, dismounted with a flip, and stuck her landing next to Birnam. Her blinding smile held the diploma.

The grandstand shook with a standing ovation.

Joining the celebration, Morning envied the mastery of her powers, and pitied the cadet who had to follow her.

Rachel descended the staircase spiraling down the middle of the tower as Birnam called the next name. "Morning McCobb."

IVLEAGUE

HOME

Dear Visitor,

Welcome to IVLeague.us, the website of the International Vampire League.

To learn more about us, please visit our open pages. To log in and access restricted areas you must be a graduate of Leaguer Academy and a member of the IVL.

In the future, we hope to open the site to everyone, including all people of mortality. Our term for those of you who are both handicapped and blessed with aging is "Lifers." (If you wonder how aging can be a blessing, see immortality.)

We hope you will explore IVLeague.us with an open mind. We offer it with an open heart.

Peace and tolerance,
Luther Birnam
President of the International Vampire League

2

Winging It

Morning tried to step forward and begin visualizing the CD that he and his guidance counselor had decided on: a great horned owl. But hearing his name had hit him like a blow to the solar plexus. Before moving he had to pry open his lungs.

"Morning McCobb," Birnam repeated.

Morning sucked in air, his legs unlocked. "Here!" he shouted as he lunged forward. An explosion of laughter scorched his ears. Breaking into a disjointed run, he laser-focused his mind on the image of a great horned owl.

He had picked the great horned owl for a couple of reasons. One, if he had to finish his graduation with a lame end-zone dance he was going to CD into something no one else had thought of. And two, one of his favorite masked heroes was Nite Owl II, from the classic graphic novel *Watchmen*.

He retreated further inward, shutting out all sound and sensation but the black screen of an empty mind. So far, so good. A second later he felt something ruffle his hair, followed by a blur of feathers—a great horned owl flew past him into the darkness. He had been tagged. Now he had to tag the owl. Changing into another form was like having a flying dream in an underground labyrinth. If you could catch the creature you set free in the wormholes of your mind, you could absorb the creature's cell-set and transform into it.

Going vampire came with its share of surprises, but nothing had surprised Morning more than how difficult CDing really was. All the superheroes in comic books and movies made physical transformation look as easy as lowering the top on a convertible—hit an internal button and presto-chango, your body turned into Wolverine or the Hulkling. But CD 101 had taught him how much more complicated cell differentiation was, not to mention how many things could go wrong. If you performed the sequence out of order, or visualized the wrong target and tagged it, the mutation malfunctions were endless.

If you really screwed up, it could be your last CD ever. It wasn't like being Beast Boy from DC Comics. When Beast Boy shape-shifted into an animal, he kept all his mental faculties and could even speak. For vampires, CDing was much scarier. After you CDed, all you retained was a shadow-conscious. And if your shadow-conscious forgot you were anything but the creature you changed into, say, a cricket, you went into CD blackout. There was no coming back from CD blackout. Once a cricket, always a cricket.

Considering the dangers of CDing, Morning was glad this was his last one. After graduation, Leaguers weren't allowed to CD. It was all part of the Leaguer mission to blend seamlessly, harmlessly, and secretly into Lifer society.

Morning sped through the blackness of his mind-labyrinth after the owl. He slalomed around corners, shot up tunnels, and dove down shafts as he drew closer to his prey. Swooping into another tunnel, he was startled by the sensation of feet springing against the ground. Wet ground. Intrusive sensations weren't good.

He struggled to ignore the feeling of pounding feet and focus on the bird's chuffing wings. It only got worse. The sound of wings turned into splashing slaps. The owl disappeared around a corner with a laughing cry. Then the blackness shattered and the graduation ceremony flooded in.

A cold sensation pulled his eyes down. He was standing knee-deep in Leaguer Lake. His white robe floated on the water like the wings of a large moth.

"Mr. McCobb," Birnam sounded from above, "we don't have all day."

Tittering laughter wheeled around him. Morning squeezed his eyes shut and plummeted back into the labyrinth where his prey had escaped. He was startled by a ticklish brush against his ear. Certain it was the great horned owl mocking him with another touch, he shot out a hand to tag it. He saw a puff of dust, the flutter of whitish wings, and realized, too late, what he had touched.

His white robe settled on the water like a collapsing volcano. In the plume of air erupting from the center, a creature fluttered up.

The crowd gasped.

Morning had accomplished one of his goals. He had CDed into something no vampire had ever thought of.

A great white moth.

He pounded at the air as he took the long flight to the

top of the tower. Just as he'd feared: another humiliating day in gym. But it could have been worse. The searing embarrassment that made every hair on his body feel like a bee's stinger meant he had retained his shadow-conscious. He would live to see another form. That is, if Birnam didn't squash him.

As the fluttering moth drew closer, Birnam looked down with a curious smile. "Morning has chosen to impress us by displaying *two* Forms. He has accomplished the Sixth Form: the Flyer."

Reaching the top of the platform, Morning saw a white-robed arm reach out. It seemed more inviting than threatening. He welcomed the perch. He would need a moment to gather his strength and focus on his return to human form.

Birnam watched the large moth settle on his robe and almost disappear against the mottled pattern of fold and shadow. "He has also taken the Second Form: the Hider."

The explosion of applause rattled Morning's feathery antennae. It also gave him the surge of energy he needed. He lifted off Birnam's arm, taking flight. He flooded his shadow-conscious with the image of a mirror holding his human reflection. Then he forced a vision of his arm reaching forward. It touched his reflection.

In a puff of wing dust, Morning CDed back to himself. As the applause faded, he found Mr. Birnam's intense eyes pinning him to the spot. He instantly thought something else had gone wrong. Had his Epidex failed to re-externalize? He stole a glance down. No, he was sheathed in black. Returning to Birnam's eyes, which now seemed deep in thought, Morning fought the urge to grab his diploma and sprint down the stairs.

Birnam's face finally creased into a smile. "Mr. McCobb has done us a great service." He turned to the crowd. "He reminds us that even though the Academy is here to guide vampires from the dark wood of their Loner past, each of us must find our own unique path out of the dark wood, the *selva obscura,* and into the light." Birnam turned and handed Morning his diploma. "Congratulations. You are now a Leaguer among Leaguers."

Morning didn't remember walking down the platform or retrieving his robe from the lake. But he must have done these things because he was back in his place at the end of the semicircle, with his damp robe sticking to him like plastic wrap. He was numb to the cold, and the other cadets performing their CDs seemed like a hazy stampede of creatures. What kept looping through his mind was the way Birnam had looked at him. And the creepy feeling that came with it: that even though his final CD was over and he clutched his diploma, it wasn't over.

An ovation jolted Morning out of his gnawing anxiety. All the graduates, back in their robes, now held diplomas. The last one was descending the stairs.

Mr. Birnam stepped to the edge of the platform. "Before I administer the Leaguer Oath, let me tell you how much closer we are to the day we emerge from our greatest dark wood, the *selva obscura* of our secrecy—the day we reveal our true nature to people of mortality."

The crowd inhaled a collective breath.

As Birnam continued, his voice cracked with emotion. "In my ancient bones, I feel the day we live openly among Lifers approaching." He turned to the end of the semicircle.

"I know this because when I look at you"—he stared directly at Morning—"I see, rising in the east, the first light of Worldwide Out Day."

Morning's skin tingled with goose bumps. It wasn't his wet robe that chilled him. It was the icy touch of Birnam's words.

IVLeague

THE LEAGUER WAY

Our code of conduct is summarized in the oath every cadet takes when they graduate from Leaguer Academy.

THE LEAGUER OATH

On my honor,
I will obey the New Commandments of Leaguer Law,
Abide by the laws of my country,
Go among Lifers in peace,
Pursue my Leaguer Goals,
Help all and harm none while consuming,
And, when given the chance, bring Loners to the Leaguer Way.

3
The Call

After taking the Oath, the newest throng of Leaguers hurled their diplomas in the air, creating a fountain of twirling batons. But unlike Lifer graduates who wildly throw their caps, Leaguers considered it bad luck if they didn't catch their diploma when it came back down.

No one was more surprised than Morning when his diploma slapped back into his palm. He broke into a smile; his anxiety vanished. Birnam's strange looks and words were probably nothing, he told himself. Just another case of his wild imagination turning shadows into monsters.

Graduates eagerly slid ribbons off their diplomas and unrolled them. They were less interested in reading the parchment's ornate calligraphy than in seeing the attachment at the bottom. It revealed the details of their first Leaguer placement, and a grab bag of surprises: where they would live, whom they would work for, what job they would have.

Morning casually slid the ribbon off his diploma. His placement would hold only one surprise: where he would live. The rest was set in stone. Because he would always look sixteen, he'd live with a Leaguer family and do what all sixteen-year-olds were supposed to do: go to school. Then, after two years he would do what nonaging Leaguers did to avoid raising suspicions. He would relocate to another town, another Leaguer family, and another school where he would repeat tenth and eleventh grade. Every two years he would do the same, repeating the same grades over and over, forever.

Back in his Lifer days, Morning always wondered about the new kids in school who were supersmart, never studied, and moved away after a couple of years. Now he knew. They were probably vampires. They were only smart because they kept taking the same classes. After a few years of memorizing his classes, he wouldn't have to study either. It would give him more time to pursue one of the Leaguer Goals that every cadet had to settle on before slipping back into the world of Lifers. Leaguer Goals could be anything that kept a vampire feeding on human culture and not on human corpuscles. Morning thought his number one Leaguer Goal was excellent. He planned to read every superhero comic book ever written. He was a slow reader, but time was not a problem.

As he scanned down to the note on his diploma, he knew there was one place he wouldn't be going: New York City. Leaguers weren't allowed to go back to the hometown of their Lifer days. If they were recognized, there would be too many questions, too many complications.

Seeing his destination brought a smile. He knew the city well. As well as you can know a city from comic books.

After returning to his dorm room, Morning changed into sneakers, blue jeans, and a sweatshirt featuring the superhero Animal Man. Then he headed to the graduation party. The only dress code at the Academy was to dress like a Lifer. It was all part of the Leaguer strategy: *Blend in.*

The party was in the dining hall. Its formal name was the Blood Court, but everyone called it the quaffeteria. It wasn't much different than a food court that offered the fast-food gamut from Arby's to Zaro's. Except the quaffeteria offered a blood-drink gamut from the Blood Shed to Vegan Veins. And blood was exactly what the graduates craved after the excitement of the ceremony, and their energy-depleting CDs.

Morning found the party in full swing. The other graduates, with drinks in hand, had also exchanged their gowns for street clothes. Their form-fitting outfits only magnified his nerdiness. He looked like Gumby crashing an Olympics afterparty. But he was used to being a misfit. In his Lifer days he'd been an outsider too. And the motto he'd lived by then worked just as well now, if not better: *Suck it up.*

He weaved through the crowd toward Vegan Veins. Luckily, everyone was too busy chattering about their placements to tease him about his moth CD. He caught snippets of conversation. Most of the Americans were going to entertainment capitals in the United States: Las Vegas, Orlando, New York City, Branson. Foreigners were going to international capitals of fun: Rio, Paris, Monaco, Cape Town, Bangkok. The emphasis on entertainment hubs was part of Leaguer Goal Number One: replacing a vampire's bloodlust—the need to feed—with fun-lust. The megadifference between Loner vampires, who were totally old school, and Leaguer vampires, who no longer did the chomp 'n' chug on humans, was all in the Leaguer motto: *Drink Culture, Not Life.*

But Leaguers still needed blood to survive. And that's what the quaffeteria was all about.

Reaching the counter at Vegan Veins, Morning was glad to see his favorite quaffeteria lady. Dolly looked about sixty and had big ears, crooked teeth, and the lithe body of a former dancer. Morning liked her because they shared something in common. Neither of them looked like super-models.

When Dolly spotted Morning, her elfin smile stretched wide. "Hey, Morning, how'd it go?"

"I hit a couple of speed bumps, but I made it."

"I knew you would." She raised a fist across the counter. "Congratulations."

Morning lifted a fist and tapped her knuckles. "Thanks."

"How do you want to celebrate?" she asked. "With something different or the usual?"

"The usual."

She shouted an order to the drink-making station. "Tall Blood Lite, no foam, room temp."

The man at the station shouted back. "T-B Lite, bury the head, roadkill-cold."

It was another thing that separated Morning from his peers. He was the only vegan in the class. The others drank animal blood from Leaguer farms where the animals were never injured but "milked." Leaguer farms weren't any different than dairy farms, but the milk was red. Unlike his classmates, who had a history with human or animal blood before coming to the Academy, Morning had never tasted either. His time as a Loner vampire had been so short he'd never fed on anything. His first taste of "blood" was after a Leaguer Rescue Squad found him unconscious from lack of feeding. While being transported on an LRS medevac flight from New York to Leaguer Mountain, he was hooked up to an IV and pumped full of a soy blood substitute called Blood Lite. Ever since then it was the only thing that tasted good and satisfied his thirst.

"Where did they place you?" Dolly asked.

"San Diego." Morning grinned.

"That's a fun city."

"Yeah." He tapped the superhero on his sweatshirt. "It's where Animal Man started."

His drink arrived in a tall cup with a lid and a straw. He grabbed a quick slurp. The clear straw turned magenta. He didn't realize how thirsty he was until the smooth, bright taste of Blood Lite filled his mouth.

"Hey, McCobb," a voice called behind him.

He turned and saw Dieter Auerbach and Rachel Capilarus approaching. Rachel had her arm wrapped around Dieter's bulging bicep. "Hey," Morning echoed as he checked out the bare band of Rachel's perfect stomach. He pried his eyes away and looked at her only imperfection: the jock on her arm.

Dieter smirked down at him. "Congrats on becoming a loser, I mean a Leaguer."

As Rachel tossed her head back in laughter, Morning glimpsed the roof of her mouth. It had arched ridges like the ceiling of a cathedral. The vision of Dieter violating that temple with his tongue made Morning wish he had a girl on his arm too: Buffy the Vampire Slayer. "Thanks," he deadpanned. "I hear I wasn't the only one they lowered the graduation standards for."

Dieter's hand tensed into a fist, but Rachel stopped the piston from firing. "Dieter, if you want to draw blood, go over to Crimson Keg and get a refill."

As Dieter grunted, Morning silently thanked Rachel for saving him from unauthorized cosmetic surgery.

Dieter's smirk returned. "Okay, McCobb, everybody wants to know. You ended up as a moth, but no way you were going for that."

"Yeah," Rachel added. "What was your CD going to be?"

The curiosity in her voice made him want to tell her the truth. But alone, not with Dieter there. He shrugged. "I did exactly what I wanted, a moth."

"Yeah, right," Dieter scoffed.

"What's so bad about a moth?" Morning said, sticking to his lie. "You heard Birnam. I did two for one, a Flyer and a Hider."

Dieter wasn't buying it. "Who would wanna do a creature that's drawn to one of our enemies, fire?"

"I would," Morning insisted.

"Why?" Rachel asked.

"So I could singe my wings in the flames and mutate into a half-vampire, half-moth superhero named Moth-Fire, who gets his power from drinking fire and then flies around the world saving Leaguers like you."

Rachel's head rocked back again in laughter. Morning grabbed another glimpse inside the vault of her mouth. Before he could fantasize about what he might do in that temple, a tone sounded from the PA, signaling an announcement. The room quieted.

"Would Morning McCobb please come to the headmaster's office. Morning McCobb to the headmaster's office."

The crowd responded with a teasing "Ooooh."

Morning was stupefied. What had he done wrong? Okay, he'd screwed up a few things during his CD, but he'd gotten his diploma, had taken the Leaguer Oath, and was ready to go to San Diego and *drink culture, not life.* What more did they want from him?

He tossed his Blood Lite in a trash can and started through the gauntlet of snickering cadets.

Dieter hit him with a parting shot. "Go get 'em, moth-boy."

Laughter jolted the room back to party mode. Morning hurried toward the exit. Just before he escaped through the doorway, a hand brushed his elbow. He spun around to see who else wanted a shot at him. He was stunned to find Rachel.

She gave him a warm smile. "Good luck, Moth-Fire."

"Thanks," he muttered.

As he hustled down the empty hallway, Morning felt like he'd been struck by lightning. Whatever awaited him in the headmaster's office didn't matter. For all he cared, this could be his last day on earth. He had entered the party as the class freak; he was leaving a superhero. At least in the eyes of the one person whose notice he desired: Rachel Capilarus.

HOW TO SEE A VAMPIRE
IN THREE EASY STEPS

1. Get up.
2. Find a mirror.
3. Look at your first vampire.

Okay, you'll be looking at an ex-vampire.

How can you be an ex-vampire?

Every mammal begins life as a vampire. When you were growing and cell-differentiating in your mother's womb, you weren't playing video games. You were feeding on your mother's blood. You didn't feed on her with fangs; you drank her blood with a straw known as an umbilical cord. Then you were born and they cut the straw off.

If you still don't believe you're a former vampire, contemplate your belly button. It's where they cut off your straw of bloodlust. It's the birthmark of the vampire in all of us.

4
The Interview

Like the rest of the school, the headmaster's office was done in Spanish mission style: dark wood beams, simple lines, adobe, painted-desert colors.

Morning stepped through the doorway. Behind a large desk, the headmaster's high-backed swivel chair was turned away, facing a bay window overlooking a rock garden. Morning cleared his throat. The chair didn't move.

His gaze lowered to a twisted bonsai tree rising from a sunken planter in the desktop. Studying the minitree's gnarled trunk and its sparse bunches of dark green needles, he recognized it as a bristlecone pine. For many Lifers a rabbit's foot was lucky; for vampires it was the wood of the bristlecone pine. It was considered lucky because, next to vampires, bristlecone pines lived longer than anything else on earth. Some lived for more than five thousand years.

Morning reached forward to touch the tree for good luck. The chair swiveled. He snatched his hand back. Even more startling was the man in the chair.

"The headmaster let me borrow his office," Luther Birnam said with a friendly smile. "I apologize for pulling you away from the party."

"It's okay." Morning tried to mask his shock with indifference. "I'm not big on parties."

Birnam gave him a sympathetic look. "I imagine it's difficult when everyone is older and more mature than you."

"They look more mature, but they don't act it." Morning wished he could snatch the words back. He had just violated another Leaguer slogan: *No Biting, with Fangs or Words.*

To his surprise, Birnam chuckled. "It sounds like you've learned to hold your own."

"I try, sir."

Birnam clicked the mouse on the desk and glanced at the computer screen. "I've been reading your file. I was surprised to see you've only been a vampire for ten months and two days." His eyes shifted back to Morning. "Do you know why that's so unusual?"

Morning knew why, and he knew Birnam knew why. What he didn't know was why Birnam was asking a question he already knew the answer to. He decided to play along until he figured out what was going on. "It's surprising because in this day and age dweebs like me don't get turned into vampires."

Birnam laughed. "I wouldn't have put it that way, but you're right. So tell me, why are you such a rarity?"

Morning was struck by his choice of words. He'd been called a lot of things but never a "rarity." Even more curious was why the president of the IVL kept asking questions every Leaguer knew the answer to. "It's basic vampire history, Mr. Birnam."

"Yes, it's a no-brainer, but if you don't mind"—he spread his hands in an imploring gesture—"humor me."

Morning wished he'd brought his diploma. He wanted to wave it in front of Birnam and shout, *Look, I graduated! I'm done with tests.* But then he would never get out of Leaguer Mountain. He told himself to suck it up and recite the catechism that Birnam wanted to hear. Luckily, it came from the one class he'd gotten an A in: Twentieth-Century Vampire History. "I'm weird because after World War V, the vampire war between Leaguers and Loners during the second half of the last century, Loner vampires got a lot more selective about who they turned into vampires."

"Blood children," Birnam added.

"Right." Morning plunged on. "Before the war, Loners turned all sorts of people into blood children. From my friend Dolly, the old lady who runs Vegan Veins in the quaffeteria"—he played the flattery card, hoping to cut this pop quiz short—"to Luther Birnam, the visionary who created the Leaguer Way, commanded the Leaguer Army during the war, and, after defeating the Loners, wrote a treaty that has kept the peace between Leaguers and Loners ever since."

"I like your choice of examples. Please go on."

So much for the flattery card ending the quiz. Morning took a breath and continued reciting chapter and verse from vampire history. "After the war, the Loners who survived and refused to become Leaguers numbered less than a hundred. They realized they were an endangered species and that their traditional lifestyle was facing extinction. So they decided to rebuild the Loner ranks with an Aryan race of vampires. They vowed to only make blood children from the young and most beautiful mortals."

"Why did they target the young and beautiful?"

Morning repressed an eye roll. The pop quiz was turning into a friggin' test. "They targeted them because youth and beauty add up to self-obsession. And Loners believe that the self-obsessed make the best bloodsucking fiends."

"Why?" Birnam asked.

Morning rattled off the answer he'd memorized during finals week. "Because there is no act more selfish than bloodlust: feeding on and killing a fellow human being."

Birnam asked his next question with a satisfied smile. "And how has the Loner plan of replenishing their ranks with Aryan vampires been working?"

"Not very well. Their newest crop of vampires usually give the old method of hunting and feeding every night a shot for a few months, or even a few years, then most of them realize hunting is too much work and too much of a hassle. That's when the Leaguer Rescue Squads get their hooks in 'em, and they come to the Academy, learn the Leaguer Way, and get a steady, hassle-free supply of their minimum daily requirement: three quarts of blood-product." By the look of Birnam's pleased expression, Morning knew he was acing the oral exam. To be certain, he went for extra credit. "Bottom line, what the Loners didn't realize is that vampires are people too. And if you can get your groceries from the local blood co-op, why waste your nights trapping and sapping?"

Birnam nodded. "Very good. You know the basic story of every cadet who's come here and become a Leaguer."

Morning shrugged. "Almost every cadet."

"Ah yes." Birnam lifted his eyebrows. "Then there's you."

"Yeah." Morning frowned. "The Loner who turned me

28

got the 'young' part right, but he had a sketchy definition of 'beautiful.' "

Birnam chortled. "I'm glad you have a sense of humor about being a SangFU."

Morning's jaw tightened.

"They taught you what that means, right?"

"Yes, sir," he mumbled.

Birnam opened his hands, asking for more.

Morning couldn't believe the quiz was popping from history to biology. And he was tired of being under Birnam's microscope. "*Sang* means blood, and *FU* means"—as much as he wanted to shout what *FU* meant, he swallowed the urge. "You know what *FU* means."

"Flubup," Birnam offered.

"Close enough." The tension in Morning's jaw spread to his chest. "But yeah, that's what makes me a 'rarity.' I'm a SangFU." He smothered his growing impatience with sarcasm. "I got bitten by fangs that went to sink 'n' drink, but somewhere between swilling 'n' killing, the vampire messed up and turned me into a big fat mistake."

Birnam's eyes remained fixed on the young cadet.

Morning shifted uneasily and tried to suck back the heat rising in his face.

Birnam leaned forward, resting his arms on the desk. "I don't believe in mistakes. I believe everything happens for a reason. Do you know that you're also a SangV?"

The term surprised him. He had never heard it in any of his classes. "What's a SangV?"

"A blood virgin. You've never fed on animal or human blood. You've never touched anything but Blood Lite."

He wanted to tell Birnam about the time he snuck a sip of a classmate's animal-blood drink to see what he was missing. But there was no point in confessing anything until he figured out why he was there. "Okay, I'm a SangV too. Is that a problem?"

Birnam motioned to the chair next to the desk. "Have a seat."

Morning obeyed.

Birnam tapped his fingers together. "When you were a Lifer, what did you want to be?"

Morning slumped. If this grilling was going back to his pre-vampire years it could take forever. Without the powers of Dr. Chronos to hit fast-forward, he went with the only weapon he had: keeping his answers short. "When I was a kid I wanted to be a grown-up."

Birnam eyed Morning's rail-thin frame with a bemused smile. "That may be what you want now, but it's not what you wanted to be when you were nine."

Morning glared at the tiny tree on the desk. That was his other weapon: only responding to questions.

Birnam gestured to the computer. "There's no use hiding anything. It's all in your file."

"So why don't you read it?" Morning demanded as his growing irritation sabotaged his battle plan. "Why do you keep asking me questions you already have the answers to?"

Birnam ignored his petulance. "Because reading a counselor's version of your life isn't the same as hearing it from you. Tell me, what did you want to be when you grew up?"

Realizing he couldn't win, Morning went with his only other weapon: indifference. He monotoned the truth. "When I was little I wanted to be a superhero, but when I realized I didn't have any superpowers, I decided to become the next best thing, a firefighter. I started taking an EMT certification course, but then at sixteen years, four months, and eleven days, I got bitten. The next thing I knew, I was in the Academy."

"If you ask me," Birnam offered, "every vampire who learns to rule his appetites and conquers bloodlust is a superhero."

"No way!" The leash on Morning's frustration snapped. "*Not* doing something doesn't make you a hero." He jumped out of the chair and paced. "*Doing* is what makes you a hero. Heroes don't sit on their butts and play video games, heroes take action. There's no way Leaguers can be superheroes. We're just a bunch of vampires who've traded bloodsucking for *product*-sucking! It's right there in the Motto: *Drink Culture, Not Life.*"

He caught his breath, but he couldn't cage the bitterness in his voice. "And that's fine, that's what I'll do. I've got my Leaguer Goals." He thrust a finger at the computer. "You can read all about 'em, but since you wanna hear it from me, here they are. I'm going to read comic books, I'm going to play video games, I'm going to get myself a Star Wars stormtrooper suit, join the 501st Legion, and march in the Rose Bowl Parade every year! I'll be a good Leaguer like everyone else, and I'll do it because I don't have a choice!"

Unfazed by Morning's outburst, Birnam slowly stood.

Morning didn't know what to expect. For all he knew, Birnam's eyes were going to turn into pools of fire and zap him with red-hot lasers, and he'd burst into flames.

Birnam was eerily calm. "What if I gave you a choice?"

Morning didn't move. "What choice?"

"What if I gave you a second chance to achieve your dream: to be a superhero?"

Morning blinked. "I don't get it."

"I want you to be the first vampire to reveal yourself to Lifers."

A chill shot through him. The same chill he felt when Birnam had stared at him at the end of commencement and talked about Worldwide Out Day. "You mean, come out?"

Birnam nodded.

He couldn't believe what he was hearing. This had to be a last joke they were playing on him before he left the Academy. "You're kidding, right?"

"I'm never been more serious in all seven hundred and eighty-three years of my life."

Morning stared, dumbfounded. "But why me?"

"I've been looking for someone like you for a long time: young, innocent, nonthreatening, someone who's more victim than vampire. You challenge every myth and fear of what Lifers think vampires are. But most important, you've never been tainted with bloodlust. You're a SangV."

"Not really!" Morning blurted. "I tasted animal blood. I snuck a sip of Bled Bull from someone's bottle at a party."

Birnam's forehead knitted. "Did you like it?"

"It made me hurl."

Birnam's expression relaxed into a smile. "Even better. Everyone loves a hero with a weakness. You'll be a vampire superhero who's animal-blood-intolerant. No," he added as his smile widened, "hemo-intolerant."

Morning squinted in confusion. "I don't follow. How is coming out going to make me a superhero?"

Birnam's serious expression returned. "Think about it. As the first, you'll be a hero to all Leaguers. More important, if Lifers accept you for what you are, and if you blaze the trail to the day we all come out, we'll no longer have to *hide* our powers. We'll be able to use our powers to help people. You'll be the first vampire to be a superhero."

As his words sank in, Morning's insides spun with wild exhilaration. The boring, obedient future he was dreading had suddenly been swept away. Birnam was offering him more than the chance to revive a buried dream. He was giving him the chance to live again!

THE LEAGUERS'
NEW COMMANDMENTS

1. You shall not age.
2. You shall not drink anything but properly milked animal blood, or artificial blood substitutes.
3. You shall not frighten Lifers with your powers.
4. You shall not destroy your maker.
5. You shall not destroy, or make, a blood child.

5

Catching a Ride

Back in his dorm room, Morning tried to shut out the sound of cadets outside the door. They were exchanging raucous goodbyes before boarding buses that would take them on the first leg of their journeys to new hometowns.

He sat on his bed and flipped through his tattered copy of *Watchmen*. He had read it so many times the graphic novel's vividly colored pages and blood-soaked panels had faded. But while the colors had lost their punch, the story hit him with a disturbing immediacy. *Watchmen* was the saga of masked heroes being murdered by a supervillain. Now that Morning had impulsively accepted Birnam's challenge to be "a hero to all Leaguers," each gruesome death of a masked hero in *Watchmen* seemed to foreshadow his own destruction. If he did become the first vampire to come out, there was no shortage of forces that would rather destroy him than see vampires accepted as the newest minority with special needs.

His grinding doubts were interrupted by another bois-
terous farewell out on the walkway. It reminded him that
he could still chicken out. Before leaving the office, Birnam
had told him that if he had second thoughts he only had to
walk out of Leaguer Mountain with the others, get on the
bus headed for San Diego, and begin the quiet, secretive
life of a Leaguer. There would be no shame in choosing
comic books, video games, and a Star Wars stormtrooper
suit over what might be a suicide mission.

Outside his room, the goodbyes grew further apart.

Birnam had also told him that he would instruct the
driver of the San Diego bus to wait an extra five minutes in
case Morning got cold feet.

The walkway fell silent.

The bell in the clock tower rang twice, echoing off the
mountain's dome. Morning snatched his backpack off the
bed and started out. He stopped at the door and looked at
the book in his hand. The cover of *Watchmen* was an extreme close-up of a yellow smile button. It featured one
black oval of an eye, crossed by an arrow-shaped splatter of
blood. As he gazed down at it, a smile tugged at his mouth.
He tossed the book on the bed. It was still his favorite novel
of all time. He just didn't think it was a good idea to begin
his journey with a book that ended in a lowering curtain of
blood.

Morning stepped onto the walkway and climbed down
the three ladders that provided the only access to the
Academy's cliff-dwelling dormitory. Carving the students'
dorm into the inside wall of the mountain served a dual pur-
pose. The long climb up and down was a constant test of a
vampire's urge to CD into a Flyer and skip the ladders. Not
yielding to temptation was the keystone of the Leaguer Way.

As he hurried across the empty parade grounds and

passed the grandstand, an old man cleaning the stands saw him and called out, "Better step on it, Morning, you're gonna miss your bus."

He stopped and recognized Reggie, the school's janitor. "I already did."

Reggie looked baffled. "You did?"

"Yeah," he answered. "A little change in my Leaguer Goals."

The janitor shot him a disapproving frown. "You're not even out of the mountain and you're changing your Goals?"

Morning flashed a smile. "I was gonna be a stormtrooper in the Rose Bowl Parade. Now I'm gonna be Luke Skywalker."

Morning hurried down a lighted tunnel until it ended at a rough-hewn wall of rock: Leaguer Gate. He stepped under a red light protruding from the wall and pressed a large button. A door in the rock slowly opened.

Walking through it, he stepped onto a dust-covered stage at the rear of a dilapidated western saloon. He looked down and marveled at the lack of footprints in the dusty floor. A half hour earlier, graduates had walked through the saloon on their way out of the mountain. He glanced up at the sprinkler heads in the ceiling. They didn't spray water, they sprayed dirt to cover all traces of vampires coming in and out of the mountain.

As he pushed through the half of a swinging door still hanging in the saloon entrance, he triggered a motion sensor. The sprinklers released a fresh cloud of track-covering dust.

Morning raised an arm against the harsh desert light. In

the last ten months, the only times he'd stepped outside the mountain had been on field trips for Vampire Health, during the section on solar phobia. All vampires were "born" with two things: bloodlust and an irrational fear of sunlight. But their fear was no different than a nonswimmer's fear of water. The nonswimmer overcame his fear by learning to swim. The vampire overcame his by learning to "sunbathe." Conquering solar phobia began with a sunlamp, moved to a tanning bed, escalated to a sunrise, and climaxed with a high-noon walk in the desert sun.

When Morning's eyes adjusted to the light, he looked down a dusty street choked with tumbleweed. The secret entrance to Leaguer Mountain looked like any other ghost town in the Sierra Nevadas. The silence was broken by the *thwop* of a helicopter. The chopper kicked up a dust cloud as it landed in the street. Its rotor torqued down, the dust cleared, and Morning recognized the pilot in the glass bubble. Mr. Birnam was right on time.

IVLEAGUE

SUNSCREEN OR SUN SCREAM?

One of the few things you Lifers got right in your books and movies about vampires is our abject fear of sunlight. Well, half right. Let us shed some light on our solar phobia.

Long ago, we were scared of sunlight for good reason. We were a nocturnal race; we only came out at night. Our dread of daylight was so irrational, so psychosomatic, that if we were exposed to it our skin would burn. And if exposed to it long enough, our apoplectic panic would ignite us in a fireball.

If you find such terror and its fiery result hard to believe, let us remind you of a similar but milder reaction in Lifers. Have you ever seen a student go to the front of the class to make a presentation, and be so terrified that his skin grows red and splotchy? Or worse, breaks out in hives? Multiply that fear a thousandfold, and you might burst into flames too.

Sometimes, people do burst into flames. You call it autoimmolation. But it's as rare as the few vampires who still suffer from solar phobia. We call these vampires <u>Loners</u>. If you ever suspect someone to be a Loner, hit them with sunlight. And stand back.

Leaguer vampires don't avoid the sun or seek it out. It's not like we can get a tan. Our skin replenishes itself too quickly. The only "sunscreen" we Leaguers need (so we don't sun scream) is SPF: Solar Phobia Fixer.

6

Second Thoughts

A half hour later, Morning and Birnam boarded a jet on an abandoned runway in Death Valley.

Morning had never flown in a private jet before. It was like being in someone's plush living room. He sat on a leather banquette across from Birnam. After takeoff, a pretty Leaguer flight attendant appeared and served Morning a can of Blood Lite, room temperature. She gave Birnam an iced drink she called "Antelope O-Negative, on the rocks."

Birnam raised his glass. "To your mission."

As Morning clanked Birnam's glass with his can, it hit him how his number one mission at the Academy was about to be turned on its head: from trying not to be noticed to stepping into the spotlight, from being freak of his class to being freak of the world. Then he remembered the question that, in his nervous excitement, he had totally forgotten to ask. "Where are we going?"

"We're flying into history." Birnam took a swig of his drink. "Having any second thoughts?"

"Not really."

Birnam feigned surprise. "Really?"

He exhaled. "Okay, about a million."

"All right, let's deal with them."

Morning started down his list. "When I come out, so will the vampire slayers."

"It's been so long since Lifers believed in us, they've forgotten how to slay a vampire. They think all it takes is a wooden stake. They've been watching too many of their own movies." Birnam swirled the ice in his glass. "What's your next worry?"

"To prove I'm a vampire I'll have to take one of the Six Forms, right?"

"Right."

"But that violates the Loners' third commandment: Thou shalt not leave a mortal with memory of thy darkest powers. The punishment for breaking their commandment is destruction, and if anyone knows how to slay a vampire, Loners do."

Birnam nodded. "Yes, that is a concern. But I know how Loners think, and they're going to face a very tough choice. If they destroy you for coming out, they'll break the peace treaty that's held for so long, and they'll reignite the war. With their diminished numbers, they wouldn't stand a chance. They'd face total annihilation. I'm sure they'll pick the lesser of two evils: letting you go unpunished."

"You're sure of that?"

Birnam studied him with a knowing smile. "I can't tell you everything, but there are a few Leaguers who have Goals that involve passing themselves off as Loners and spying. The intel I'm getting from them says this is going to be a slam dunk."

Morning wasn't sure where he'd heard that promise before, but something about it bugged him. "Okay, even if it's a slam dunk, will I have protection, you know, like bodyguards?"

"No."

"Why not?"

"For the same reason Jackie Robinson didn't have bodyguards when he integrated baseball. For the same reason the first woman cadet to attend West Point didn't have bodyguards. You'll be all by yourself because we need to see if the world is ready for the change, if they're ready to accept us." The chair leather creaked as he leaned forward. "Morning, the mission *is* dangerous. You *are* a guinea pig. And if you're having serious doubts, you don't have to do it. I'll be disappointed, but I'll understand. If you want, we can turn around right now, fly to San Diego, and I'll take you to the biggest comic-book store in town so you can start on your Leaguer Goals."

While his insides churned like a cement mixer, Morning's eyes didn't break from Birnam's. "I left my copy of *Watchmen* at the Academy."

"Do you need another?"

He knew this was his last chance to back out. A thousand voices in his head screamed, *Don't do it!* But something in his gut said, *You have to.* It was a chance to reclaim his life, even if it ended in a lowering curtain of blood. "No," he said with a nervous smile. "Why *read* about superheroes, when you can *be* one?" Then he raised his last worry. "If I am attacked, can I defend myself?"

"You know the rules," Birnam said, referring to the

Leaguers' third commandment. "No frightening Lifers with your powers. But if you're facing destruction, you can use one of the Six Forms to escape, as long as no one gets hurt." He leaned back. "Does that cover all your concerns?"

"Except for the one about forgetting to wear my Epidex."

Birnam laughed and drained his drink. After pulverizing an ice cube, he held Morning with hard eyes. "Now, let me tell you *my* biggest worry. It's greater than a Lifer rediscovering the secrets of vampire slaying, or a Loner wanting to punish you for violating an old commandment. The greatest threat to your mission doesn't come from without." He pointed at Morning's chest. "It comes from within."

Morning's face scrunched. "Within?"

"You claim you've never felt it, but its seed still lurks inside you. Bloodlust."

Morning breathed a sigh of relief. For a second he'd thought Birnam was going to hit him with another dark secret he didn't know about. "I know the seed of bloodlust is always there. It's the first thing we learned in Bloodlust Management. But we learned techniques to keep it in check."

"Yes, and those skills are about to be severely tested."

"They won't be tested any more than if I'd gone to San Diego, and lived a closeted life in the middle of a bunch of Lifers."

"Oh, yes, they will."

"How?"

"The answer lies in the definition of bloodlust." Birnam opened his hands. "Let's hear it."

Morning bristled at being tested again. Why couldn't Birnam just get to the point? He rattled off the answer. "Bloodlust is more than a craving for a particular taste, like hot cocoa after sledding. It's a deadly cocktail of thirst and envy. The thirst is for the liquid we need to survive. The envy is for the human dreams we had to abandon when we became vampires."

"That's right." Birnam nodded. "Cradle-to-grave mortals are blessed with something we no longer possess: a deadline, the ticking clock of life that whips desire and ambition into fantastic human dreams. Immortality is a clock without hands. It robs us of the very things a short life span inspires: will, aspirations, dreams. All we have left is envy. Envy of Lifers for their zeal and passion to achieve their dreams before they die. Yes, bloodlust is an act of jealous rage, but there is one other thing that makes it such a powerful urge. Human blood carries the very *taste* of what we've lost: the ambrosia of human aspiration."

Birnam's lips parted in a quick smile, and Morning could have sworn he glimpsed the emerging tips of fangs.

"Even talking about it can be dangerous," Birnam added.

"Then maybe we shouldn't talk about it," Morning suggested, hoping to drop a subject that was giving him a headache. "Besides, if thirst and envy are what kick-start bloodlust, now there's even less reason to worry about it. Why should I be jealous of some Lifer's dream when you're letting me go after my old dream of being a superhero?"

"Because chasing a dream is not achieving it. That's what makes you a double experiment, both for Lifers and Leaguers."

Morning wagged his head in confusion. "I don't understand."

"No Leaguer has ever been allowed to return to the dreams that died when he became a vampire. There's no telling what other desires and cravings it might stir up inside you. That's why I've chosen you. Your bloodlust is buried deeper than any Leaguer I've ever known. Keeping it buried will be your ultimate test. If you succeed, Worldwide Out Day will become a possibility. If you fail, and succumb to bloodlust, we will never live peacefully and openly among Lifers."

Morning tried to dodge the enormity of Birnam's challenge with a quip. "So you're saying I've got two choices. Be the superhero, or be the supergoat."

Birnam acknowledged his flippancy with a smile. "Pretty much. Now, do you want to know where we're going?"

Morning was thrilled to change the subject. "Where?"

Birnam gave him a sly grin. "Your hometown."

"New York?"

Birnam nodded.

Morning fought the urge to do an end-zone dance that included all Six Forms and half the species on earth. "Cool."

HOME   ABOUT US   NEWS   COMMUNITY   CONTACT US

AN APOLOGY

"We're human beings with the blood of a million savage years on our hands. But we can stop it. We can admit that we're killers, but we won't kill today."

—Captain James T. Kirk

On behalf of all Leaguers, the IVL offers this apology. We deeply regret the pain and suffering vampires have inflicted on mortals over the centuries. We are not the first people to have practiced blood cannibalism, nor shall we be the last. This in no way excuses our barbaric behavior in the past. But the past is not prelude to the future. We are a changed race. We have seen the evil of our ways, defanged ourselves (through a strict program of Bloodlust Management), and will never drink human blood again.

That said, and in the interest of full disclosure, we admit there are a few—less than a hundred—Loner vampires in the world who have not rejected the old ways. We're working on them. In the meantime, be assured that Loners are so rare that the chance of being bitten by one is less than the chance of being bitten by a shark, or winning the Mega Millions jackpot.

7

Penny Dredful

After Birnam went over a few more details about his mission, Morning, exhausted from a day of surprises, fell into a deep sleep. Birnam had another Antelope O-Negative and immersed himself in his favorite card game: solitaire.

As the jet banked over the southern tip of Manhattan, Morning's eyes blinked open. He stared out the window. The setting sun gilded the towering buildings. Passing over the spiky golden crown of the financial district, he imagined he was looking down on a great tree, with its glass leaves burning in autumn glory. Then the tree's gaping flaw slid into view—the pit of shadows where the World Trade Center towers had once stood. Seeing the wound still there, after so many years, jarred him awake.

Morning remembered 9/11 all too well. He'd been nine. The Saturday before the fateful day, Sister Flora drove him from his group home on the Lower East Side, the St. Giles Group Home for Boys, to a foster home in New Jersey. He spent the weekend with his new foster family. Then, on Tuesday, the towers fell, along with his new foster father. Unhinged by grief, the mother couldn't separate the arrival of Morning and the death of her husband. As soon as Sister Flora could get across the river, she fetched Morning. He rode on the wave of rescue workers, EMTs, and firefighters rolling into the city.

In the days that followed, he watched them work the mountain of destruction like a colony of heroic ants. He followed every detail of their efforts to find survivors. They inspired him to perform his own rescue: to wrestle his imagination from the grip of comic-book heroes and imagine what a living, breathing hero might look like. That was when he traded the image of himself as Nite Owl III for the image of a New York firefighter.

But now his old dream of becoming a superhero had been miraculously rescued from the rubble of his fate. Which reminded him, he needed to think of a name when and if his superhero dream came true. Super-Vamp? Leaguer-Man? Creature of the Right?

As Long Island Sound slid into view, his name game was interrupted by Birnam placing a silver case on the seat beside him. "It holds a week's supply of Blood Lite," Birnam explained. "And a cell phone. If you need anything, call me. I'll be there for you twenty-four/seven."

Morning smiled at the thought of another name. Blood Lite-Year.

They took a town car into the city. It was dusk by the time they reached the West Village and arrived at the offices of Diamond Sky Public Relations. Because of the late hour, they had to ring the buzzer. The frosted glass door was opened by a short woman with freckly skin and a bonfire of red hair. She wore a stylish green pantsuit and appeared to be about forty. Ms. Penny Dredful, the owner of Diamond Sky PR, led them through the empty reception area and explained that her secretary had left for the day. She ushered them into her cluttered office. The walls were crowded with pictures of clients she'd represented over the years.

"Thank you for agreeing to meet with us, Ms. Dredful," Birnam said, "on such short notice."

"Please, call me Penny," she corrected. "There's a reason I didn't call it Dredful Public Relations."

Morning instantly liked her. Not only was she the kind of fast-talking New Yorker he'd missed in the last ten months, her outfit was the same color as the Green Lantern's.

Birnam gave her a friendly smile. "Why did you name it Diamond Sky?"

" 'Twinkle, twinkle, little star, how I wonder what you are. Up above the world so high, like a *diamond* in the sky,' " she recited. "I'm in the business of making people sparkle. So, which one of you is my diamond in the rough?"

Birnam gestured toward Morning. "Meet Morning McCobb."

Morning watched her cheery mask for a twinge of disappointment. Nothing slipped through.

She eyed the gawky string bean of a teenager sitting on the other side of her desk. "Hello, Morning."

"He's a vampire," Birnam announced.

Without skipping a beat, she waved at the picture-covered walls. "I've handled everyone from a professional wrestler named Two-Headed Harry to an Elvis imperson-ator who claimed he was the real Elvis, back after thirty years of alien abduction."

"That's why we picked you," Birnam explained. "The more unusual the client, the more you rise to the occasion."

She laughed. "A vampire joke."

Birnam tossed her a quick smile. "Only if you believe vampires rise from the grave. You see, Morning has some-thing Two-Headed Harry and alien-abduction Elvis don't. He's not an impersonator. He's the real thing."

It was Penny's turn to flash a smile. "The customer is al-ways right. But could I make a suggestion on the costume?"

"Actually, no," Birnam said politely. "This is how he dresses."

"Okay," she conceded, "we'll do the slacker vampire thing."

"We were thinking more on the lines of the *Leaguer* vampire thing."

Penny's brow knitted. "Isn't he too old for Little League?"

Birnam opened the briefcase on his lap. "It's all right here, Penny." He pulled out a glossy presentation folder and handed it across the desk. "Here's the playbook."

Penny's cheeriness vanished as she lifted her hands away from the folder. "Whoa now, Mr. Birnam. *Here's* the 'playbook.' I figure out how to put the diamond in the sky. I come up with the plan that sends this morning star blazing across the firmament of celebrity. It can be for fifteen min-utes or fifteen years, that's all negotiable. But whenever Morning's last twinkle is swallowed by the Black Hole of Has-beenia, I'm still going to be here. I have a reputation to protect. And *no one* tells me how to do my job."

Birnam gently placed the folder on Penny's desk and turned the open briefcase toward her.

Glimpsing the contents, her eyes widened. The neatly wrapped bundles in the briefcase were the same color as her pantsuit. "Like I said"—her smile returned—"the customer is always right."

Birnam nodded happily. "I knew I picked the right woman for the job."

"Shall we begin tomorrow morning?"

"Sounds good." Birnam rose from his chair and extended his hand. "I know you and Morning will make a great team."

Shaking hands, Penny glanced at Morning, still slumped in his chair. "Me and Morning? Won't you be here tomorrow?"

Birnam gave Morning a tight smile, like a parent leaving his firstborn at college. "No, he's all yours now." He turned and walked out.

Penny scooted around the desk and followed him into the reception area. "Wait a minute, where is he staying?"

Birnam opened the glass door and turned back. "He may not look like it, but he can take care of himself. Before he became a vampire, he was an orphan in this city."

"But—"

But Birnam was gone.

Penny hustled back into her office. Morning hadn't moved. "Do you have friends in the city?"

Morning spoke for the first time. "Not really."

"Oh, c'mon. How can you not have friends?" She opened a safe behind her desk.

"Friends don't stick when you keep bouncing from trial family to trial family."

She turned back and studied him. "You seem like a nice kid. Why didn't someone adopt you?"

"Before I was a vampire, I was really quiet. Too quiet."

"And now you're what? A back-slapping party-animal vampire?"

"No, I'm just a little less quiet."

"Good." She shut the cash-filled briefcase, shoved it into the safe and spun the lock. "Then putting you up in a hotel won't be a problem."

"A hotel?" he asked, faking an anxious expression. Morning actually liked the idea of staying in a hotel. Anything was better than the stuffy dorm room he'd been trapped in for almost a year. But persuading Penny to let him stay at her house was the first task Birnam had given him. The reason was simple. The sooner Penny got to know and trust him, the sooner he could CD in front of her and convince her she was dealing with the real thing, not some faux vampire.

Penny crossed her arms. "Yes, a hotel. Where else am I going to put you?"

"Your house."

She looked aghast. "You can't stay with me!"

"Why not?"

"For one, you're a vampire."

Morning grinned, exposing his perfectly straight, fang-less teeth. "Do you really believe that?"

"Of course not."

"Then why can't I stay with you?"

She waved her hands in exasperation. "Because I don't have sleepovers with my clients. Even when they punch my guilt buttons about being orphans."

Sensing her weakening resolve, Morning dipped into

the backstory Birnam had provided on Penny. "Mr. Birnam told me that when you were my age you believed in vampires. You even pretended to be one for a while. My people have always liked goths and vampire-wannabes. We call them 'the faithful.' "

Her face tightened with suspicion. "How does Birnam know that?"

"When he hires a PR person, he does his homework. He said you have an extra bedroom."

Her jaw dropped. "How does he know *that*?"

"Well, since he's a vampire too, he probably—"

"He's no vampire, he's a Peeping Tom!"

Morning gazed up at her. She was flushed with anger. Birnam had warned him about the various stages Lifers might go through before they accepted him for what he was. Angry denial was one of the first. Then he remembered Birnam's last words of advice. "The playbook is only a suggested path out of the *selva obscura* of secrecy. If a tree falls across your path, go around it."

Morning stood up. "You know, it's only for a night." He shouldered his backpack. "If the St. Giles Group Home is still open, they'll put me up. I think I still have a friend there." He picked up the silver case of Blood Lite. "See you tomorrow."

He crossed the reception area. Penny appeared at her office door, shaking her head with a scowl. "Okay, you win. But for one night only, then we find a hotel."

"Really?"

"Really." She stepped back into her office, then reemerged with her purse.

"Aren't you forgetting the playbook?" he asked.

She ducked back in and grabbed the folder.

As she locked the glass doors to the office, she chuckled to herself. "Now that I think of it, I did put up Two-Headed Harry one night. He left his fake head in my apartment and I had to FedEx it to him before his next bout." She dropped the keys in her purse and lifted a cautioning finger. "Try not to leave your fangs, okay?"

"I don't have fangs."

"Right." She headed toward the elevator. "Tell that to my daughter."

Morning tensed. "You have a daughter?"

She answered his startled expression with a smile. "Well, I'm glad there's something you and Mr. Birnam don't know." Reaching the elevator, she punched the down button. "Don't worry, my daughter's bark is worse than her bite."

As they rode the elevator, Morning was sure Birnam had known about Penny's daughter, but for some reason he hadn't mentioned it. Given all of Birnam's blather about bloodlust and ultimate tests, Morning had to believe the daughter was a tree Birnam was intentionally throwing across his path.

WHAT DO VAMPIRES
REALLY WANT?

Leaguers want the same things any minority wants that has suffered the slings, arrows, and stakes of persecution.

OUR SHORT LIST

1. Respect.
2. Equal rights.
3. To make staking a hate crime.
4. To put our holidays on the calendar.
5. To have a parade on Vampire Pride Day.

8

Portia Dredful

Portia gripped the fat cheeseburger with its overhangs of lettuce, bacon, mushrooms, and raw onion. Her jaw yawned open, and she chomped down. Burger juice rained onto her plate.

Almost seventeen, Portia didn't look a bit like her mother. She got her looks from her father. Which was the only thing she got from him these days. When she was thirteen, her mother had hit the husband eject button, and Dad hadn't stopped flying until he landed in Australia. Portia was six inches taller than her mother, with olive skin. Her languid figure was a mushroom stalk under a mad cap of curly, dark brown hair. Two of the few things her father managed to get right were the nicknames he had given Portia and Penny: the Gypsy and the Gremlin.

As the Gypsy savored her first scrumptious bite of cheeseburger, the locks on the apartment door clacked. Her mother bustled into the kitchen, followed by a skinny kid in a hooded sweatshirt and jeans. Normally, Portia would have gotten the first word in, but her tongue was burger-tied.

"This is my daughter, Portia," Penny said. "She's a recovering vegetarian."

Portia swallowed and spoke to the scrawny teenager. "You've obviously met Penny. She's a recovering mother." Her dark eyes shifted to her mother. "Your burger's on the stove. Is this my punishment for not waiting for you? You bring home a stray?"

"His name is Morning McCobb. And he, my darling daughter—"

"Lemme guess." Portia gave him a quick once-over. "He's either a chess prodigy or winner of the latest reality show, *America's Next Top Geek*?"

Morning was torn between lobbing a comeback about him winning *Top Geek* only because she wasn't allowed to win two years in a row, and wanting to thank her for being no Rachel Capilarus. Birnam no longer had to worry about him busting out in bloodlust and hanging his fangs on the first Lifer girl he met. It's not that he thought Portia was ugly; she was okay. She just wasn't a girl who would make him forget the poster hanging in the Bloodlust Management classroom: *Just Say No to Chugalugs.*

"You're not even close," Penny informed her daughter with a tiny smile. "Morning is a vampire."

"Right," Portia deadpanned, then positioned her burger for another bite. "Another freaky client from Diamond Sky PR, as in Pesos and Rubles."

"As in Pays the Rent," Penny countered. "So be nice."

Portia stood up and shoveled a second cheeseburger onto a bun on a plate. "Okay, I'll give him your burger."

Morning tried to stop the mother-daughter bout from escalating any further. "That's okay, I don't eat"—they both turned to him—"meat."

"Of course you don't," Portia said, slapping the bun top on the burger. "You're a vampire." She lifted it and squeezed juice onto the plate. "But we've got plenty of drippings."

"Portia," Penny cautioned, "don't be rude."

"Rude? Who's being rude?" She dropped the burger back on the plate. "It's my night to make dinner. You don't show. You don't call. Then you come home with some goth who doesn't even know how to dress the part." She glared at Morning. "I mean, what's your angle? Are you the coming of the antivampire?"

Morning returned her glower with a pensive look. "Yeah, that's one way of looking at it." Before she could fire her next shot of venom, he turned to Penny. "You know, maybe I should stay at a hotel."

Portia's eyes bugged wide. "What? He's staying *here*?"

"Just for one night," Penny explained.

"Mom, I have to study. I can't babysit him!"

"Nobody said you had to. I'll entertain him."

"Why should you entertain him when he could be a lot more entertained in a hotel room?"

"He's too young to stay in a hotel by himself."

"You put *me* in a hotel room by myself."

"That's because you snore and I needed a good night's sleep."

"Oh, great!" Portia eye-rolled. "Now he's going to spend the night with his ear plastered to the wall waiting to hear me snore."

"Don't be silly."

"Don't be naive, Mom! He's a teenage boy so saturated with testosterone he thinks anything a girl does is a turn-on!"

Their cross talk was interrupted by the metallic pop of a ring top. They both snapped toward the sound. Morning's silver case rested on the countertop. He held a small can with no label. Birnam had given him several unlabeled cans of Blood Lite for use before he came out to the world. He stuck a straw in the can and took a drink. The straw turned magenta.

"What's that?" Portia asked.

He swallowed. "It's like a protein drink." He gave her an impish smile. "We're all recovering from something. I'm a recovering eater."

Penny laughed.

Portia didn't know whether to laugh or call Bellevue to have the kid who really thought he was a vampire carted away in a straitjacket, with a two-jacket option to have her mother taken away as well for bringing home such a whackjob.

Morning took another sip and stared at Portia. It was the first time he'd seen her when she wasn't talking or chewing. She was prettier than he'd first thought.

Portia stared back. Just because he'd cracked a good joke and thrown the ball back in her court didn't mean she was going to look away. What really bugged her was the difference between his eyes and the rest of him. Everything about him—his gangly arms and legs, his plank of a body, his disheveled mop of hair, and his whiskerless face—said nerdy, attitude-riddled kid trying to slog his way across the messy flypaper of teendom. But there was something in his dark brown eyes that didn't go with all that. It was like his eyes were older than the rest of him.

Before she could decipher who he was, and what he was up to, she took her ball and left the game. "While you and the"—she air-quoted—" 'vampire' are down here yukking it up, I'll be studying."

Morning noticed that she air-quoted with just her index fingers. He wondered if in the ten months he'd been away from the city single-digit air-quotes had become the new thing.

She grabbed her plate and climbed the spiral staircase off the kitchen. Portia was defaulting to her number one rule when meeting a guy for the first time: *Assume the worst.* Or more explicitly, every guy you meet is coming to bat to get to first, second, third, or all the way home.

As she closed her bedroom door, she realized another weird thing about the domestic invader. He was so laid-back he seemed to be coming to the plate without a bat. It could mean one of two things. Either he was sneaky-clever, or he was gay. For the moment, she was leaning toward sneaky-clever, because, she had to admit, his crack about being a recovering eater *was* witty.

Back downstairs, while Penny ate her cheeseburger and Morning sipped his Blood Lite, she asked him about his life. He told her about his years at the St. Giles Group Home, and the countless trial months he'd had with foster families that never panned out. He told her about his favorite nun at St. Giles, Sister Flora, and how she joked about installing a revolving door to accommodate his comings and goings.

It was the kind of getting-to-know-him talk that Morning had hoped would set the stage for him CDing into one of the Six Forms and showing Penny he wasn't some goth kid with fang envy. He was the real deal. But her daughter had complicated things. As much as he wanted to blow Portia away for being so bitchy, Birnam had stressed how important it was for his first CD to be nonthreatening, to keep the freak-out factor to a minimum. If he came out now, and Penny couldn't keep it a secret, there was no telling what Portia might do. If a teenage boy sleeping in the guest room grossed her out, her reaction to a vampire doing the same would probably involve carving one of her bedposts into a stake. And the last way he wanted to end his first day back in Lifer-land was with a dart in his heart.

After dinner, Penny left Morning in the living room to watch TV, and then retreated to her office off the living room. He examined their DVD collection: romantic comedies, old seasons of *Grey's Anatomy*, along with a strange mix of foreign films and offbeat documentaries. He was amazed they didn't have one superhero blockbuster. No *Batman*, no *Spider-Man*, no *X-Men*, nothing. Obviously, they were culturally deprived. He turned on the TV and channel surfed until he found the animated movie tribute to *Watchmen*, *The Incredibles*.

After studying for her AP English test, Portia spent the next hour cruising the Web for short student films and video essays. She still hadn't found a topic, a theme, or even a glimmer of inspiration for the ten-minute video essay she had to make as part of her application to NYU Film School and the other top-notch film schools that *had* to accept her. She had just started her junior year at LaGuardia High School of Music and Art and Performing Arts, so she still had time. But making an audition film that's drop-dead genius can take a lifetime. She only had a year.

When the sound of a jacked-up action sequence from *The Incredibles* blared from downstairs, she remembered the weird guy who had a thing for a drink that looked like a Pepto-Bismol–beet juice smoothie. The guy who would soon be sleeping in the next room. The guy who was going to subject her to strange and disgusting noises in the middle of the night. The guy who had inspired her to check the lock on her door three times.

Not finding anything inspirational on docsthatrock. com, Portia Googled "Morning McCobb." Maybe if she discovered he was an escaped felon, called 911, and had him in handcuffs before she brushed her teeth, she could save herself and her mother from being splattered across the front page of *The Post*. The latest victims of the Magenta Milk Killer.

She got one hit. It was from the website for *The Lower East Side Voice*. She clicked on it. A newspaper article filled the screen. The date was from the mid-nineties. There was a picture of a transit cop holding a skinny toddler. The toddler was reaching up and trying to take off the cop's hat. She read the caption below the photo. "Officer Newsome and Morning McCobb." The article's headline bannered, "Rescue on the 'Williams Bird Bridge.' " She read on.

If not for the heroic actions taken by Officer Phil Newsome, we would be mourning the last morning of little Morning McCobb. Last Monday, three-year-old Morning escaped from the St. Giles Group Home for Boys, evaded concerned citizens for three blocks, and ran into the middle of the A.M. rush-hour traffic coming off the Williamsburg Bridge. Waving his arms and shouting, "Go 'way. Not your bridge! Go 'way!" he was almost struck by several swerving vehicles. Directing traffic near the base of the bridge, Officer Newsome sprang into action, ran into the oncoming traffic, scooped up Morning, and saved him from serious injury or worse.

After the toddler was reunited with a panicked Sister Flora from St. Giles, the nun explained what was behind Morning's strange behavior. The night before, when Morning mispronounced Williamsburg Bridge as "Williams Bird Bridge," Sister Flora made up a bedtime story about the Williams Bird Bridge and why pigeons fly. Before the story put little Morning to sleep, it also planted a bizarre notion in his impressionable mind: The bridge had been unfairly taken away from the pigeons. The next morning, the outraged toddler took it upon himself to correct this injustice. So he charged onto the "Williams Bird Bridge" to reclaim it for the pigeons. Fortunately, Officer Newsome charged after him and saved Morning's first heroic act from being his last.

Portia read the article twice before she realized why she was so fascinated with this little squib of a story. What if her video essay was about this incident? Like a minidocumentary of then and now. She could do a dramatic recreation of the event, and then mix it with interviews with Morning, Officer Newsome, and Sister Flora. It would be *so* Ken Burns. But she needed to know more. Especially about the bedtime story the nun had told Morning. What kind of story would motivate a three-year-old to run into traffic?

Portia grabbed her Sony Handycam, unlocked her door, and stepped into the hall. The TV downstairs was now off. The only noise was her mother's voice on the phone in her office. She glanced down the hall. The door to the guest room was shut. Light spilled from underneath it. He'd gone to bed, but he was still awake.

She moved to his door and raised a hand to knock. She stopped. She couldn't believe what she was doing. It was *so* stupid. If she knocked and asked him about Sister Flora's bedtime story, he would totally take it the wrong way. She'd be standing there in her baggy sweats and NYU sweatshirt, but all he'd see, in his testosterone-steeped stupor, would be a Victoria's Secret model who had *knocked on his door!* A Victoria's Secret model who had knocked on his door, *and* wanted to film something!

Retreating to her room, she muttered, "It can wait till morning." She chuckled at her unintended joke and re-locked her door.

IVLEAGUE

FAQs

CAN VAMPIRES HAVE CHILDREN?

No. We're a sterile race. Which is a good thing. An immortal race that could breed would soon turn the world into a mosh pit of immortals. Sterility is the price we pay for immortality.

WHAT IS IMMORTALITY?

An ancient way of being. Many species started out immortal. While a few species survive today that can live for hundreds, even thousands of years, mortality evolved in most species for two reasons. (1) It saves them from overwhelming their habitat. (2) Aging and death allows each generation to adapt and evolve in an ever-changing environment.

In this way, people of mortality are a more evolved species than immortals. But we too can adapt to ensure our survival. Whereas vampires were once the most feared race on earth, we have evolved into a benign and peaceful people. Today, we are no more threatening than an apple orchard.

9

Morning Mystified

Early the next morning, when Portia's alarm joggled her awake, she thought it was a dream that her mother had endangered their lives by bringing home a stranger and letting him sleep in the guest room. Then she saw the article from the *Lower East Side Voice* that she'd printed and left on her desk. It all came back to her, especially the part about the untold story of what had motivated little Morning to throw himself into traffic on the Williams Bird Bridge. And the fantastic idea she'd come up with for her video essay.

After pulling on jeans and a sweatshirt, she ate a bowl of cereal in the kitchen. Except for bird racket coming from the back garden, the apartment was quiet. Her mother was still in bed. No surprise there. She was a night owl. But the silence coming from the upstairs was irritating. She noisily rinsed her bowl and clattered it into the dishwasher. Then she realized that even if she woke him up, of course he was going to pretend to sleep in. To keep up his vampire act, he wouldn't get up until after sunset. Which was perfect. After school, she'd fire up her Handycam, park herself outside his door, and when he emerged, pepper him with questions about the Williams Bird Bridge. It would be so *60 Minutes*.

But to pull it off there was another bridge that needed mending. Before leaving for school, she slid a note under the guest room door.

> *Morning, Morning,*
> *Wait—wait! Don't tear this up 'cause you've heard that doofy joke a gazillion times, and 'cause you must hate me for being so rude last night. I'm blaming it on PTS (Pretest Stress). Being rude, not the lame joke. There's no excuse for that. Anyway, having a "vampire" as a houseguest is a lot cooler than the last one we had, Two-Headed Harry. (Don't ask.) Soooo . . . mi crib es su crib, and all that.*
> Your new roomie,
> Portia
> *PS Look forward to fangin' out—oops—I mean* hangin' *out with ya later.*

Morning didn't have to pretend to sleep in. The previous day had been long and exhausting, even for someone with the recuperative powers of a vampire. But his stay in horizontal heaven was cut short by Penny pounding on the door. She told him to hurry up and get dressed. He barely had time to swill a Blood Lite before they were out the door.

Morning squinted against the sun brightening both sides of the narrow street. Penny hailed a cab. He stumbled into the backseat after her. He was barely awake, and only because he'd read Portia's note. Her change of mood was an eye-opener, especially the part about "mi crib es su crib." That could be taken a lot of different ways. When Penny gave the driver an address on the Lower East Side, Morning's brain jolted to full alert. "We're going to St. Giles?"

"Yes."

"Is that the first move in Mr. Birnam's playbook?"

"No," Penny answered with a frown. "Your friend, or whatever he is, has a twisted sense of humor. His so-called playbook is blank."

Morning laughed.

She shot him a testy look. "Did you know that?"

"No." He immediately got Birnam's joke. A vampire had never been outed. How could there be a playbook for a game that had never been played? "But that's a good thing," he added. "Now you get to write the playbook as it goes."

"Yes, for as long as it goes."

"Why are we going to St. Giles?"

"It's a surprise."

Anticipation surged through him. "I haven't seen Sister Flora for almost a year."

"Sorry, Morning," she said. "When I called last night, they told me she's moved on to other things."

He deflated. The nuns at St. Giles came and went, but Sister Flora had been there since his first day. As far as he was concerned, she was the only reason to go back. "C'mon, what are we doing there?"

Penny gave him an enigmatic smile. "Writing the first page in the playbook."

He stared out the window and thought about the other playbook. The one between him and Birnam that Penny knew nothing about. This book was also blank, except for the first page: to CD in front of Penny. Last night had been the wrong moment to come out. He would have to bide his time until the right moment presented itself.

The cab turned off Delancey Street's crowded boulevard and nosed down a narrow canyon of tenement buildings.

Seeing his old street stirred up a riptide of feelings. It was the place he thought of when people asked him where he was from. And it was a prison. A prison he had thought he'd escaped from so many times, but each time he'd looked at it for the "last time," he had been returned after flunking out of another family.

The cab pulled to a stop in front of a small stoop. The building that housed St. Giles looked the same as the other six-story brick tenements on the block. The big difference was the occupants: nuns and an unruly bunch of boys ranging from infants to teenagers short of their eighteenth birthday, when they "aged out" of the foster care system.

As Morning followed Penny onto the stoop, he glanced up at the wire web above the door. It protected a half-moon window with ST. GILES GROUP HOME FOR BOYS stenciled on the glass. A black handball was still wedged in the wire where one of the Mallozzi twins had thrown it while trying to break the window. Morning wondered if the Mallozzi twins had finally found a real life version of their perfect foster family: the Sopranos.

Penny pushed open the door. "Wait here a sec," she instructed. "I'll be right back." She stepped inside the entryway and rang a buzzer.

He didn't mind waiting. If Sister Flora wasn't there, it wasn't like there was anyone else he wanted to see. And if the Mallozzi twins had not been successfully placed in a crime family, he didn't want to run into them. Even though they were two years younger than him, they were much bigger and the neighborhood bullies.

He surveyed the tenements on the other side of the street. The bright splatter of fall flowers in windowboxes took him back to a day he had tried to imagine countless times. It was a summer morning, sixteen years earlier, when he had been stranded on the stoop for the first time. As Sister Flora told it, his mother, or someone, left him on the stoop in one of those plastic handbaskets used in grocery stores. A note was pinned to his baby blanket: "Please take care of me." When Sister Flora opened the door and discovered the baby, she said, "Good morning." The baby responded with a happy smile, so she started calling him Good Morning. She dropped "Good" during his terrible twos. McCobb became his last name in the St. Giles tradition of assigning surnames from the orphanage's founders.

Morning's time travel was interrupted by the gun of an engine. He spotted a white van speeding down the street. A satellite dish rode on top. As it jerked to a stop in front of the stoop, he read the big logo on the side. HOUND TV. His eyes darted around the street looking for the slashes of yellow tape he'd probably missed. But there was no police tape cordoning off a crime scene. Hound TV, a local all-news channel, was famous for its crime reporting, and for showing grisly footage none of the other channels would show. "We report, you recoil" was how one New York comedian put it.

The driver of the van hopped out and disappeared

around the back. A handsome man with a helmet of blond hair emerged from the passenger side. His face was tan-in-a-can orange. Morning recognized him as one of Hound TV's star reporters, Drake Sanders.

"Is this St. Giles Group Home?" Drake asked.

"Yeah," Morning said. "Did someone die?"

"Nah, we're doing a three-hankie piece, backup for the day there's a corpse shortage." Drake stopped at the bottom of the stoop and struck a dramatic pose. " 'With no red gold flowing anew, tears of silver will have to do.' " Then he hit Morning with his megawatt smile. "Tele-journalism is what I do, poetry is who I *am*."

The driver, now with a camera on his shoulder, joined Drake, followed by a woman carrying a microphone with a big "H" on it. "Where's the princess of PR?" the camera guy asked.

Drake glanced down the street. "Must be running late."

Penny came out the door and onto the stoop. "Hey, Drake. Ready to go?"

"This better be good, Penster," Drake said as he grabbed the mic from the soundwoman. "But I can't promise airtime. You know how it works. Gory bumps gooey every time."

Surprised that Drake seemed to know her, Morning glanced at Penny. "What's going on?"

"We're doing a press conference about your miraculous return to St. Giles." Before Morning could object, Penny grabbed his arm. "Gimme a sec," she told Drake as she pushed her client into the entryway. "Morning, this is New York. Everyone dressed in black with purple hair claims to be a vampire. I had to go with a different angle to get the media outlets here."

He waved outside. "You mean all one of 'em."

She held his shoulders like a steering wheel. "Listen, I trusted you enough to let you stay in my house last night. Will you trust me enough to do this interview? I promise you, it's a lot bigger than it looks."

"I know it's a lot bigger. I'm a vampire. If you want, I'll prove it to you right now."

Penny gripped his shoulders. "Please, don't use the V-word on camera. If you do, our little media play will go up in a cloud of BOWGAS. You know what BOWGAS is? It's short for the Book of Who Gives a Shit."

Morning remembered Birnam's warning about another stage Lifers might go through in their first encounter with a vampire. Total dismissal. There was only one cure for it. His own version of gas. He shut his eyes and laser-focused on a gray mist. As he dove into a mental wormhole, a loud sound snatched him back.

Drake's head poked through the opening door. "Penster, every nine minutes there's a death by unnatural causes in the city of sob stories." He tapped his watch. "You got three minutes before my police scanner starts to wail."

"We're good to go," Penny said, guiding Morning outside.

He wondered if he was ever going to get the chance to come out.

The cameraman started shooting as Drake joined them on the stoop. Drake began with a transition to an absent anchorwoman. "Thanks, Kristin. I'm here on the Lower East Side, at the St. Giles Group Home for Boys, for an incredible moment in the life of this young man, Morning McCobb. This is his friend Penny, and she's going to fill us in. Penny."

Penny talked to the camera. "Last November, Morning McCobb left St. Giles for a Thanksgiving meal in a real home, and then mysteriously disappeared for ten months. Unlike so many stories about missing children that end tragically, this one is about to end happily. In fact, we've arranged a surprise reunion with the nun who raised Morning since he was a baby."

As Morning realized he'd been set up, Penny reached back and opened the door. "Sister."

A stout old nun wearing a gray pantsuit barreled outside and wrapped Morning in a bear hug. Tears streamed down her face as she alternated between laughter and thanking God. Morning answered her joyous embrace with his own. It felt like he hadn't seen her in years. He tried not to cry in front of the camera. But Sister Flora squeezed a couple of tears out of him anyway.

Drake pushed the mike toward her. "Sister, what was your first thought when you saw Morning?"

"It's a miracle!" she exclaimed as she finally let go of him. "Seeing his face again is the wondrous work of God."

"Do you have anything special you'd like to say to him?"

"Besides wanting to take my ruler to him for not writing or calling?" Everyone laughed at her joke, including the dozen onlookers gathered on the sidewalk. "Yes, I do have something to say." She took Morning's hand and beamed at him. "My dear boy, today the pigeons took back the Williams Bird Bridge."

"What's that mean?" Drake asked.

"A little secret between me and Morning," Sister Flora said with a chuckle. "But I've got a question."

"Go ahead," Drake urged.

She wiped away her tears and held Morning with somber eyes. "We heard a terrible rumor about your disappearance."

"Really?" Drake perked up. "What was that?"

Flora cleared her throat. "We heard, and I pray it's not true, that you were turned into a vampire."

The question stunned Morning. As far as he knew, a Leaguer Rescue Squad had swept into the house where he'd been turned, and had removed all evidence that he'd ever been there. The only thing Sister Flora had been told was that he had disappeared without a trace.

Penny jumped in. "All right, let's wrap this up."

"No, no." Drake shot a mischievous glance at the camera. "I think our viewers would love to hear the answer. Is it true, Morning? Did you become a vampire?"

Morning half-heard the question. He was staring at the face he had spotted at the back of the small crowd. Luther Birnam. With a reassuring smile, Birnam gave him a thumbs-up. Morning had no doubt what the gesture meant. It was time. A private exhibition for Penny was no longer in the cards. He leaned into Drake's microphone. "Yes, I am a vampire."

Snickering laughter darted among the onlookers.

Sister Flora crossed herself. "Dear God."

A high thin voice announced, "If you're a vampire, then we're Batman and Robin."

All eyes snapped to the voice.

Morning recognized the newest onlookers bulldozing to the front of the crowd. John and Paul Mallozzi had gotten bigger. They had also gotten tattoos on their huge arms. Their arms read, from left to right:

```
D              P
O    X    R    A
N              T
T              H
```

"Yeah, and besides," Paul added in a thin voice like his brother's, "vampires can't go out in the sun."

"That's a myth," Morning said.

"Listen to him," John snickered. "He disappears, and comes back with a listhp."

"A vampire with a listhp?" Paul said in mock horror. "That musth mean he'th a bloodthucking fiend!"

Morning didn't see the twins double over in laughter, or hear the crowd join in. He had dived into the inky labyrinth of his mind, where he chased a serpentine swirl of mist. For his first outing, he had chosen the least threatening form of all: the Drifter.

As the Mallozzi twins straightened up, Morning's shirt and jeans tumbled to the ground. Everyone on the stoop jumped away from the pillar of fog where a skinny teenager had just stood.

The cameraman almost tripped, steadied himself, and kept shooting the ribbon of mist as it drifted toward the twins.

Drake and Penny gaped as the terrified onlookers edged away. Except for the Mallozzi twins. They were frozen in slack-jawed dunderment, riveted to the band of mist as it rose up and tilted into a flat cloud over their heads.

Inside the haze, Morning kept his dim shadow-conscious focused on the most important thing while doing the flimsy and dangerous Drifter: not blacking out. If he did, the story of the first vampire to out himself would end in the H_2O equivalent of autoimmolation: autoprecipitation. A watery grave indeed.

Luckily, holding the Drifter for any length of time was not Morning's forte.

As the Mallozzi twins gaped up at the oval mist like extras in *The War of the Worlds,* the cloud thickened. A split second later, it rematerialized into Morning and crashed down on the twins, knocking them to the pavement.

Morning disentangled himself from the screaming boys, popped up, and brushed off his Epidex. It wasn't graceful, but it was convincing. He was out.

10

Spin City

Morning's version of crowd surfing on the Mallozzi twins had numerous effects on the dozen witnesses.

Sister Flora fainted and was caught by Drake Sanders, which was just as well because she covered up the dark spot on his pants where he had wet himself.

Penny finally closed her mouth, opened her mind, and understood why Birnam's playbook had been empty. It was no joke, Morning was uncharted territory. And he was *her* client.

While the terrified onlookers backed away from the monster who had turned into mist and back again, the Mallozzi twins scrambled to their feet and performed a rarity. They ran in opposite directions. "Dont X" and "R Path" were now a divided highway.

What follows after smooth-sailing reality is abruptly capsized in a freak accident is profound confusion. For some, the chaotic scramble to right the mental ship can take a minute. For others, it can take a lifetime. For Penny, it took seconds. She picked up Morning's shirt, pants, and shoes and hurried into the street. Before Drake could re-boot the part of his brain that held terms like "exclusive interview," Penny hustled Morning away from the scene.

Morning looked back to find Birnam, but he was gone.

When they reached Delancey, Morning scrambled into his pants and shirt as Penny hailed a cab. Popping his head through his shirt, he spotted the Williamsburg Bridge rising at the end of the street. He wanted to run out onto the bridge and celebrate his historic outing, but Penny pushed him toward a cab as it screeched to a stop. They jumped in.

Morning vented the rush of adrenaline charging through him in an explosion of laughter.

Penny eyed him with a mixture of fear and bewilderment. "What's so funny?"

"The Mallozzi twins," he managed between snorts. "You should have seen their faces." A thought shut down his laughter. "Oh man, now they're going to be gunning for me."

"Don't you mean, staking for you?"

He glanced at Penny. She was pressed against the door on the other side of the seat. His best-laid plans of not scaring her, or anyone else, during his first outing hadn't exactly worked out. And if Penny looked like she wanted to melt into the car door, when Portia found out she was going to totally freak. So much for "mi crib es su crib." But it wasn't his fault, he told himself, it was Birnam who'd given him the green light. He gave Penny a sheepish smile. "I guess you believe me now, huh?"

She nodded decisively. "Oh yeah."

The first chords from the *2001: A Space Odyssey* theme sounded from her purse, making her jump. She dug out a cell phone and thrust it across the seat. "It's yours. It fell out of your pocket when I grabbed your clothes."

He'd totally forgotten about the cell. The four chords sounded again. He took it, flipped it open. "Hello." He handed the phone to Penny. "Mr. Birnam wants to talk to you."

She took it and put it to her ear.

Birnam heard her suck in a breath. "Cards on the table, Ms. Dredful. Morning and I are from the International Vampire League."

Penny was still getting her bearings. "Vampires have their own league?"

"Not as in baseball," he offered. "We're like a big family."

"And what do you want from me, Mr. Birnam? To play Marilyn Munster, the normal one in a house of monsters?"

Birnam laughed. "I wouldn't put it that way, but yes, that's what we need. A talented woman with big ideas, big skills, and big hair."

She arched an eyebrow. "Are you sure that's all you need?"

"Penny, we don't drink human blood anymore."

"Don't PR a PR person."

"It's true. But the rest of the world isn't going to believe it."

"So you want me to make Morning the harmless poster boy for, what did you call it, the International Vampire League?"

"Exactly. If you're successful, we'd be happy to make you an honorary member. That's a nonbiting offer," Birnam said with a chuckle. "So what do you say, Penny? Are you up to the job?"

Penny did a quick pros and cons list.

Cons:

(1) The client, Birnam, was another smug, ego-riddled powerbroker, the Donald Trump of vampires, whom she would have to suck up to—which was better than the other way around.

(2) The product, Morning, was about as sexy as chicken soup.

(3) The clientele, vampires, had a habit of leaving behind corpses.

Pros:

(1) Birnam seemed to have deep pockets, and the story of the first vampire was a gold rush waiting to happen.

(2) Representing a real vampire might make her daughter use the words "mother" and "cool" in the same sentence for the first time ever.

(3) Repping Morning would make her famous, even put her in the history books. There weren't many PR people in the history books. She owed it to the profession.

This reminded Penny of one more item on the con side.

(4) If she didn't take the gig, one of her competitors would.

That sealed the deal. "Mr. Birnam—"

"Luther, please."

"Mr. Birnam," she insisted, "as long as it remains safe for my daughter and me to associate with you and your kind, you won't be disappointed."

"Excellent."

"But the second your boy pops his fangs and gets glassy-eyed over Portia or me," she growled like a mother lion, "I promise, you're the one who will be disap*pointed*. Do you get my meaning?"

"Point taken," Birnam replied with a chortle. "We're playing high-stakes poker. And you're holding the stakes."

The phone went dead. She handed it back to Morning and scrutinized him. "Is the world ready for you? Are *you* ready for it?"

He looked past her, at the passing street and the bustle of New York. It felt good to be home. But this time he wasn't a nobody. His suck-it-up days were over. Now he was going to lay it down, vampire style. Okay, Leaguer style. "Yeah," he said with a wide grin. "I'm ready."

By the time Drake Sanders procured a new pair of pants, interviewed several of the eyewitnesses, and got back to the studio to edit the story, it was midafternoon. The only eyewitnesses he didn't interview were Penny, who wasn't returning his phone calls, the Mallozzi twins, who were nowhere to be found, and Sister Flora, who had retreated inside St. Giles. The group home's spokessister claimed Sister Flora was too busy praying for Morning's soul to talk to the press.

After returning to her apartment, Penny pulled all the curtains and posted Morning in the living room in front of the TV. She told him to call her when Drake broadcast his story and then retreated to her home office to brainstorm a new PR plan.

Morning popped a Blood Lite and drained it. The mist CD had wiped him out. He opened a second can and nursed it as he watched the afternoon soaps.

Shortly after four, Hound TV interrupted *The Bitches of Brunch* and aired Drake's story.

Morning called Penny out of her office. They watched the interview on the stoop, the taunting Mallozzis, the moment Morning seemed to disappear, him floating over the twins, then returning to human form and falling on them. The story cut to Drake standing on the sidewalk, looking solemn.

"What this reporter and more than a dozen people just witnessed was the first vampire to come out of the casket."

As Drake began interviewing a wild-eyed onlooker,
Morning glanced up at Penny. "What happens next?"

"We wait for the spin."

"The spin? What do you mean?"

"Did you literally 'come out of a casket'?" she asked.

"No."

"See, Drake's already got the story wrong. Now it's
everyone else's turn to do the same. That's spin. After
they've all gotten the story ass-backward, we'll set it
straight."

Penny was right. Over the next two hours, the story of a
missing orphan turning into a misting vampire kept shape-
shifting in the fog of news.

During the five o'clock news, the local stations each
twisted the "vampire story" in their own way. WABC reported it was a hoax concocted by special effects wizards at
Hound TV. WNBC claimed it was a publicity stunt by an
unknown magician making a grab for fame and fortune.
And WCBS, after discovering that the street where it took
place had been sealed off by the police, turned it into a
story about freedom of the press and America's slide
toward authoritarian rule.

The truth behind the WCBS story was less dramatic. Sister
Flora had called in her markers at the local police station, and
had the media circus in front of St. Giles swept off the street.

By six o'clock, about the only person in the city who had
not heard a version of the vampire story exited a viewing

booth in the Paley Center For Media on Fifty-second Street. Having calculated that Morning would not emerge from his room until after sunset, Portia had gone to the museum after school to knock off some homework for her Twentieth-Century Television class.

As she stopped at the security desk in the lobby, she jumped when she heard Morning McCobb's name. She looked around. There was no one else in the lobby but the half-dozing guard and a bank of television sets. As she scribbled her name on the sign-out sheet, she went into worst-case-scenario mode. Either Morning was capable of some kind of voodoo ventriloquism, or she was having a Joan of Arc moment, or—and this was the worst possibility—the image of Morning that had danced through her mind all day was now *talking*.

Hearing his name again, Portia spun toward the only source of sound in the lobby: the bank of TVs.

All of the screens showed the same grim-faced anchorman delivering the network news. "Once again, the barrier protecting hard news from the flood of infomercials packaged by PR firms and sold as news was breached today." The show cut away to footage of Morning a few seconds before he turned into a mist. "We've all seen the footage by now. Morning McCobb, the alleged vampire, supposedly shape-shifting into a mist."

Portia gawked as the anchorman droned on. "After conducting our own investigation, we learned that the collaborators behind this trumped-up story include Hound TV, a public relations firm known as Diamond Sky PR, and the Archdiocese of New York, which is about to launch a major fund-raising drive for the church's foster care program."

Portia stopped listening. She felt like her brain had just

been hit with a double-barreled stun gun. *Assume the worst?* This was surpassing all previous worsts. Not only was Morning's geeky goth act just the tip of the iceberg, but her mother, the freak magnet, had finally gone too far. In the past, she'd always let her creepy clients do the TV time, but now there she was, front and center, part of the whole charade, part of a *media scandal*! At least the Greek child slayer, Medea, had the decency to kill her children quickly, Portia lamented. But her mother, Medea Dredful, was going to kill her with a thousand cuts of humiliation!

On the bank of TVs, the anchorman continued. "But why quibble with the story?" he asked with a smirk. "Everyone's a winner. Hound TV gets a ratings boost, the PR firm gets a fee, and Morning McCobb gets his fifteen minutes of fame." His voice dropped to funereal. "The only loser is the truth. And everyone who still believes in reporting it."

Portia's swelling rage over her mother's infamy dashing all hopes of her getting into any film school, ever, careened in a new direction. The only way to recover from the curse of having a mother who was a whore in the temple of journalism was to do the Jesus thing: Clean out the temple! Her video essay wasn't going to be a little *60 Minutes* segment. It was going to be a kick-ass exposé of the media-industrial complex! A story of how two forces of blatant self-interest, Hound TV and her mother, had plucked Morning McCobb off the street and turned him into the newest fake of the month. It would be so Michael Moore!

As Portia hurried out of the museum, she flashed on a title. *Sucko.*

11

Vanishing Act

The same stone-faced anchorman filled Penny's living room with his gravitas. Morning stood at a window and peeked through the crack in a closed curtain. Penny's voice drifted out of her office. She had been on the phone for the last hour. He pulled out his cell phone and speed-dialed a number.

"Hello, Morning," Birnam answered. "We're off to a fine start."

"Fine start?" Morning stammered. "Everyone thinks I'm a fake."

"Of course they do. When they've logged billions of hours watching fictional vampires doing their thing on movie screens, one vampire playing misty for them on the news is not going to turn them into true believers."

"But there were eyewitnesses."

Birnam laughed. "UFOs have witnesses too. That doesn't make everyone a believer."

Morning peeped through the curtain. "If they don't be-lieve me, then why does the street outside Penny's apart-ment look like a media block party?"

"Morning," Birnam explained patiently, "they don't even know you're in there. They're there for Penny."

"Why Penny?"

"She's the witch behind the 'alleged vampire.' And there's nothing the masses like better than a witch-burning. Believe me, I've seen a few."

Morning was in no mood to appreciate Birnam's little joke. And the fact that nobody believed him wasn't the only thing on his mind. "How did Sister Flora hear a rumor about me becoming a vampire? Did you plant that?"

"Very good, Morning. Yes, I did it to move things along." Morning started to speak but Birnam cut him off. "But that's water under the bridge. Or fog under the bridge. For now, just let things play out, and trust Penny. You're the Leaguer, she's the handler. Remember that."

Birnam hung up as Penny leaned into the room with her portable phone pressed to her chest. "Guess who I'm on hold with."

He shrugged. "Not a clue."

"Ally Alfamen."

"The host of *Wake Up America*?"

"The one and only." She gestured at the television. "We'll give the spinners of spin city till morning to get it wrong, then, first thing tomorrow, we'll set the record straight." Hearing a voice on her phone, she disappeared into the office.

Morning tried to absorb the latest development. From Drake Sanders to *Wake Up America* was a huge leap. His next appearance would have dozens of witnesses and millions of viewers. He had to plan it carefully. And there was one place he did his best thinking.

The jam of news crews clogging her street didn't surprise Portia. She was glad none of them had done enough homework to know what Penny Dredful's daughter looked like. They didn't fire up cameras and start barking questions until she walked up the stoop of the town house. She ignored them, making sure they didn't see her face. If she stayed incognito she could return later with her own camera and interview some of the media jackals feeding America its daily dose of sensation.

Moving down the hallway to the apartment door, she brimmed with excitement. Her video was getting more Michael Moore by the minute. And she was about to pounce on her two main targets: Penny Truly Dredful and Morning McFaker.

She and her mother lived in the bottom two floors of the four-story town house. The top floors were occupied by an elderly couple who traveled a lot. They'd chosen a good time to be in Europe.

Portia unlocked the door and moved into the kitchen, which looked out on the back garden. She dropped her backpack on the table and ran up the spiral staircase. On the way to her room, she noticed the guest room door was shut. She could burst in on Morning later. Right now it was more important to spring a trap on her mother. She grabbed her Handycam, went back downstairs, and was shooting by the time she entered her mother's office.

Penny looked up from her desk and saw the camera. "What are you doing?"

"How much are they paying you for passing off a missing orphan as a vampire?"

Penny stood up and started to shoo Portia out. "Okay, you think I'm crazy—again. But clients like this only come around once in a lifetime." She managed to herd Portia, still shooting, into the living room. "Now go. I have a ton to do."

The door shut in Portia's face. She turned the camera on herself and reported, "Obviously, Ms. Penny Dredful, of Diamond Sky PR, has drunk the Kool-Aid. Now, to find another Kool-Aid drinker: Mr. Morning McCobb."

She went upstairs, knocked on the guest room door, and made sure the camera was recording. There was no answer. She knocked again. No answer. She opened the door. He wasn't there. She pointed the camera at the neatly made bed and added her commentary. "What do you know? A con artist who makes his bed. The nicer they are, the more dangerous they are, right?" She turned the camera on herself again. "Or have I, Portia Dredful, seen too many horror movies? Whatever the case, I may have reason to fear for my life. Not because he's a"—she bugged her eyes in mock fear—"vampire, but because pathological liars ramp up to psychos when they get caught." She pushed a little closer to camera and whispered ominously, "I hope you're not watching this on *America's Bloodiest Home Videos.*"

As she turned off the camera, she got a creepy feeling from what she'd just said. She thought about deleting it. "Get over it," she scolded herself. This was no time for editing. That's what postproduction was about, *after* she got all the footage she could. Which reminded her, she didn't have one frame of Morning yet. *Sucko* wouldn't exactly work if she didn't have footage of the kid con artist.

After checking for him in the upstairs bathroom, she headed back downstairs. Coming down the spiral staircase, she stopped cold. The door to the back garden was slightly ajar. It was always locked. She raised her camera, got a shot, and whispered, "We have an intruder. Or one of those reporters has crossed the line." Her stomach plunged at another thought. "Or Morning has flown the coop."

The possibility was devastating. If he was gone for good, she'd never get footage of him. She cursed herself for being a coward the night before, for not knocking on his door and getting the interview. She cursed herself for going to school, for missing the story of a lifetime. She cursed herself for not obeying her first rule of documentary film-making: *Do it like the coolest newswoman to ever report from the hot spots of the world; do it like Christiane Amanpour.* No way would *she* have scurried back to her room. Christiane would have battered down Morning's door and done *anything* to get him to spill the story behind the story of his toddler death march on the Williams Bird Bridge.

"The Williamsburg Bridge!" she blurted. If the bridge meant so much to him when he was three, maybe it still did.

12

Paper Boats

Morning wore a Yankees baseball cap pulled down low and wraparound sunglasses he'd bought after escaping from Penny's apartment through the back garden. He moved along Delancey Street, past stores with their wares spilling onto the sidewalk. Approaching the street St. Giles was on, he considered a detour to see if Sister Flora was all right. But two cops stood at the barricade blocking the street. Not wanting to be recognized, he gave them a wide berth.

At the end of Delancey, rising in the sky like an invading robot was the towering Erector set of the Williamsburg Bridge. It was his favorite bridge in New York because it was no one's favorite. It was the ugly duckling of bridges. And its last paint job made it even uglier. The superstructure was battleship gray, while the walkway running through the center of the bridge was pink. The bridge's name plaque, dating from the time it was spelled "Williamsburgh," said it all. Two letters had been stripped away so it read THE WILLIAMS U GH BRIDGE.

As he headed onto the long walkway, he took off his sunglasses. The setting sun glazed the buildings and docks across the East River in burnt orange. For as long as he could remember, every time he'd left St. Giles for a new foster home, he'd gone to the middle of the bridge to say goodbye to the city. And with each return to St. Giles, he never considered himself home until he'd visited the same spot, and watched the river spill toward the Statue of Liberty. His latest homecoming wasn't any different.

Reaching the middle of the bridge, he closed his eyes and gripped the handrail. He felt the rumble of traffic from the roadway below vibrate into his legs and hands. He opened his eyes, looked beyond the Manhattan and Brooklyn bridges, and found the statue in the harbor. For Morning, she was never just the Statue of Liberty. She was the mother of New York, waving hello or goodbye to everyone who came or went. He returned her wave, and noticed she was wearing another garment to honor his return; the sunset wrapped her in a blood orange cape.

His eyes dropped to the slate-colored water pushing under the bridge, and he began another ritual he always performed on the bridge.

"Hey, Morning!"

He snapped to the voice. A girl with dark curly hair loped along the walkway. She wore jeans and a baggy cargo jacket that flapped open with each step. She looked like a brown ostrich on a bad feather day. Then he recognized her. Portia Dredful. *What's she doing here?* There's no way it was coincidence. He told himself not to ask. From their brief encounter last night, he knew he couldn't count on a straight answer.

Portia joined him at the rail, tossing him a smile. "Fancy meeting you here."

He thought her smile looked forced. "Yeah, right."

She answered his frown with mock concern. "Hey, you didn't come out here to jump, did you?"

"That would be dumb."

"Well, yeah, jumping is always dumb."

"No, I mean totally dumb." He pointed down.

She glanced over the rail. Not far below, two lanes of traffic headed across the bridge.

"If I wanted to make the river I'd have to start with a standing broad jump of twenty-five feet."

She recovered from him being right. "Okay, but vampires can do that, can't they?"

"Maybe, but whoever heard of a suicidal vampire?"

She laughed. "Good point." She reminded herself it was too early to talk about vampires. She would only end up challenging his claim to be one. That wouldn't get her anywhere. She wanted to win his trust so she could pull out her camera. She closed her jacket against the breeze. "So, what *are* you doing here?"

"That's what I was about to ask you."

"I asked you first."

He paused.

"Okay, I'll go first," she volunteered, hoping it might win her some trust points. "I thought you might be out here because I Googled you and found the story about how you tried to take back"—she did her single-digit air-quote—"the Williams Bird Bridge for the pigeons."

Morning had forgotten about the story until Sister Flora had alluded to it earlier that day. "So you figured I came out here to rally the pigeons for another assault on the bridge?"

"It's that or jump, and we ruled out jump." A subway rumbled under the walkway, launching a few pigeons into flight. She pointed at the birds and raised her voice over the subway. "See, your commandos are here, but they need a leader!"

Morning let himself smile. He glanced at her as the subway rumbled on. She was the first girl he'd met in ten months who wasn't a vampire, or drop-dead gorgeous. She didn't make his heart race, his palms sweat, and his mouth say inane things he regretted a second later. She was a regular girl. She had some major attitude, but what girl worth talking to didn't? "I came out here because whenever I come back to the city I do this stupid ritual."

"Most rituals *are* stupid," she replied, "but that's not the point. People do them because it makes them feel good. You wanna know my dumbest ritual?"

"Sure."

"Before I take a test, I shake my pencil like a thermometer because I think it'll knock the right answers down to the tip."

Morning nodded. "That's pretty stupid."

"Exactly, but it makes me feel like the pencil is on my side. I bet you can't top that for stupid."

"I bet I can." He gazed out at the river. "I look for paper boats."

Portia chuckled. "Paper boats?"

"See, I win the stupid bet."

"Maybe not," she said with a straight face. "I mean, hey, everyone knows about the Annual Paper Boat Regatta. I go every year. And I've read about drug smugglers who use paper boats to bring marijuana to New York, one joint at a time." Her eyes popped wide. "I even heard a rumor about a terrorist plot to use a paper boat to bring in a dirty firecracker."

As Morning laughed, she grinned in triumph. She was

racking up trust points. "But none of those are *your* paper boats, right?"

"My boats aren't as funny as yours."

"I hope not," she said playfully. "But I still want to hear about 'em."

His eyes returned to the water sliding toward the harbor. "When I was about seven, I got sent to a foster family in Poughkeepsie, way up the Hudson River. I didn't like the family, and pretty soon they didn't like me. So, whenever I got the chance, I'd sneak down to the riverbank and launch a paper boat with a message on it."

"Who was the message for?"

"Sister Flora at St. Giles. I figured the message would float down the river, she'd get it and come rescue me. Then one day, she called to check on me. I asked her if she'd gotten my messages. She told me that if I wanted to send her a message on a paper boat, I had to start putting rudders on 'em because a boat had to go down the Hudson, take a left at the Harlem River, and then a right at the East River to reach her on the Lower East Side."

"Why didn't you just tell her on the phone you wanted to be rescued?"

"My foster parents were in the kitchen, listening, and they liked using a belt. Anyway, after that, I launched a bunch of paper boats with rudders. But Sister Flora still didn't get the message to rescue me. So, one day, I stole a canoe and paddled a mile down the river before I got caught. But some kind of message got through because Sister Flora showed up the next day and took me back to St. Giles."

"So you come out here to see if one of your paper boats finally made it down the river?"

Morning shrugged. "Yeah, something like that."

She smiled. "That's nice."

He didn't think her smile looked forced this time. "And stupid," he added.

Portia wanted to say, *No, what's stupid is that I didn't catch one frame of your story on camera!* She kicked herself for not having a secret camera. Suddenly something else gnawed at her. The same thing that bugged her when she realized he had made his bed. What kind of con artist goes out on a river and looks for paper boats? Either he wasn't a con artist or he was such a good one he could con a mother out of her firstborn child. She kicked herself again for the triple sin of doubting whom she was dealing with, not staying on task, and not being more like Christiane Amanpour. It was time to change tactics. Being friendly had only drawn her into his web. It was time to go hardnose. "I've got another question."

Morning had enjoyed the long silence. He liked the feeling that, for a moment, he'd forgotten she was even there when he knew she was. "About paper boats?"

"No. I'm doing a school video project on my mom's business and her clients. Kind of a take-your-daughter-to-work thing. Can I tape your answer to my next question?"

Morning tensed. "I didn't know I was being interviewed."

She regretted her new tact, but it was too late: You don't go hardnose, then ask for a nose job. "My documentary teacher says even small talk is an 'interview,' " she said, air-quoting again. "And everything is 'on camera.' Some cameras roll tape"—she pointed at her eyes—"some cameras roll memory."

Morning couldn't stand it anymore; he had to ask.

"Why do you air-quote with single fingers? Is that the latest thing?"

"Hardly." She jumped at the chance to change the subject until he was more receptive. "When Americans write a sentence with quotation marks, we start with double quotes, then go to single quotes. But the British start with single quotes, than go to doubles. I think going from single to double makes more sense 'cause it's a more natural build. But if I did it like the Brits on my homework, my teachers would totally freak. So I do it the Brit way whenever I air-quote." She demonstrated with single fingers, then noticed his glazed look. "And after hearing that you probably *do* wanna jump."

He shook his head. "I've never met someone who thought so much about punctuation."

She suddenly realized the light was perfect: the "golden light" filmmakers called it. The golden light didn't wait for the right moment, it *was* the right moment. "And I bet you never met someone who was so pushy about sticking a camera in your face."

Her persistence made him remember that in about twelve hours he was going to be interviewed by Ally Alfamen in front of millions of people. If he was going come across as the relaxed, polite, honest vampire Birnam wanted him to be, he needed practice. Besides, there was something about the way Portia looked at him that he liked. He couldn't remember the last time a pair of girl eyes had looked at him with real interest.

"Okay," he said. "Lights, camera, whatev."

13

The Williams Bird Bridge

Portia yanked out her Handycam before he changed his mind. She framed him in the flip-out screen and hit record. "It seems like you have a thing for this bridge."

"Yeah, I guess I do."

"Last night, when I read the article about you trying to take back the Williams Bird Bridge for the pigeons, it never told the nun's bedtime story that made you do it. Do you remember the story?"

"I don't remember it, or even running onto the bridge and the cop rescuing me."

She deflated. "You're kidding."

"No." He shook his head. "But Sister Flora told me the story countless times."

Portia perked back up. "Cool."

He dove in. "The night before the bridge thing, Sister was tucking me in, and for some reason she told me the name of the Williamsburg Bridge. When I asked, 'Why are cars on the Williams Bird Bridge?' my messing up the name gave her an idea for a story."

"What did she call it?"

" 'Why Pigeons Fly.' "

Morning felt his chest tighten with anxiety. He ignored it. If he couldn't tell a story to a regular girl with a camera, he'd never be able to talk to Ally Alfamen, much less flirt with the next Rachel Capilarus that came along.

"Once upon a time, before pigeons knew how to fly, all the pigeons in Manhattan lived on the other side of the river, in Brooklyn. To get to Manhattan every day, the pigeons walked across their own private bridge, the Williams Bird Bridge. This was fine until the traffic on the other bridges got so bad that the cars and trucks started using the Williams Bird Bridge too. This led to a war between the pigeons and the cars. The pigeons lost the war when the mayor banned pigeons from using their own bridge and ordered them to get to Manhattan by learning to fly like the other birds, or taking the subway. Since the pigeons didn't have money for the subway, they had to learn how to fly.

"Now, according to Sister, when she got to this point in the story I wasn't convinced. So she told me that we know the story is true because every time a pigeon hits a car or a person with bird poop, they're letting us know how they feel about losing their bridge. Well, that was all the proof I needed. It made me mad that the pigeons had lost their bridge. So the next morning, I tried to be a superhero and take it back for them."

Portia zoomed in tight. "After the cop rescued you, did Sister Flora tell you the story wasn't true?"

His eyes shone with pleasure. "No. She's smarter than that. She told me that taking back the bridge wasn't a good idea because if the pigeons ever got it back, they'd forget how to fly. And wouldn't it be terrible if pigeons didn't know how to fly."

"And that was the end of it?"

"Yeah. Except for the expression me and Sister have."

"What's that?"

"Whenever we want to say something is impossible, we say, 'Yeah, right—when the pigeons take back the Williams Bird Bridge.' "

Portia didn't have any more questions, and widened the shot.

The silence made him uneasy. It was broken by a tune bursting from Portia's jacket.

She turned off the camera, dug out her cell phone, checked the ID, and flipped it open. "Hey, Mom."

"Where are you?" Penny demanded.

"On a bridge."

"What *bridge*?"

"The bridge Morning is standing on."

"Thank God! Is he all right?"

Portia's eyes darted to Morning. "Are you all right?" He nodded. "He's all right."

Penny's voice dropped an octave. "I want both of you home, this instant."

Portia chuckled. "Yeah, right—when the pigeons take back the Williams Bird Bridge."

Morning grinned and heard Penny's voice on the phone. "What's that supposed to mean?"

"Don't worry, Mom. I'll explain when we get home."

As the two of them walked off the bridge toward the darkening skyline, the silence belied their tumbling thoughts.

Morning was preoccupied with the wordless tether that seemed to connect them. It felt like a weave of two silences: the one of being alone, and the one of being with someone who didn't require talk. But there was also part of him that distrusted it. Being so laid-back with someone was too soon, too easy. And, for all he knew, the connection he was imagining only flowed one way. After all, she'd been crystal clear. She wanted his story for her video project. She was the interviewer, he the interviewee. Nothing more. It reminded him of a lame joke he'd heard back at the Academy. *What happened to the vampire who fell for the first mortal girl he met? She turned him into a sucker.*

Portia was trying to untangle her own snarl of thoughts. Yeah, she'd gotten some incredible footage of the faux vampire, but she was haunted by the feeling that her exposé of the media-industrial complex had taken a wrong turn. It was turning into a sympathetic portrait of a con guy. But that's not what disturbed her the most. She had totally believed his tales of paper boats and bedtime stories. She was even charmed by them. If that was the case, she was being sucked into his lair. Her guy credo—*assume the worst*—was flirting dangerously with the romantic abyss so many daffy girls threw themselves into: *Assume the best.* She hated that in women. One minute you're young, vivacious, got a career on cruise control, then bam!—you have a head-on with some guy who knocks your brain into the backseat, and the next thing you know you're pregnant and being towed off to the junkyard of domestic life. Just like her mother.

Just like her mother. The words blared in her head like an alarm, yanking her back to the only thing that mattered: the video essay that was going to get her into film school.

But she was right, it *had* taken a turn. From a Michael Moore rant against the powers that be, to a documentary with no ax to grind. An intimate profile of a troubled and tragic teenager. That was it, she thought. It was so *In Cold Blood*. She even had a new title. *Portrait of the Con Artist as a Young Man.*

14

The Loner

Several hours later, on the West Coast, the sunset lowered its red curtain into San Francisco Bay. Then, just as April showers push worms out of the ground, the sinking sun pushed another species to the surface.

Loners.

A lean young man in a charcoal gray jogging suit ran effortlessly through Golden Gate Park. His shiny black hair unfurled in his wake. Despite his long strides, he didn't breathe any harder than the walkers he passed in the gathering dusk. While his smooth, chiseled face made him look nineteen, his gray eyes seemed older. No wonder, they had been drinking in the world for over a thousand years.

Ikor DeThanatos ran out of the park and slowed to a silky walk. His full mouth stretched into a smile as he spotted his destination: a "refreshment stand" he often visited because of its ample supply of young blood laced with dreams. The Fog City Cybercafé.

A couple minutes later, he leaned against the counter near the window, pretending to drink a latte. He surveyed the room and the wide selection of human vessels warming their faces before glowing laptops. He spotted a pink young woman whose head nodded toward her screen, then bobbed back up. Either she had found something on the Internet worth worshipping or she was the kind of sleep-deprived, caution-deprived young thing who could be tapped for a few pints. Or, if her ambrosia was exceptional, the full five quarts.

To get a closer look at the drowsy feast arousing pressure in his gums, DeThanatos glided across the room with the pretense of fetching something from the reading rack. Halfway there, an image on a laptop caught his eye. He thought he'd seen a falling cloud of mist erupt into human form. He halted behind the shaggy young man sitting at the laptop, which now framed the image of a skinny boy in a black bodysuit.

The young man turned and threw a grin at his curious onlooker. "Did you see it?"

"Just the end." DeThanatos's voice veiled his concern. "What was it?"

"News clip. Totally cool. Wanna see it?"

"Sure."

The young man swept the cursor to the play button on the screen. "Check it out."

As DeThanatos watched the clip of Morning taking the form of a Drifter and then exploding back into human shape, his eyes seethed like small thunderheads. He squeezed his latte so hard the top blew off. Hot coffee cascaded over his hand.

By the time the young man turned and saw the coffee

spill on the floor, DeThanatos was almost out the door. "Hey, dude, chillax," the young man shouted. "It's not like it's real, it's Hound TV."

Back in Golden Gate Park, DeThanatos raced through the darkness. Reaching a giant eucalyptus tree, he pressed his back against the sinewy trunk and dug his long fingers into the smooth bark. He had to inform the others. He had to convene a Rendezvous. He tilted his head against the tree, shut his eyes, and focused the power gathering within him.

Back in the Cybercafé, a young woman in an apron lifted a mop to clean up the coffee puddle on the floor. Before she could drop the mop, the puddle ruffled. The woman's eyes snapped up. Heads jerked out of computer hypnosis. Frightened faces found others, confirming the vibration coming through the floor.

"Tremor!" she shouted. "Everyone out!"

By the time they all reached the street, it was over.

The call for a Rendezvous had been sent.

And Ikor DeThanatos was on his way to the Mother Forest.

IVLEAGUE

HOME   ABOUT US   NEWS   COMMUNITY   CONTACT US

THE OLD COMMANDMENTS

The International Vampire League no longer believes in the Old Commandments. We have reinterpreted them so that we can live peacefully among Lifers. However, in the spirit of full disclosure, here are the Old Commandments of the few Loner vampires who still roam the earth.:

1. Thou shalt not age.
2. Thou shalt not crave anything but blood.
3. Thou shalt not leave a mortal with memory of thy darkest powers.
4. Thou shalt not destroy thy maker.
5. Thou shalt not destroy thy blood child.

We leave it to vampire historians to tell the full story of how we transformed the Old Commandments into the New Commandments. But here's a hint. We consider "blood" to be a metaphor for the lifeblood of every civilization: culture.

15

Odd Bedfellows

After Morning and Portia returned to the apartment through the back garden, Penny told him to never wander off again and sent him to his room. Not to punish him. She wanted him to get plenty of sleep. They had to be at the *Wake Up America* studio before dawn.

When Portia learned about their appearance on the most popular morning show in the country, she was angry at her mother for not telling her sooner, but even more POed at Morning. They'd just spent an hour hanging out, getting to know each other, and he'd *never* mentioned he was about to be on *Wake Up America*. But she didn't bang on his door and let him have it. His little oversight only confirmed her fears as they had walked off the bridge. Con guy was quick to tell charming stories that painted him as the poor little orphan, but not so quick to share the facts that could make or break her video essay. And the horrifying fact was, if Ally Alfamen played Barbara Walters to

Morning she would totally steal Portia's *Portrait of the Con Artist as a Young Man* idea.

Portia took a calming breath, and asked herself what she often asked when teetering on the brink of panic. *What would Christiane do?*

(1) She wouldn't panic.

(2) She'd tell herself there was no point in trying to compete with Ally Alfamen and *Wake Up America*.

(3) She would ask, *What do I have on this story that nobody else does?*

The answer came in a flash. Access! Intimate access to the two main players in a trumped-up story that was about to unravel on national television.

Portia fired up her camera, hit record, and threw open the door to her mother's office. "Mom, we need to talk."

"C'mon in," her mother said calmly. "Have a seat."

Portia got over the shock of not being kicked out, and, still shooting, slid into the chair facing the desk. "You know, I've been trying to zero in on a subject for my college video essay."

Penny went back to tapping on her laptop. "Something tells me you've found it."

"Oh yeah."

"Great. What's the logline?"

"A behind-the-scenes, uncensored look at a PR agent and her client."

Penny glanced up with an encouraging smile. "Sounds terrific."

Portia wondered if her mother had taken a ditz pill. "Mom, it's about you and Morning."

Penny went back to her computer. "I'd be disappointed if it wasn't."

"It's not going to be a valentine to you, or to PR."

"Whatever gets you into film school, dear. Preferably with a scholarship."

Portia plunged on before the drugs her mother had to be on wore off. "To do it right I need to go with you to *Wake Up America*."

"I was counting on it."

Portia waggled her head in disbelief. "You were?"

Her mother shut down her laptop. "You can go on one condition."

Portia tensed, but was relieved that her mother was beginning to sound like her mother again. "What's that?"

"You sleep in my bed tonight."

"Sleep in your bed?"

"Yes. In case Morning gets any ideas, we'll both be safer."

The staggering implication that Morning might be so twisted as to have sexual feelings for her mother turned Portia's stomach. "Mom, he may be a pathological liar, but he's not a psychopath. He doesn't scare me."

Penny raised an eyebrow. "He should. He's a vampire."

Portia was speechless, except for an inner voice telling her to turn off the camera. Did she really want to go through life with a video showing the precise moment her mother went stark raving mad? But it was too late. There she was, in the middle of frame, looking as normal as a cult victim.

She lowered the camera, turned it off, and, for the first time in her life, looked at her mother like she was the child. "Okay, Mom. I'll sleep with you."

As Portia brushed her teeth, she studied her reflection. She had always wished she had more of her mother's perky good looks and less of her father's long, aquiline features. But tonight, things had changed. If her mother's DNA included the whackjob gene, maybe she was lucky she had more of her dad's package. Then there was the best-case scenario. Her mother was just going along with the vampire thing because of some PR ethics code. Unlikely, Portia reminded herself; "PR ethics" was an oxymoron.

She spit in the sink, looked in the mirror again, and asked some tough questions. *At what point does the inside look at a PR agent become too inside? At what point does a filmmaker become a cannibal gnawing on the hand that feeds her?*

A fang of toothpaste froth slid down her chin. It yanked her out of her guilt. She scooped water from the faucet, splashed her chin, then took another mouthful, swished, spit.

Returning to the mirror, she found her dark eyes hardened with resolve. Daughterly guilt wouldn't stop Christiane Amanpour, and it wouldn't stop Portia Dredful. Sure, blood was thicker than water, but truth was thicker than both.

16

A Tree Grows in Manhattan

As sunrise reddened the Big Apple, *Wake Up America* had already been saturating TV screens with color for an hour.

In the cavernous studio, Portia stood near one of the big cameras, shooting with her Handycam as Ally Alfamen began her interview with Morning and Penny.

Even though she was the most popular host on the number one morning show, Ally had the same problem so many overly attractive and articulate women had in TV journalism. No one believed she could be one of the ball-busting guys. It was the main reason she'd agreed to Penny's request to come on the show. It was her chance to show the world her newswoman chops.

The floor manager counted down. Ally set her bright red lips in a friendly smile. The camera answered with a red light.

"Welcome back to *Wake Up America*," she announced cheerfully. "Which is exactly what we're going to do with our surprise guest: give you a wake-up call on the story everybody's talking about." She turned to Morning and Penny seated on a couch. "Here's the young man behind the story, Morning McCobb, and his publicist from Diamond Sky PR, Ms. Penny Dredful. Welcome to the show."

"Thank you," Penny said.

Morning nodded nervously.

"Ms. Dredful—"

"Penny, please."

"Of course, Penny," Ally continued. "I'd be happy to make that *small change.*"

Penny answered her little jab with a catty smile. "My name often has that effect on people."

"What's that?"

"Inspiring the lowest form of humor."

The crew responded with an "oooh" as Ally's face stiffened. "Touché," she said gamely, then turned back to camera and got down to business. "As you probably know, yesterday, Morning performed a stunt that has the country guessing his real identity. Is he a magician trying to break into the big time? Is he an actor playing orphan of the month for the Archdiocese of New York? Or is he what he claims to be? A vampire." She turned to Morning. "Which brings me to something that's been bothering me about your interview yesterday."

"What's that?" Penny asked.

"Everyone knows a vampire's greatest enemy is sunlight. Yet you decided to come out of the casket in bright sunshine. If you're a vampire, how can that be?"

Off camera, Portia zoomed tighter on Morning.

He cleared his throat and spoke for the first time. "The

111

only vampires who can't handle sunlight—who suffer from solar phobia—are the very few who still drink human blood."

"So that makes you a vampire who *doesn't* drink human blood?"

"Right." He was glad to set the record straight. "Never had a drop in my life."

Ally's face pinched in feigned confusion. "Let's see if I've got this right. You're a vampire who doesn't avoid sunlight, doesn't drink human blood, but *does* turn into a cloud of mist?"

He nodded. "Yep."

She turned to camera and addressed her audience. "Which is exactly what we're hoping Morning will do now, and blow away all those naysayers who believe"—she turned back to Morning—"that you are, for lack of a better word, a fraud."

Penny leaned forward, but Morning beat her to the punch. "Actually, Ms. Alfamen, I'd rather not do the Drifter, I mean, the mist thing. It scared some people yesterday, and the last thing I want to do is scare anyone."

Ally reached out and patted him on the knee. "Oh, Morning, I'm sure you're perfectly harmless. Please, humor us."

Ignoring her patronizing tone, Morning dropped his chin to his chest to concentrate.

There was a long pause.

Too long for live television.

Ally turned to Penny. "What's he doing? Is he going to cry?"

Penny opened her hands. "I have no idea."

Ally had seen enough. "Well, folks, there you have it.

Sometimes it's not pretty, but on *Wake Up America* we wake you up with the truth. Whoever, or whatever Mr. McCobb is, he's certainly no—"

A sharp, crackling sound snapped her attention to Morning. He seemed to disappear in a puff of white light. In his place was a small apple tree, no more than a sapling, in full white bloom. Its roots gripped the couch. His button-down white shirt ringed the base of the tree. Two of the longer roots wore his jeans.

Penny gaped wildly at the tree. His second transformation was as mind-blowing as the first.

Ally's eyes blinked incessantly as she tried to make sense of what had happened.

At first, Portia thought some circuit had fried in her flip-out viewfinder, until she looked past the camera and saw the white-blossomed tree where Morning had been. Her filmmaker instincts were overwhelmed. Her camera now shot a close-up of a cable snaking along the floor.

The studio was so quiet you could hear an apple blossom drop. One did.

Ally slowly stood and took a shaky step forward. She still didn't believe the guest she had planned to take to the woodshed had turned into wood. To be certain she had to touch it.

Morning couldn't see, but he had the senses of a tree, as well as a glimmer of shadow-consciousness. He knew he'd taken the First Form, the Hider. Then his dim awareness perceived something reaching for him. It felt threatening.

Ally's hand trembled as she reached for a blossom-covered branch. The branch mirrored her fear with its own

113

quiver. The blossoms suddenly dropped like dislodged snow. The tree creaked as its girth and height expanded.

It was too much for Ally. She screamed and ran off the set. Her wake-up call had turned into a nightmare.

Penny white-knuckled the other side of the couch.

Portia still shot the floor. Her mental ship was more than capsized, it had disappeared in the Bermuda Triangle.

Then it all ended in one swift motion. The tree bent over like it was trying to touch its roots. When it snapped back up, Morning was back in his human skin and his Epidex. His pants were still on, but his shirt encircled his waist like a life ring.

In the pandemonium that followed, several things occurred.

The show's many producers reverted to what they did best. They focused on job one: the mental health and well-being of Ally Alfamen.

The crew didn't know if Morning was the next Houdini, a quick-change artist from another dimension, or precisely what he claimed to be: a vampire. But they did know the difference between a major and minor autograph opportunity. They swarmed around him.

Still slightly dazed and drained from his CD, Morning couldn't escape. He submitted to the barrage of pens and markers. As he scrawled his signature on scripts, hats, and coffee mugs, he couldn't shake the unsettling feeling that his CD had been far from perfect. He felt like a gymnast who performs a difficult move, almost loses control, but gets away with it.

Portia remained in drop-jawed shock-lock. Her arms hung limply at her side. Her camera dangled uselessly from one hand.

Unable to hold back a Cheshire-cat grin, Penny stepped next to her. Torn between the exaltation of knowing Diamond Sky PR was about to soar to a new galaxy, and motherly concern, she touched her daughter's arm. "Are you okay?"

Portia snapped out of her catatonic stupor. "Mom!" she blurted with a wild gesture, almost clocking herself in the head with her Handycam. "Is he for real?"

"It seems so."

"Why didn't you tell me?"

"I tried."

"I mean *really* tell me!"

Penny graced Portia with a knowing look. "Sweetheart, you're sixteen. There's going to be a lot of things I *really* tell you that you won't believe." She glanced at the excited crowd engulfing Morning. "Now, if I were you, I'd get some footage of his first fan swarm."

"Ohmigosh!" Portia raised her camera and got a shot as the meaning of Morning's legitimacy sank in. The potential for her video essay had just catapulted past a Michael Moore exposé, past the greatest documentary Christiane Amanpour could ever imagine. But only if she cut a major deal. "Mom, here's the thing," she declared, still shooting. "From here on, wherever you're taking Morning, I'm going too. The documentary I can make will pay for college *and* my first feature."

"So it takes a vampire to get you interested in Take Your Daughter to Work Day?"

Portia ignored the dig. "Or week, or month, or whatev, I'm going with."

Her mother nodded. "Okay, as long as you go as a filmmaker *and* my assistant."

"Deal."

As the throng of autograph hounds broke up, and a producer tried to get the show back on the air with the male host, Penny had gained an assistant but lost a client.

Morning had disappeared.

17

The Fire Knight

Morning shoved through the exit door into an alley. Hurrying toward the street, he yanked out his cell phone and speed-dialed.

"Hello, Morning," Birnam answered cheerily. "I just saw your second outing. I thought the tree was a brilliant touch."

"No it wasn't!" Morning shouted. Pedestrians turned and looked. He hustled down the sidewalk and lowered his voice. "Didn't you see what happened? I almost grew into one of those trees in *The Wizard of Oz*. If I had an apple I probably would have beaned Ally with it. But it's not like I needed one to scare the crap out of her."

"I think she overreacted."

"No," Morning insisted, "*I* overreacted. I did exactly what you told me not to do: frighten a Lifer. But that's not the worst part. I felt something in my shadow-conscious take over. I *wanted* to scare her. For all I know, next time

I'll CD into something that really hurts someone! I don't wanna do this anymore, Mr. Birnam. I wanna go to San Diego and disappear."

There was a long pause.

"Are you still there?"

"Yes," Birnam said calmly. "I understand why you're upset, but let me explain something, and listen carefully. Our third commandment, to not frighten anyone with our powers, is an ideal. We strive for it, but we can never completely achieve it. Because of our past, and because we're different, there will always be someone who's scared of us. But you're going to show the world that the Lifers' fear is more about *them* than us."

Morning rushed down the sidewalk, so immersed in the call he didn't notice the man standing in the doorway of an electronics store. Birnam watched Morning hurry by, then returned his gaze to the bank of TVs in the window. They all replayed the same clip: Morning's transformation into an apple tree. "And I might add," Birnam said into his phone, "after your last performance, it's too late."

"No it's not," Morning protested. "I could—"

"By the end of the day, hundreds of millions of people will know who and what you are," Birnam said sternly. "Turning back now is as impossible as turning back into a Lifer. Like it or not, you're our first ambassador to people of mortality. What you do in the next few days will determine the future of our race. You said it best, Morning. You can be a superhero or a supergoat."

The connection went dead. Morning stopped and jammed the phone in his pocket. He wasn't sure what to do: go back to the studio or keep going, keep running. Then something across the street caught his eye. An

American flag hung in the still air above a huge bay door. It was a firehouse. He frowned at the memory of another Lifer dream that had been cut short: becoming a firefighter. The urge to visit the old ambition pulled him across the street.

The sun sliced into the open bay, illuminating the front of a pumper truck. Its red paint and silver chrome sparkled from a recent washing. A tongue of water darkened the sidewalk.

Down the street, Birnam watched his troubled "guinea pig" scurry across the wet sidewalk and disappear into the bay. There was no point in stopping him. He knew Morning's temptation to reclaim the past would come in all colors, shapes, and sizes. And until he faced *all* his temptations, the great experiment wouldn't be over.

The firehouse was silent except for the drip of water. Morning figured the firefighters were upstairs having breakfast. Their bunker gear hung on the wall in a long row.

He stared at the row of bodiless suits. Each hanging figure was topped by a wide-brimmed black leather helmet with the fire company's red insignia on the front. Underneath each helmet hung a black bunker coat with three yellow and white reflective stripes across the back, hips, and hem. Thick black trousers reached down from under the coats, stretching toward boots waiting on the floor.

He mouthed the names firefighters used for their bunker gear: *Personal Protective Equipment, PPE, turnout.* "Turnout" was his favorite. It said action, dashing off to the rescue. Which, for Morning, is what the suits looked like they wanted to do. Like the costumes of all superheroes, the outfits seemed to have a life of their own. The neon yellow stripes quivered in anticipation, like bumble-bees gathered in a hive. He imagined the alarm sounding, and the suits—unable to wait for the flesh and blood that rode inside them—jumping off their hooks, dropping into their boots, leaping on the truck, and speeding off to fight the fire themselves.

As the fantasy wailed through his imagination, an even wilder vision careened through him. What if he could be-come both? A superhero *and* a firefighter.

He almost laughed at the absurdity of it, and scolded himself. He hadn't entered the firehouse to indulge in fan-tasies. He'd come to revisit the family he had once hoped to adopt when he turned eighteen.

He moved around the other side of the fire engine, past the cab and crew cab. The expanse of detail took him back to the hours he'd spent memorizing the weaponry on one of these war wagons. He glanced up at the neat bed of folded fire hose. "Two-and-one-half-inch crosslay matidales ready to go." He scanned the gleaming chrome of the pump panel. "Discharge gauges with crank wheels to adjust GPM, gallons per minute. Intake gauges and bleeder valves." He touched the most massive valve protruding from the panel like a chrome horn. "Six-inch steamer valve." He slowly walked along the back half of the rig. "Storage compartments, irons box, a five-hundred-gallon tank capable of pumping twelve hundred and fifty GPM." His eyes caught the long steel nozzle protruding from the top of the truck. "Rear-mounted deck gun." Swinging around the back, he stared up at the bed of heavy hose folded like a giant stack of fettuccini. "Five-inch LDH, large-diameter hose."

"With an accordion fold," a voice sounded.

Morning's heart almost shot out of his chest. Spinning

around, he found an old fireman sitting in a chair against the wall. He had a bushy white moustache, and his swept-back hair was as silver as the chrome on the engine. His face was a craggy wall of old leather. He wore bunker trousers, held up by wide blue suspenders, and an FDNY T-shirt. A paper wrapper with a half-finished egg and cheese roll rested on his knee.

"I'm sorry," Morning blurted, "I didn't know—"

"You didn't know I was here, but it seems you know a few things about my rig." The fireman's voice graveled with smoke damage.

"Yes, sir, I do." Morning was relieved the man didn't seem to recognize him.

The fireman gave him a friendly wink. "All right, let's see what you know. If I'm the one that just washed her down, who am I?"

"The chauffeur," Morning answered.

The old man's mustache spread into a smile. He pointed his meaty hand at the engine's running board. "The chauffeur says have a seat."

Morning sat on the chrome running board.

Taking a bite of his sandwich, the fireman chewed and talked at the same time. "Lemme guess, you wanna be a firefighter, right?"

He wasn't sure how to answer. "I've thought about it."

"Have you thought about it enough to know whether you wanna be a firefighter or a fire knight?"

The term caught Morning by surprise. He thought he knew firefighter lingo inside and out. "What's a fire knight?"

"A firefighter knows the equipment; a fire knight knows the code."

"The code?"

"It's all right here." The fireman plucked at the FDNY emblem on his shirt. "Know what this is?"

"The fire department logo."

"More than that, it's a Maltese cross." He took another chomp of sandwich.

Morning stared at the stubby cross with FDNY worked into it. "I thought it was a four-leaf clover."

The fireman laughed and sprayed sandwich dust. "It's your lucky day, son, 'cause I'm here to set you straight." He tapped his shirt. "The Maltese cross has been the symbol of all firefighters since 1095."

"What happened then?"

"The First Crusade."

Morning watched the fireman place the sandwich on his knee. Obviously, this was too important to chew through.

"The Knights of St. John were fighting the Saracens in a battle to take back the Holy Land. As the army of crusaders advanced on the walls of the Saracen city, the Saracens started catapulting glass bombs at them. When the bombs broke they released a stinky, jellylike liquid. Then, when the crusaders were soaked in the stuff, the Saracens launched a volley of burning arrows which ignited the liquid."

"Was it napalm?"

"No, a crude form of gasoline. Hundreds of knights were burned alive, while other knights risked their lives to save crusaders from fiery deaths. When the battle was over, the Knights of St. John were recognized for their heroism and given a badge of honor in the shape of a Maltese cross. The Maltese cross was chosen because the Knights of St. John were from the island of Malta."

The fireman pressed his hand to his chest. "Any fire-fighter who wears the cross knows three things. He lives in courage, a ladder rung from death. He lives knowing he may lay down his life to save others. And he lives knowing his life is protected by all firefighters. That's the code. When you live by it, you're a knight at the fire table."

Morning was transfixed. And stunned that he'd never heard this before. It wasn't in the books. It was something you learned after being initiated into the brotherhood.

The fireman lifted his sandwich and took a bite. "If you still wanna be a fire knight when you turn eighteen, come back and see me."

The words slapped Morning out of his reverie. You had to be eighteen to get into the Fire Academy. Being sixteen forever didn't cut it. He could never live by the code, or sit at the fire table.

"Morning!" a voice shouted from the sidewalk.

He jumped up and saw Portia standing outside in the sun. His skin prickled with anger. If he were Plastic Man he would have shot out a thirty-foot arm and cuffed her for butting in.

"Whoa," the fireman said, eyeing Portia, "that's a harsh way to start the day. Is that your girlfriend?"

"No." Morning doused his irritation, and extended a hand to the fireman. "Morning is my name."

Shaking hands, the fireman's wrinkles deepened as he searched for where he'd heard it before.

Morning started out. "Thanks for the story."

"Come back anytime," the fireman called after him. "The chauffeur will give you a ride."

Joining Portia on the sidewalk, Morning told himself that Birnam was right. It was too late—too late to be a fire knight; too late to be anything but the first vampire to come out, for better or worse, for superhero or supergoat. And for whatever Portia was about to hit him with.

She surprised him by apologizing. "I'm sorry I shouted, but I—I—" She cleared her throat and reminded herself this was no different than when Jake Gyllenhaal had visited her school. If she could talk to Jake Gyllenhaal when it felt like he was holding her heart in his hands, she could talk to Morning McCobb when it felt like he was holding her entire future in his hands. "I thought I might never see you again." She cringed and shot up a hand. "Don't take that the wrong way." She caught a quick breath and tried to collect herself. Gyllenhaal had been a cakewalk compared to this. "Look, I'm a little nervous, and I just wanted to say, I'm sorry I didn't believe you."

Her confession blew away his lingering annoyance. Under her tough-girl armor maybe there was a human being after all. He shrugged. "Hey, if I were in your shoes, I wouldn't have believed me either."

She dug into her jacket and pulled out his Yankees cap and sunglasses. "You better put these on."

She was right. Passersby were beginning to stare. He slipped on the hat and glasses.

"We should walk," she added. "It's harder to recognize a moving target." They started back toward the studio. "Do you mind if we do something?"

"What?"

"Hit the reset button. I want you to forget that I thought you were some lowlife trying to take advantage of my mother."

He pressed an imaginary button on his forehead. "Bzzt. Reset."

"And I'm going to totally forget about the video project I *thought* I was making."

"What was that?" he asked.

"Portrait of the Con Artist as a Young Man." He laughed as she hit her own reset button. "Bzzt. Forgotten."

As much as she wanted it to be that easy, she knew it wasn't. If rule number one when it came to guys was *assume the worst,* when it came to this guy, she no longer knew what *worst* was. The guy she had thought was coming to the plate without a bat was not doing it because he was sneaky-clever or gay. He didn't need a bat. He had fangs. The only comforting thing about that was knowing he hadn't sunk them into her or her mother in the last thirty-six hours. Maybe he wasn't the bloodsucking fiend he claimed he wasn't. Whatever, the chance to make an up-close-and-personal film about the first outed vampire far outweighed the risks. For now. But pulling out the camera would have to wait. As well as asking him everything he knew about vampires. First she had to earn his trust by talking to him about everything *but* vampires.

With her nerves calmed and her strategy clarified, she began. "Do you have a thing for firehouses?"

"No," he lied. "I thought someone recognized me on the street and I ducked inside."

"After this morning, it's going to be impossible to hide."

"Yeah, I know."

Before she could lob another question, a limo screeched to a halt in the street. Penny hopped out of the back. "Get in!" They obeyed. Inside, Penny leaned toward the driver. "Take us to Teterboro."

"What's Teterboro?" Morning asked.

"A private airport," Portia answered, turning to her mother. "Where are we going?"

Penny's eyes darted to the driver's rearview mirror. She caught him watching before his eyes slid away. "We're going on tour."

"But, Mom," Portia protested, "I need to pack."

Morning raised his own objection. "And I need my—"

Penny shushed him. "Your protein drink, I know. It's in the trunk, along with Portia's suitcase."

She stared at her mother. "So you knew all along—"

"That I'd need an assistant I could trust? Yes. It's all part of the playbook." Penny turned to Morning. "And here's what I need from you." She punched each word. "No. More. Wandering."

He sighed. It sounded like being the first ambassador to people of mortality was going to be a 24/7 gig. "Okay, no wandering."

18

The Rendezvous

In the White Mountains of California there is a sparse forest of bristlecone pines. Mortals call it Patriarch Grove. Vampires call it the Mother Forest.

Since midnight, when a gibbous moon began climbing the star-choked sky, Loners had been arriving in the forest. They came in flying forms, from bats to vultures. Some still perched silently in the bald, twisted branches that made bristlecone pines look more dead than alive. Others had shape-shifted to human form, and stood in the rocky grove wearing nothing but moon shadow and starlight.

Being naked didn't bother the men, women, and few children. Loner vampires weren't shy; they didn't care what anyone thought of their bodies. It's not like they were in the business of attracting a mate. Besides, when you could transform into thousands of creatures, the human skin was just another cloak in a closet the size of the animal kingdom.

What did trouble the growing throng, and had them whispering in small groups, was not knowing why the Rendezvous had been called. After all, their night of hunting had been cut short by the silent alarm. Those close to San Francisco felt the call like mortals feel the shudder of an aftershock. Those farther away sensed it the same way elephants pick up sounds below the range of human hearing. They felt a subtactile quiver of the earth, dropped whatever they were doing, or drinking, and flew to the Mother Forest.

It was the first Rendezvous in almost fifty years. The previous one had been a Grand Rendezvous of all Loners in the world, and it ended with the armistice that ended World War V.

The Loners lost the long war because they were a scattered band of solo warriors fighting an organized army of vampires led by Luther Birnam. The lone predator can thin the herd, but he can never wipe out the entire group. While Loners had considered banding together in a killer pack, they also knew that a pack of Loners was no better than an army of generals: all would lead, none would follow. So, before being wiped off the earth, the Loners negotiated a truce with the Leaguers. And all of them signed the peace treaty. All but one.

Ikor DeThanatos had been the first to arrive in the Mother Forest. Having made the trip as a peregrine falcon, he remained in Flyer form. He perched on a bare branch belonging to the oldest tree in the grove. It was called the Matriarch. From there, he had watched the flock of Loners swell to over fifty.

The falcon's turretlike head, armed with steel gray eyes, swiveled to the eastern horizon and perceived a paling beyond the ridge. Hearing the whoosh of wings, he turned as a golden eagle landed on the branch of another tree. More Loners were still on the way, but to allow time for everyone to return to safety before sunrise, the Rendezvous had to begin.

He swooped down off the branch, transformed midair, and landed silently on the rocky ground.

The closest group of Loners turned to him. One of them recognized DeThanatos. His name was Bosky. He was short and square-built, and his torso was covered in a thicket of dark hair.

"DeThanatos," he said with a mocking smile. "What's it been, a century, or two?"

"Not long enough."

Bosky ignored the surly answer. "You were missed at the armistice."

DeThanatos sneered. "When the war begins again, why give Birnam the privilege of knowing my face?"

Bosky raised his bushy eyebrows, and his voice. "Oh, do you know something we don't?"

"Yes." DeThanatos was done with sparring. "I saw it on streaming video."

"*Streaming* video?" Bosky exposed a partial fang. "Please, you're making me thirsty."

Several vampires laughed.

Bosky's eyes narrowed. "You called the Rendezvous, didn't you?"

DeThanatos started up a rocky slope.

Dark shapes silently swooped down from treetops, expanded, and dropped gracefully to the ground in human form. By the time DeThanatos turned and looked down the slope, the clearing in the grove was crowded with curious and agitated vampires.

"Who convenes this Rendezvous?" a voice called, officially beginning the gathering.

"I, Ikor DeThanatos, called you to the Mother Forest."

And with that, the formalities were over. Loner vampires didn't stand on ceremony. They liked to get to the point. "Why?" several shouted.

"Haven't you seen it?" DeThanatos asked.

"Seen what?"

Their ignorance didn't surprise him. Loners weren't big on current events unless the current was red and flowing. "A boy, a Leaguer boy," he explained, "shape-shifted into a Drifter, a mist, and he was caught on video."

The vampires stared in breathless shock.

"He has made himself known to mortals," DeThanatos announced, dispatching any doubts. A wave of alarm swept through the crowd. "He has broken the third commandment. He must be punished!"

Bosky stepped out from the crowd. "You mean destroyed."

"Yes, according to ancient law."

Bosky started up the slope toward DeThanatos. "That's *our* law, not Leaguer law. If you had bothered coming to the treaty-signing you might know the terms." He turned and reminded his fellow Loners. "We agreed to let Leaguers live by their New Commandments as long we could live by the Old Commandments."

"And you wonder why I wasn't there," DeThanatos mocked. "Our sacred laws aren't carved in clay, they're carved in stone! There is no 'old' or 'new.' There are only *the* Commandments!"

Bosky continued his appeal to the crowd. "We also vowed to slay no more Leaguers. If we enforce the law and punish this boy, we'll break the peace!"

"And the Leaguers will resume the war!" someone hollered.

"A war that will destroy us!" another yelled.

As the crowd shouted in agreement, a sandhill crane sailed in, flared its wings, transformed into a woman, and landed on the slope near DeThanatos. "Are you talking about the boy named Morning McCobb?" the latecomer asked.

"Yes," DeThanatos hissed.

"About an hour ago, he did it again," she announced. "He took the Form of a Hider on television."

The crowd rumbled with concern.

"What did he become?" DeThanatos demanded.

"A tree."

The Loners gasped.

DeThanatos saw his opening. "He not only breaks sacred law, he threatens our deepest secrets!"

"He threatens the Mother Forest!" someone bellowed.

As the crowd shouted for Morning's destruction, Bosky strode up the slope, coming even with DeThanatos. "Wait!" he thundered over the mob. "To shape-shift in front of a mortal once might be an accident. To do it twice can only mean one thing. Luther Birnam is finally making his move."

DeThanatos scowled. "What move?"

"I've heard Leaguers talk about a plan to emerge from the *selva obscura*," Bosky explained. "To shed their secrecy and try to live in open coexistence with mortals."

The Loners clucked and laughed at the absurd notion.

DeThanatos wasn't amused. "What if they succeed? Imagine what mortal scientists could learn if they had a chance to examine one of us. Imagine what will happen if mortals relearn the secrets of vampire slaying."

131

As fear rippled though the crowd, Bosky countered. "Birnam won't let that happen."

"What makes you so sure?" someone yelled.

"Because he's not suicidal," Bosky declared. "He's far worse. He's shape-shifted into the lowest form of all: a politician. His bloodlust has mutated into power-lust, and he will never risk the army of Leaguers that feed his power." Bosky had the crowd's undivided attention. "I believe the day Leaguers come out and make themselves known to mortals could be the beginning of a new night for us."

"What do you mean?" the vampiress asked.

Bosky's voice rose with excitement. "Imagine it. What if the mortals accept Leaguers as harmless, law-abiding citizens with—how do they like to say?—'special needs.'"

The crowd shared a ghoulish laugh.

Bosky grinned, revealing a fine pair of fangs. "Maybe that's not a bad thing for those who practice the old ways." His eyes gleamed. "Imagine how much easier it will be to hunt if mortals think vampires are harmless. Their guard will be down. Imagine how much easier it will be to satisfy our bloodlust when we become Loners in Leaguers' clothing."

The crowd sounded their approval.

DeThanatos shouted over them. "I don't need more disguises to hunt. I can drink or kill anytime I want. You're no different. We must enforce sacred law! It's what has kept us alive for tens of thousands of years, honoring the Commandments!"

Bosky answered his finger-wagging lecture with a hearty laugh. "DeThanatos, sometimes you really sound your age. What are you now? A millennium-something?" He rode the surge of laughter. "You're so old-fashioned.

Sacred laws, Commandments, blah-blah-blah." He turned to the crowd. "I prefer the term favored by today's mortals: core values. And the only *core value* I've ever had is this: to serve myself and my appetites." His voice rose, inciting the crowd. "So if Luther Birnam wants to put his Leaguers on display, and make hunting that much easier for us, I say, let him do it!"

The mob of Loners shouted in agreement.

Before DeThanatos could protest a voice sounded, "Who ends this Rendezvous?"

Bosky bellowed the traditional answer. "I, Theodore Bosky, declare that we depart the Mother Forest."

The crowd ballooned outward; vampires transformed into flying forms and rose into the air. Within seconds, there was nothing but a veil of dust settling to the ground.

Still on the slope, Bosky glanced at the graying behind the eastern ridge. He flashed DeThanatos a full-fanged grin. "Good to see you again, Ikor. Sappy hunting." He laughed as he strode down the slope. His thick torso compacted, his arms punched wide, and a condor lifted off the slope. His huge wings kneaded the air, cutting a majestic silhouette against the paling sky.

DeThanatos loped down the hill toward the Matriarch. The great tree's trunk, over thirty feet wide, was not one trunk. It was seven trunks twisted around each other to form the mother of all bristlecone pines.

Reaching it, he pressed his hand against the bare reddish bark. "Sacred Mother," he intoned, "on your seven trunks, on the cradle and grave of the Old Ones, I, Ikor DeThanatos, the last true vampire, will enforce your immortal law."

As sunlight streaked the top of the tree, DeThanatos

shriveled into the Fourth Form: the Climber. Where his hand had rested on the trunk was now a tarantula. The huge spider crawled into a dark crevice of gnarled pine. He would spend the day sleeping in the Matriarch's protective fold. At sundown, he would begin his hunt for Morning McCobb.

19

Small Talk

The private jet carrying Morning, Portia, and Penny reached cruising altitude and leveled off. The jet belonged to Gabby Kissenkauf, the host of *The Night-Night Show* in Los Angeles.

Penny sat in the front of the roomy cabin. She was on her cell phone talking to a *Night-Night* producer about Morning's appearance on the show the next evening. It was going to be taped at the grand opening of Okeanos, a huge new aquarium in L.A.

In the back of the jet, Portia returned to her seat with a bottle of water from the snack bar. Morning sat across the aisle. He was wearing *The Night-Night Show* sweatshirt he'd found in the goody bag that had come with their flight.

During the limo ride to the airport, Portia had done some multitasking. She had stuck to her starter plan of keeping it to small talk with Morning, even when he'd asked to see her video of his interview with Ally Alfamen. While he had a good laugh over her oblivious shot of a camera cable on the floor, she had brainstormed a new title for her documentary on Morning McCobb, the first outed vampire. *Out of the Casket.*

Portia opened her bottle of water, glanced out the jet window, and reminded herself that there was no point in firing up her laptop—which her mother had thoughtfully packed for her—and designing the opening credits to "A Portia Dredful Film" unless her small-talk plan led to more footage of her star.

She pulled out her Handycam, pointed it out the window, and got a shot of the countryside below.

Morning watched her. "What are you shooting?"

"Clouds."

"Can I give you a tip?"

Still recording, she shot him a dubious look. "Oh, so you're a vampire *and* a cinematographer?"

"No, but after the camera-cable-on-the-floor thing, I just wanted to make sure you were shooting more than the wing."

She threw up a hand. "Go ahead, make fun, but this video project is going to make or break my college application."

"What kind of college asks for a video essay?"

"Film school."

"You wanna be a filmmaker?"

"Yeah." She eye-rolled. "Doesn't everybody?" She stopped shooting and lowered her camera. "What do you want to be when you grow up?"

He looked away with a rueful smile. "Maybe you didn't get the memo. I'm not the growing-up type."

"Oops," she said. "I forgot, vampires are like Peter Pan. They never get older."

"Yeah."

"Wizzywig," she added.

"Wizzy-what?"

"It's a computer term. Short for What You See Is What You Get."

"Yep, that's me." He opened his arms in hapless resignation. "What you see is what you get."

"But you weren't wizzywig before a vampire came along and—"

"Of course not."

"Can I ask you about it?"

His mouth tightened. "About when I was normal, or when a vampire came along?"

She took a swig of water. "To be honest, I want to know about both."

He shrugged away his tension. "They're both boring stories, especially the one about me getting turned."

"Oh really? As boring as the ones about paper boats and the Williams Bird Bridge?"

"Just about."

She lifted her camera. "If it's so boring, can I tape it?"

He pulled back. "What makes you think I'm going to tell it?"

"Well, if it's such a *boring* story you certainly don't want to tell it to Gabby Kissenkauf on national TV. I mean, nobody survives bombing on *The Night-Night Show.* Not even a vampire. So, here's what I think we should do for each other."

"I can't wait to hear this."

"You tell me all your stupid and mind-numbing stories,

like how you became a vampire, and save your best stuff for the spotlight. That way, everyone gets what they want. You become the first vampire superstar, my mother becomes the most famous PR agent since George Bush, and I make a quiet little documentary about you that wins the Oscar."

He shook his head over her chutzpah. He also realized how short a documentary on him might end up being. After all, the welcoming committee in L.A. might include a bunch of Loners, armed with stakes, eager to turn his next CD into Cell *Destruction*. If that was the case, the least he could do was help Portia get into film school by giving her a little more footage. "Okay, fine, but don't blame me if you and your camera are disappointed."

She flashed a triumphant smile. "That's what I like about you, Morning. Your 'disappointments' keep getting bigger and bigger." She turned on the camera and found him in the viewfinder. "So, Morning McCobb, one day you're cruising along as a normal teenage kid, the next you're undead."

"I was never undead."

"No?"

"It's one of the things about us that's not true."

"Undead equals untrue," she chimed in. "Got it. So what are you?"

"When you become a vampire you don't die and rise from the grave. You get really sick. You crawl into a corner and *wanna* die, and you almost do because your insides are being rearranged. Then you feel better, and you think you're back to normal. But then your gums hurt, and you have this overwhelming thirst for blood. That's when you go, whoa, this is new."

Portia raised a hand behind her camera. "Okay, I got the basics, but can you go back to the beginning, you know, the day or night you got turned?"

Morning was already there, flashing back on the horrifying moment he realized his body craved blood. That was when he decided not to succumb. That was when he decided to starve himself to death rather than drink blood.

Through the viewfinder, she saw the change in his face. It was taut, pained. And his eyes seemed to have retreated to a nightmare. She suddenly realized she was asking too much too soon.

She flicked the camera off and set it on the seat. "Listen, if you don't want to talk about it, don't. You don't even have to talk to me." She threw a hand toward the back of the jet. "Want something from the snack bar? If you want, we can just sit here, eat candy, throw peanut M&M's at each other, and get fat." She cringed. "Oops, forgot again. You don't eat, you don't get fat, you don't change." Her eyes popped wide. "Ohmigod, you *don't get fat*!"

Her verbal spasms pulled him back to the present. He watched, baffled, as she yanked a notepad from her tote bag and scribbled something on it.

She ripped the paper off the pad, and shoved the note and pen across the aisle. "You have to sign this."

He took the note and read it. "Should I, Morning McCobb, ever be tempted to turn Portia Dredful into a vampire, I promise not to do it until she has a chance to lose seven pounds." He rocked back in laughter.

"Not funny," she mock-protested. "If I ended up seven pounds overweight forever, I'd kill myself."

He signed the paper and gave it to her. "Please, turn on

your camera. At least when I do the talking I know where the conversation's going."

"You sure?"

"Sure."

She grinned. Christiane Amanpour couldn't have done it better.

20

Passing the Deuce

Portia opened the camera's flip-out screen, started recording, and tried to keep it light. "Was it a dark and stormy night?"

Morning chortled and ran a hand through his hair. "No, it was last Thanksgiving. I was living at St. Giles, and there are these host families that invite orphans to come to their home for a real Thanksgiving. I got invited to a house on Staten Island. I took the ferry out there, and the husband picked me up at the ferry landing. When I got to the house and met the wife, I realized they didn't have kids. I was their kid for the day. We had a huge meal and watched a football game. The couple was about to take me back to the ferry when they noticed I'd broken out in red spots. The woman said it was chicken pox."

"You never had chicken pox when you were little?"

"No. That's what they found out when they called Sister Flora. And because there were a dozen little kids at

St. Giles who hadn't had chicken pox, Sister asked the couple if they'd keep me for a few days until I wasn't contagious. They agreed. We made turkey sandwiches for dinner, and they let me sleep in their spare bedroom. It wasn't just a bedroom. It had a crib, with a mobile over it. The walls were painted with puffy clouds and airplanes, and there was an Elmo night-light."

"It was a nursery for a baby that wasn't coming."

"Yeah. It even had those glow-in-the-dark stars on the ceiling. I remember staring at the stars and thinking that if there was a God up there in the stick 'em stars, he was a weird dude. He gave me to a woman who didn't want me, but he wouldn't give a kid to someone who really wanted one."

Portia zoomed in a little tighter. "So what happened next?"

Morning searched for the right words. "Thanksgiving isn't just a holiday for mortals. There are some vampires who like feast days, or nights, as much as anyone. Especially when their human turkeys are fat, happy, and filled to the brim."

"You mean with blood?"

He nodded. "He fed on the couple first."

"How do you know that?"

"When I woke up and saw him standing over my bed, his chin was covered in blood."

Portia squinted with disgust. "What made you wake up?"

"I don't know if I imagined it or it really happened, but I think it was a burp."

"He burped?"

"Yeah. Then everything happened superfast. I saw a flash of fangs, I felt something hit my chest, and I got yanked out of bed like a bag of cookies grabbed off the shelf."

"You were dessert."

"Pretty much. He struck faster than a snake. I tried to scream, but the air rushed out of me without a sound."

"What did it feel like? I mean, having someone drink your blood."

"I remember feeling two things. I was terrified and struggling to get away, but he was superstrong. Then there was this other part of me, the like-a-movie part of me, that was just watching it happen."

"What did that part see?"

"It's like my whole body had turned into a punctured tire. It felt like it was caving in on itself. Even my brain felt like it was collapsing. I knew I was about to black out."

"Did you think you were dying?"

"Yeah, and I probably was. Until the accident."

"What accident?"

Morning frowned at the absurdity of it. "Backwash."

"Backwash?"

"The vampire was so bloated from feeding on the couple, and on me, that he burped in the middle of feeding. Some of the blood that was in his mouth long enough to be tainted backwashed into my neck."

Her face scrunched. "Gross. So that's why you became a vampire, backwash?"

"Yeah. When it's done intentionally, it's called passing the deuce."

"What's the deuce?"

He touched his neck with two fingers. "The fang marks of a bite, and, if a vampire wants to make another vampire, it's passing the virus that lives in vampire blood."

"You mean like AIDS?"

"Yeah, or like being bitten by a tick and getting Lyme disease. The vampire virus infects a mortal, makes them very sick while it spreads through their body, and creates a different creature."

Portia was mesmerized. "Kind of like the metamorphosis of a caterpillar to a butterfly?"

"Yeah, but not as pretty," he said with a twisted smile. "Especially when you're a backwash accident. There's even a word for it. SangFU."

"What's that mean?"

"Blood flubup, if you wanna be nice about it."

"What about the vampire who turned you? Was he around—"

"When I realized I wasn't dead? No, he'd disappeared. I never got a close look at him. I wouldn't know him if he was sitting next to me."

"So what happened next?"

"When I finally came to, I left the bedroom and saw myself in a mirror. I looked like anyone who'd been sick for a few days. And I wrote off the vampire thing as a nightmare, or some hallucination I had from the chicken pox. But then I looked for the spots on my face. They were completely gone. The only spots I found were the two on my neck."

"The deuce."

"Yeah." He smirked. "A leopard can't change its spots, but a vampire can. I traded the chicken pox for the vampire pox."

"What about the couple?" Portia asked. "Were they vampires too?"

"No, they were dead. That's when I decided I'd rather die than do that to anyone."

"But you were a vampire. How did you have the willpower to resist what you'd become? How could you starve yourself to death?"

"I don't know. Maybe it's because I'm a SangFU. Maybe I'm missing something." He slid her a grin. "Maybe I'm bloodlust-challenged. Whatever, I went to the basement, found a hammer and nails, and nailed myself in the room with the ceiling stars. And I stayed there until I blacked out."

Two questions popped into Portia's head: If Morning had been at the couple's house, why wasn't he a suspect in their double murder? When she Googled him, why didn't his name come up in the reporting about the murder? But seeing how tired he'd begun to look, she shelved her questions and kept the focus on his turning. "But you didn't die. Someone got you out of that room." A lightbulb flared in her head; she couldn't kill her curiosity. "And someone must have eliminated the evidence of you being there! Otherwise you'd be a suspect in a double homicide!"

Morning nodded, impressed. "True." But telling her who had scrubbed his presence from the crime scene, who had convinced Sister Flora that he'd run away before the murder, and who had bought the Sister's silence in the matter with a generous contribution to St. Giles was not something he was ready or authorized by Birnam to divulge.

"Well?" Portia exclaimed, exasperated with the long silence. "Who got you out of the room?"

He answered with a weary smile that he didn't need to fake. Telling his story of being drained and rearranged had sucked him dry. He opened his silver case on the window seat, slid out a label-free can of Blood Lite, and pulled the tab. "I promised to tell you the boring stories. Don't you think I should save some of the good stuff for Gabby Kissenkauf?"

She wanted to punch him in the shoulder. Hard. But maybe punching a thirsty vampire wasn't a good thing. She turned off her camera, even though she was still in the throes of story-lust. "You're right. I mean, we're flying on his jet and all. I guess he deserves something."

Watching him take a long swig from the unmarked can, she had a million more questions about what he was drinking, where it came from, and on and on. But another thought cut to the front of the line. If vampires weren't dead or undead, her new title, *Out of the Casket,* had just kicked the bucket. She needed a new one. *The Accidental Vampire, An Inconvenient Tooth,* and *Thanksgiving Bites!* came quickly to mind. But they were either too retro or too flip. She needed a title that sounded good with "Oscar-winning."

VAMPIRES VS. HUMANS

THE BIG DIFFERENCE

Our minor differences—drinking vs. eating, immortality vs. mortality, fangs vs. retainers—get down to one big difference. Cells. No, not cell phones.

STEM CELLS

You've heard of them. They're the supercells you begin with when you're a speck of life in your mother's womb. Your stem cells divide, differentiate, and explode into the complex human organism you become. But during your transformation from fetus to full grown, your stem cells change from miracles of morphing to monsters of monotony. If cells in a grown-up could talk they might sound like this: "You want me to divide into a brain cell? Fuhgettaboutit! I do nose hair cells, dat's it!"

But vampires never lose these miraculous morphers. We are walking pillars of stem cells. It's why we possess the ability to "differentiate" into so many forms. It's why we can regenerate ourselves for as long as we chose to live.

You are clay, molded in childhood, dried in youth, and fired in the kiln of aging. We are clay that never dries, that never solidifies.

However, this hardly makes us a superior race. It only makes us different.

21

The Night Visitor

After arriving in Los Angeles, Morning, Portia, and Penny were whisked off to the luxurious Babylon Hotel and escorted to the presidential suite, compliments of *The Night-Night Show*.

The penthouse suite consisted of a palatial central sitting room flanked by two bedrooms that needed a dozen Persian carpets to cover the floors. Morning took one bedroom, while Portia and Penny shared the master bedroom.

From the moment they arrived, security was provided by the hotel's version of the Secret Service. Which was needed because word had gotten out that "the vampire kid" was staying at the Babylon. Besides the media trucks and news crews in front of the hotel, there were paparazzi and an array of vampire fans, from black-clad goths to a vampire-themed cheerleading squad called the Blood-curdling Screamers. There was also a group of protestors from End Times Community College. While half the students loudly accused Morning of being the Antichrist, the other half worked the crowd trying to sell memberships in the school's Rapture Miles Program. It promised mileage points to the chosen ones who would be shuttling back and forth between earth and heaven during the End Times.

To avoid contact with the fans and foes down on the street, Penny and Portia ordered room service for dinner while Morning downed another unlabeled Blood Lite. Between mouthfuls of filet mignon, Portia peppered him with questions about his mysterious drink of choice and the locked case he kept it in. While he dodged most of her questions, he admitted it was an "artificial blood protein drink," and the only beverage he had ever liked as a vampire. When she asked to taste it, Penny told her to finish her steak or she wouldn't get desert.

After Penny briefed Morning on their appearance with Gabby Kissenkauf the next day, she sent Morning to his bedroom, and insisted that Portia come with her to theirs.

He welcomed the break. It had been an exhausting day that had started before dawn in New York and was ending three thousand miles away in L.A.

After stripping down to T-shirt and boxers, he slipped between the bed's cool linen sheets. The scenes of the day swirled through his head. Scaring Ally Alfamen. Meeting the old guy in the firehouse. Learning about the Maltese cross and the knights of the fire table. And there was Portia.

He was surprised how much he liked hanging out with her, tossing words back and forth. It had never been something he was very good at, but with her it came easy. He wasn't so sure about her take on him. He wondered how much she was faking the friendliness because she wanted something from him: his stories. At least she was up-front about it. He had to give her that. She wanted to make a movie about him. But he didn't like thinking of her as some story vampire. He pushed her out of his mind by going back to the best part of the day.

The firehouse. And the crazy idea he had about becoming a superhero *and* a firefighter. Then an even weirder notion drifted into his head. What if he could CD into exactly that? Like the supersuits he'd imagined earlier. He slipped into the black labyrinth of his mind, and laser-focused on the image of a firefighter's bunker gear hanging on the wall. A moment later, something knocked his shoulder and flew past him. He'd been tagged by the black and yellow armor of a fire knight. He raced after it, careening through the darkness. As he hurtled around corners and down holes, the blackness began to streak with red. He dismissed the tiny red comets as if they were nothing but neon ladybugs. As he swung around a sharp turn pursuing the fire knight, he zipped past a swarming nest of red bugs. He realized they weren't bugs; they were glowing embers. His mind-labyrinth was smoldering. As he shot up a shaft after the knight, the red-streaked blackness exploded into flames.

Morning woke with a yelping start and realized he'd fallen asleep. It was only a dream. His skin prickled with heat; he was clammy with sweat. He threw off the covers and jumped out of bed.

He opened the nearest window. A breeze pushed through it, cooling his skin. He looked down at the street and noticed that the carnival of press, fans, and protestors had vanished. Either they'd gone home or the End Times had kicked into serious gear and they were earning their first Rapture miles.

Climbing back into bed, he tried to shut down his

senses. But there was a gnarl of tension in his jaw and a dull ache in his gums. It was like a sensation he used to have as a Lifer, after a night of grinding his teeth. *Great,* he thought, *after two days of hangin' with Lifers again, I go back to grinding my teeth.*

He turned toward the window. The bothersome sensation went away. Just outside the window was a yellow and white awning. Beyond it the lights of the Hollywood Hills twinkled. Over the faint noise of traffic drifting up from the street, he heard a steady ding. He figured it was a piece of awning hardware being blown against the aluminum frame. It sounded like the clang of a pulley against a flag-pole. It became a percussive lullaby as he watched lights snuff out in the distant hills.

A few minutes later, the gathering darkness claimed his last flicker of thought and buried him in sleep.

When the window framed just a few scattered lights, an object slid into view. It jutted down like the sharp nose of a spaceship, then it lengthened into a thick cane of twisted wood. Next came the knot of rope it was secured to. It was a massive stake.

The wind thumped it against the window.

Morning rolled onto his back. His eyes fluttered open. He stared at the ceiling and listened to the gentle knocking. Dismissing it as the awning, he fell back to sleep.

A blanket of mist slid down the outside of the window, curled through the opening, and glided down the wall like a stingray. A moment later, a naked figure, facing the window, rose up. He had the wide back and narrow hips of a swimmer. He reached out the window, clutched the wooden stake, and deftly flicked away the knot of rope. Pulling the stake inside, the man turned toward the bed.

Ikor DeThanatos.

Morning groaned.

The vampire instantly crouched to the floor.

Morning resumed the rhythmic breathing of sleep.

DeThanatos rose and stepped to the bed. He looked down at the young vampire and sneered with contempt. The boy had violated immortal law. He had made sacred secrets known to mortals. He had endangered the existence of all vampires.

He clutched the stake in both hands and raised it over his head. He would plunge it through the boy's heart, impaling him on the bed like a moth with a pin. Then he would fetch the other tools from the roof and carry out the sentence the law demanded for commandment breakers: annihilation.

As the slayer gathered his strength for the impaling, something swirled in his gut. It snagged his attention, but he dismissed it. He had stopped to feed during the journey to Los Angeles; his gut was probably objecting to flying on a full stomach.

DeThanatos rebraced to plunge the stake. Pain shot through his viscera like a jagged blade of lightning. He defied it, lifting the stake higher. His face contorted. The searing pain sapped his strength, draining his resolve. DeThanatos felt like he was the one impaled. He was. On the stake of confusion.

Of all the human races, vampires possess the greatest powers of mind over matter. But in one instance, a vampire's body will trump his will every time. When a mortal is turned into a vampire, one of the biggest changes is in the gut. The gut becomes a second brain. This second brain controls two things: bloodlust and the survival instinct.

The horrendous realization of why his body was betraying him shifted DeThanatos's gut-wrenching pain to knee-buckling nausea. He brought the stake to the floor, steadying himself. He dropped to his knees and gasped for air. Clutching the top of the stake, his glazed face fell on his hands. As he caught his breath, the nausea dissipated.

DeThanatos lifted his head and glared at the sleeping boy. He wasn't any boy. He was *his* boy. A blood child he had never known.

Then the memory came. The previous Thanksgiving. The feast of two adults, and a teenage boy with red spots. He recalled the juicy gluttony. But in his ravenous rapture he couldn't remember when he had accidentally pushed blood back into the boy, spawning a blood child. A SangFU.

Only one thing was certain. His gut had stayed his hand and stopped him from breaking the fourth commandment: Thou shalt not destroy thy blood child. The punishment for doing so was swift. Instant conflagration. His second brain had saved him from the fireball of annihilation.

Staring down at his blood child did nothing to weaken DeThanatos's resolve. If anything, knowing that this vampire traitor was *his,* made it stronger. Yes, the boy had received a stay of execution. But not for long. While immortal law forbid the destruction of a blood child by the maker's hand, it said nothing about a hired hand.

22

The Swimmer

As Penny and Portia ate breakfast in the sitting room, Morning checked out the scene in front of the Babylon. The throng of media, fans, and End Timers had returned and doubled in size. Like a block party, it spilled into the street and stopped traffic.

Holding a cup of coffee, Penny joined him at the window.

"How are we going to drive through that?" Morning asked.

"We're not," she replied. "We're going over it."

A half hour later, they rode the elevator to the hotel's helipad and climbed into Gabby Kissenkauf's private helicopter. It would take them to the new, state-of-the-art aquarium that had been built on the ocean, north of Los Angeles.

As they flew over the giant water-spouting gate announcing OKEANOS, Morning asked, "What kind of name is that?"

Portia was shooting a bird's-eye view of the new attraction. "According to the Greeks, Okeanos was the great river that flowed around the world and connected all the oceans." She shot him a smile. "I did my homework."

Unlike *Wake Up America,* which was aired live, *The Night-Night Show* was taped during the day and shown later the same night. And the show was always taped in front of a live audience.

The Aquatorium Theater seated five thousand people arcing around an aquatic stage designed to resemble an ocean cove. Beyond the Aquatorium, the real ocean stretched so seamlessly to the horizon you couldn't tell where the man-made cove ended and the ocean began. Despite the sunny weather, the retractable roof over the grandstand was closed to contain the balloons scheduled to rain down at the proper moment.

The double treat of the Okeanos grand opening and seeing Gabby Kissenkauf tape a segment had filled every seat in the house. It overflowed to standing-room-only when the rumor spread that Gabby had a surprise guest: Morning McCobb.

A crescent of rocky beach created an apron between the audience and the cove. Because it would take so long for the emcee and the animal trainers to walk to the middle of this faux beach, elevators had been installed to deliver them from below the rocky sands.

When three heads appeared behind a long rock, the crowd pointed and cheered as Gabby Kissenkauf, Morning, and Penny rose into view. The trio sat in high director chairs with Morning in the middle. He wore a jean jacket over an Okeanos T-shirt, tattered blue jeans, and sneakers. Penny had chosen an emerald green dress that jumped out against the watery blue background.

From the front row of the grandstand, Portia captured their entrance on her Handycam. Behind her, cameras flashed like metal in a microwave.

Gabby possessed a Humpty Dumpty face, a paintbrush of salt-and-pepper hair, and the impish air of a class clown who'd never grown up. His cranberry-colored sports coat was offset by a yellow and purple tie. He began the show with his standard opening line. "So, where y'all from?"

The audience answered on cue, shouting their home states.

After Gabby made a few opening jokes about his network exiling him to an island and "putting him out to ocean," he transitioned to his guests. "Until yesterday, I thought *I* was gonna do the Moses thing, part the waters and open Okeanos solo, but it turns out there's a new guy in town who can out-Moses Moses. And here he is, Morning McCobb."

The crowd erupted.

Startled by the noise, Morning glanced down at his sneakers on the chair's footboard. His left foot was tapping nervously. He stilled it, then waved at the sea of flashing cameras. It was one thing to be stared at by the cyclops of a TV camera, it was another to feel the roar of a monster with ten thousand eyes.

"Morning is going to assist me in the grand opening," Gabby continued, "along with his publicist, protector, and hopefully not his pincushion, Penny Dredful."

The audience laughed and gave Penny a round of applause.

"But before we cut the ribbon on this amazing aquarium, I say we cut to the chase." Gabby leaned toward the audience with a wink. "I don't know about you, but until yesterday I thought I knew a thing or two about vampires. But now I'm really in the dark. I mean, when I think of vampires, I think Dracula, Lestat, Michael Jackson." The audience laughed and he kept up his befuddled act. "But when I look at Morning, and what he's done in the last twenty-four hours, I'm thinking, this guy is a vampire version of Rosa Parks." He paused, then continued his setup. "You know, the African American woman who refused to ride in the back of the bus. But Morning refuses to ride in the back of the hearse." Gabby rode the wave of laughter to his next punch line. "I mean, I don't even wanna call him a vampire. I wanna call him an Undead American."

When the laughter died down, Morning found his voice. "Can I say something?"

"Please!" Gabby encouraged.

"There *are* undead people in the world, but vampires aren't undead."

"Oh, really?" Gabby said with singsong curiosity. "Who's undead then?"

Morning wiped his palms on his jeans, and hoped he could remember all the answers he had rehearsed with Mr. Birnam. "People who die, like on an operating table, and then get brought back to life are more undead than vampires."

Gabby nodded, impressed. "Okay, that makes sense. But if you didn't die, how did you become a vampire?"

Morning was glad he'd rehearsed this one with Portia. But he had to make it shorter. "When you're bitten by a deer tick and get Lyme disease, it changes how your immune system works. When you're bitten by a vampire and get vampire disease, it changes how your whole body works."

157

Gabby leaned forward and cleared his throat. "And one of those changes is a thirst for blood."

Morning nodded. "Yeah."

"Aha!" Gabby exclaimed. "So that part's true."

"Yes." Morning reached into his jacket. "But I only drink an artificial blood substitute made from soy." As the crowd hooted in disbelief, he pulled out a magenta-colored can. "No, really, it's called Blood Lite."

The crowd convulsed with laughter. Portia zoomed in for a close-up of the can's curly white letters spelling BLOOD LITE. It was the first one she'd seen with a label.

Gabby stared at the can in bemused disbelief. "Where do you get that?"

Morning shrugged. "You have to know where to shop." For the first time the eruption of laughter that followed didn't jar him. In fact, he liked it. They were laughing at his joke, not Gabby's.

"Okay, okay, we're on a roll here." Gabby dug something out of a jacket pocket and flipped it to his guest. "What about garlic?"

Morning caught the garlic bulb and held it up. "Doesn't bother us one bit. I still like the smell of it."

"So you don't fear it?"

"We're scared of garlic for the same reason everybody else is. It can give you wicked bad breath." The ten-thousand-eyed monster laughed again.

Gabby whipped out a crucifix and pushed it at his guest. "What about this? Do anything for you?"

Morning eyed the cross. "It's a nice cross, but it doesn't bother me. I mean, as a Christian symbol the cross has only been around for a couple thousand years. Vampires have been around a lot longer than that. Why should we suddenly start getting creeped out by a cross? And besides, if we recoiled every time we saw one, we'd be a dead giveaway in the library." He answered Gabby's quizzical look. "We'd be the ones getting jiggy every time we looked at the letter *t*."

The crowd piggybacked their laughter with applause.

Morning grinned. This was getting more than easy, it was fun.

Gabby shoved a hand mirror toward him. "What about mirrors? Can you see yourself?"

Morning found his face in the mirror and checked his hair for cowlicks. "Yeah, I can see myself."

"Okay, but what about the thing about vampires avoiding mirrors?"

"It's true," he acknowledged. "We avoid them."

Gabby raised his arms in triumph and turned to the audience. "Hey, we got one right!"

"Yeah," Morning interjected, "but the only reason we avoid mirrors is because we've lost the main reason for looking in one. We never change. It's not like we're going to discover a pimple or a new wrinkle."

Gabby lifted his hand dramatically. "Ah, but what if you look in the mirror and discover a stake through your heart? Do you crumble and turn to dust?"

"Well," Morning hesitated, "destroying us isn't that simple."

Gabby leaned closer, pretending to share a secret. "C'mon, Morn. Between you and me, a peg in the ol' ticker is worse than a splinter, right?"

Morning's foot began to tap again.

Penny jumped in. "Maybe we should change the subject."

"But I have a thousand more questions," Gabby protested.

"I thought you had an aquarium to open," Penny said with a reproachful smile.

Gabby's face lit up. "Water! I forgot about the water thing. Vampires hate it, right? Especially holy water. It's like battery acid."

Morning threw a look over his shoulder. "If I hated water, would I be here?"

Gabby laughed. "Good point."

"Actually," Morning added, "we need water more than you. If we couldn't stand water, we couldn't survive." He answered the host's puzzled look by raising his Blood Lite. "All blood, even soy blood, is eighty-three percent water."

Gabby hopped out of his chair and started down the fake beach. "Okay then, if water's no problem, let's get to what everyone's been waiting for."

Morning and Penny left their chairs and walked down the crescent beach in the opposite direction from Gabby.

Gabby addressed the audience. "It's time to take our positions, cut some ribbon, and open Okeanos with a splash." Arriving at one end of the cove, he reached into the water and pulled up a yellow ribbon.

At the other end of the cove, Penny lifted her end of the ribbon. They both pulled until the one-hundred-yard stretch of yellow popped out of the water and wavered above the surface.

At the cove's outermost point, Morning stepped off a rock and appeared to walk across the water.

The crowd gasped and reveled at the wonder of it. He was walking along the far edge of the cove, but the seam-

160

less illusion between the huge tank and the real ocean made it look as if he were water-walking. Reaching the center of the horizon, he turned to the crowd.

Holding the ribbon taut, Gabby pointed at Morning dramatically and exclaimed, "Look! It's a fog! It's a tree!"

Morning dove into the still water. In the middle of the expanding circle of ripples, his clothes floated to the surface. A moment later, a bottlenose dolphin shot out of the water in an arcing leap.

"It's Morning McCobb!"

The crowd roared.

Morning performed two more leaps and worked his way back to the center of the cove.

"Drumroll," Gabby called as he raised his end of the ribbon high in the air with the help of a pole.

Joining Penny at her end of the beach, a dozen drummers began a drumroll. Having secured her end of the ribbon to a pole, Penny raised it fifteen feet above the water.

The dolphin shot out of the water in the middle of the cove and soared toward the yellow ribbon. At the apex of his leap, he snared the ribbon in his mouth and broke it. As the severed ribbon fluttered to the water, the dolphin knifed below the surface. Balloons rained down from above. The Aquatorium exploded with applause.

Under the water, Morning's shadow-conscious was unsure if the vibration quivering through him was the thrill of performing, or the tremor of sound traveling through water. He only knew he had one more move before he could score this CD a perfect ten.

He saw the reef of gawking faces behind the wall of glass providing an underwater view. They had seen his CD into a dolpin. Now he had to demonstrate to the viewers up on the surface that a boy jumping in the water and leaping out as a dolphin wasn't just a magic trick.

He pumped his tail and gathered speed. He locked one eye on his reflection in the observatory glass. He transformed the reflection of a speeding dolphin into the image of himself missiling up through the water. He broke the surface at the edge of the beach, shot into the air, and thrashed into human form. He glanced down to make sure he was wearing his Epidex and to judge his landing. His Epidex was in place, but he was startled to see the sandy beach covered with shifting balloons. Sticking his landing on a moving surface wouldn't be easy.

He popped through two layers of balloons, miscalculated where the sand would be, landed off-balance, and fell on his butt.

The crowd couldn't have cared less. They gave him another thunderous cheer and ovation.

Morning leaped to his feet, took a bow, and gave himself a nine-point-five. As he straightened up, he spotted Portia in the front row, shooting away. She flashed a smile and gave him a thumbs-up.

His insides ballooned with pride. He changed his score to nine-point-eight.

23

The Flyer

While Gabby emceed the Aquatorium's inaugural show with a cast of trainers and hundreds of marine animals, Penny hoped to slip out of Okeanos unnoticed. After retreating below stage, she, Morning, and Portia hopped in a VIP courtesy cart with tinted windows.

When they arrived at the receiving area below the park's helipad, Penny realized she had underestimated the hunting skills of Morning's growing legion of followers. A couple hundred teenage girls and some boys pressed against a makeshift barricade manned by a half-dozen security guards. As soon as the crowd saw the VIP cart pull up, they let out a collective scream. They didn't know if Morning was behind the tinted windows, but the possibility was worth a scream. Penny had seen enough flocks of crazed fans to make a quick assessment. The security guards stood as much chance of controlling the crowd as weekend cowboys holding a herd of wild mustangs in a toothpick corral.

And there was a good stretch of open ground between the cart and the stairway that led to the helipad.

"Can we get any closer?" Penny asked the driver.

"Sorry, this thing won't go over a curb," he said. "And the ramps haven't been installed yet."

She turned to Morning. "It takes luck and talent to become a star. But if you want to be one for more than a day, there's one more thing you need."

"What's that?" he asked.

"A good forty-yard dash."

The driver lifted a remote. "When you get there, I'll pop the gate. After you get through, it locks automatically."

Portia yanked her camera out of her bag and started shooting. Morning's first fan dash was a must. The cart's doors flapped open and the trio ran for the gate. The fans screamed, "There he is!" Fortunately, they did more jumping up and down, arm-flailing, and screeching than barricade-busting. As she ran, Portia got a shaky shot.

Seeing that the barricades were holding, Morning rewarded the screaming mob with a wave. Their reaction was odd. They gasped. A split second later he knew why. The blow came from behind and almost knocked him over. Two arms encircled his chest. He regained his balance, reached around, and pulled at the clinging body.

It was a teenage girl, on the chubby side, with major goth makeup and short brown hair. She was panting from her sprint and blindside tackle. Still clutching him, she threw her head back, exposing her pale neck, and cried, "Take me!"

Stunned and at a total loss, Morning noticed the security guard running toward him and the faces behind the barricade. They resembled a wall of masks. Their expressions ranged from envy to fear.

164

Penny grabbed the girl's arm and started to pull.

"Mom, don't," Portia protested from behind her camera. She answered her mother's look with a gesture to the crowd. "We're not in danger. He's a star. He's gotta learn how to deal with this." She censored her biggest reason for seeing this play out. This was Morning's first invitation to the all-you-can-drink buffet, and she was getting it on film.

Realizing her daughter had a point, Penny let go of the girl and waved off the approaching security guard. "It's okay. We'll handle it."

Morning averted his eyes from Portia's camera. He didn't want her catching the anger boiling inside him. He fought the impulse to do one of two things: swat her camera away for putting him on the spot or chomp into the girl's flesh. Not because he had popped a couple of fangs and wanted to feed, which he hadn't. There was piece of him that wanted to give 'em what they wanted, confirm their worst fear, and slap Portia with the sensational footage she craved.

A voice cried from the crowd: "Go ahead, Morning. Take her."

He stared at the girl's alabaster neck, and the spot where her pulse tapped a steady beat. His throat tightened. From revulsion at the thought of plunging into her flesh or anger at Portia, he wasn't sure. He only knew he wasn't who they thought he was. And that his worry about Portia was true. She was more story vampire than friend.

He glanced up at Penny. "Gimme a Sharpie." She pulled a marker from her purse and handed it to him. He pulled off the cap with his teeth and autographed the girl's neck: *MM*.

The girl moaned with pleasure and fainted in his arms.

The crowd released a collective sigh mingling disappointment and adoration.

Morning turned and glared at Portia's camera. The tension crept back into his throat. "I don't take, I like to give."

His dark eyes and cutting edge jarred Portia out of her trance. She turned off the camera. She started to say something but was cut off by a cry from the crowd. "Sign me!" It mushroomed into a chant. "Sign me! Sign me!"

Penny scanned the crowd with a worried look. "Let's go."

Morning handed the limp girl to the security guard. The threesome started toward the gate. Before they got halfway, the crowd surged forward, toppled the barricades and rushed forward like a wave licking up a beach. The trio sprinted for the gate.

Portia reached it first and tugged at the handle. It was still locked. "Open it!" she shouted back at the driver standing near the courtesy cart.

Having gotten out to watch Morning sign his first neck, the driver had left the remote in the cart. He reached through the window.

It was too late. While the leading charge of fans trapped them at the gate, the rest continued their stampede forward. Morning, the Dredfuls, and the first wave of fans were slammed against the gate and the wall by a human bulldozer. A bulldozer whose blade could push no farther but pressed with greater and greater weight. Lungs emptied in protest. Their pleas were drowned out by the shrieking chorus of "Sign me!"

Flattened against the gate, Portia could barely breathe. Being taller than the girl welded to her, all she could do was turn her head toward Morning. He was smashed face-first into the gate. Portia watched in horror as the girl pinned to Morning's back lost consciousness. A second later, the girl's lips tinted blue. Unable to fight the rib-breaking weight on her chest and the iris of darkness collapsing her vision, Portia expelled her last breath. "Do something!"

Hearing her, Morning pressed his head back, dragged his face across the chain link, and found Portia saucer-eyed with fear. He didn't know what to do. He couldn't scream loud enough to make the human battering ram stop. He didn't have the strength to repel it. He saw her eyes roll back. He couldn't believe a moment before he'd resented her. And the last thing he might ever say to her had been sarcastic and bitter. Her head dropped onto a coiled bun of auburn hair. The sight of her cheek, blanching in the nest of hair, sparked an idea.

He squeezed his arms up the rough edges of the gate and wrapped his fingers through the chain-link. He pulled with all his might. He squirmed up and away from the crush until he got high enough to prompt a scream from the back of the mob. "There he is!" He shut his eyes and dove into the wormholes of transformation.

A moment later, his T-shirt flattened against the fence, except for a lump the size of a small bread loaf. His empty shirt collar delivered a feathery gray head with a pink beak. Two wings popped out, and a pigeon flapped away from the gate.

As the fans who had seen Morning's transformation screamed with delight, the pigeon flew over outstretched arms trying to touch him. The yearning arms and bodies surged backward like shells and stones chasing a wave back into the ocean. Released from the crush, the bodies at the wall decompressed, lungs ballooned with air.

Penny watched the pigeon fly over the park. But she didn't have time to marvel at what Morning had done. The limp bodies around her wavered in the expanding space. She caught the closest one. Her daughter.

She lifted her chin and shook it. "Portia!"

Portia's eyes opened and swam into focus.

"Are you all right?"

"Mmm," she moaned with a nod. Her eyes took in the scene of chaos and crying girls. "Is it over?"

"Yes."

"Is everybody okay?"

Penny glanced at other girls being revived. "I think so. Maybe a few bruised ribs."

Portia's eyes clouded with confusion. "Where's Morning?"

"He had to fly." She ignored her daughter's baffled look. "And so do we." She grabbed the handle to the gate, which finally opened, and pushed Portia through it.

Before leaving Okeanos, the pigeon circled back to see if anyone was hurt. Everyone was on their feet or sitting up. The bird wheeled over the ocean, and flew down the coast. While he let the hardwiring of his pigon brain set a course back to the hotel, Morning's shadow-conscious fixed on a decision.

24

Change of Heart

Fortunately, the maid who cleaned the Babylon's presidential suite took so many pictures for the "Famous People Slept Here" art show she dreamed of hanging in a Melrose Avenue gallery, she never got around to closing the window in Morning's bedroom.

The pigeon flapped through the opening, CDed back, and Morning collapsed in a chair. The dolphin transformation had been tiring, but the last CD and the long flight had totally wasted him. His body ached, his mouth felt like Death Valley, and his gut growled for nourishment.

He caught his breath, fetched two Blood Lites, plopped back in the chair, and chugged the first. Putting the can down, he noticed an acrid smell. He raised his arm, took a whiff. His face scrunched in disgust. He smelled like a chicken coop. Not a surprise. Being able to shed a creature's skin but not its scent was a sign of exhaustion.

He showered, changed into a fresh shirt and jeans, and

speed-dialed a number on his cell. He was glad to get Birnam's voice mail. That way he wouldn't be interrupted as he delivered the speech he'd composed in the shower. "Mr. Birnam, when you see me on *The Night-Night Show* tonight everything's going to look like it's going great. But you won't see what happened afterward. I almost got a bunch of girls killed. It's only a matter of time before something worse happens. I can't do this anymore. I'll do whatever it takes, move to the jungles of Borneo, I don't care—I quit. If you don't come get me at the Babylon by midnight, I'll disappear on my own." He didn't want to end on a threat. He liked Mr. Birnam. He just had the wrong vampire to break the ice with mortals without breaking skin. "Please come soon."

Morning jackknifed the phone shut and opened the second Blood Lite. Within minutes, bone-weary fatigue rocked his head back in sleep.

He awoke to the thudding whop of a helicopter rattling the window. His eyes blinked open. He sat bolt upright. Recognizing the sound of the chopper, he sagged back in the chair. It was Gabby's big chopper, not Birnam's.

He had hoped to avoid a goodbye scene with Penny and Portia. He thought about changing back into the pigeon and hiding on the roof until Birnam came, but the possibility of being too weak to fly and plunging into the hands of the protestors who thought he was the Antichrist made saying goodbye the lesser of two evils. He heard the door to the suite open, voices, and then a gentle knock on his door.

"Morning," Penny called. "You in there?"

He got up and opened the door. Behind Penny, he saw Portia detach the battery from her camera. "Everyone was okay, right?"

Penny nodded. "Just shaken and bruised. It would have been a lot worse if you hadn't done what you did."

Portia locked the battery in her charger and it beeped. "You saved a bunch of lives."

He shrugged. "Yeah, right."

Portia caught his sour look. "Oh, do you regret it?"

"Not the saving part."

Penny eyed him with concern. "You want to talk about it?"

He shook his head. "Not really."

Penny wasn't convinced, but she knew enough about teenagers, even eternal ones, to know sometimes they needed to stew in their own hormones. "Then we won't." She turned away. "I need to firm things up for tomorrow's gig. Next stop, Las Vegas."

Before he could tell her not to bother, Portia took her mother's place. "I wanna talk about it."

He put a hand on the doorframe. "Sorry, no cameras allowed."

"No cameras," she agreed.

He didn't budge.

"C'mon, Morning. Can't a girl thank a guy for saving her from being turned into girl pâté?"

His scowl softened. He was going to miss her morbid sense of humor. He dropped his arm and turned back to the room. "I'm expecting a visitor."

"I'll leave when he, she, or whatever comes." As she followed him in, her mother began talking on the phone. Portia shut the door behind her.

"House rules," Penny called.

Portia reopened the door, reentered the sitting room, and headed for the minibar. "Mom, an hour ago, he had a chance to jump a girl's veins and he didn't even pop a fang. He's a mensch."

Penny held a hand to her phone. "I don't care if he's a eunuch. House rules."

Portia heaved a put-upon sigh, grabbed a soda from the fridge, and hurried back to Morning's room before he changed his mind and bolted the door. She plopped on a couch opposite his chair. "Guy in any bedroom, the door stays open," she explained. "House rules." She took a swig of soda.

Morning sipped his Blood Lite.

An uncomfortable silence followed.

"Okay, lemme try this," Portia offered. "A penny for your thoughts, and I'm not talking about my mother."

He half-smiled at her dumb joke. "I was thinking that when you got squashed, the nosy filmmaker got squeezed out of you."

She cocked her head. "Oh, why do you think that?"

"Just now, you didn't ask about my visitor."

"Well, I wouldn't want to disappoint your impression of who you *think* I am, so"—she feigned a hard-boiled squint—"who's your visitor?"

"That's better. Now I know you're a hundred percent okay."

"Hey, no one got hurt. No harm, no foul." Her brow knitted pensively. "Actually, that's not true. There was a"— she did a single-finger air-quote—"fowl. You."

He chuckled.

She shook her head in mock disgust. "Very bad joke. I'm sorry I missed it. Your pigeon, not the joke." She stopped herself, took a drink. "Have I persuaded you I'm a blithering idiot yet?" She shot up a hand. "Don't answer that. Okay, here's the deal. I'm trying to cheer you up. But I don't get it, why so glum? You just saved a dozen damsels in distress. You should be walking on air. I mean, what's the

172

problem? Are you mad at me for shooting your encounter with that girl?"

"No," he lied. There was no point in getting into that. There wouldn't be any more moviemaking.

"Then what's bugging you?"

He looked out the window. "Every time I change, something happens that wasn't exactly planned, that's out of my control. I flattened the Mallozzi twins. I scared the crap out of Ally Alfamen. And today, things got a lot worse."

"It wasn't your fault."

"Of course it was."

"It was an accident."

"It could happen again."

"It won't because my mother won't let it happen again," she assured him. "From now on, if we don't have proper security, we don't go."

He chuffed with disdain. "Oh, great, we get to live like caged animals."

His pissy mood finally provoked her sarcasm. "Oh, it's more than a cage, Morning. It's got a little turnout area where you can wallow in self-pity all you want."

Her words stung. The same wave of rage rose inside him, like when he wanted to smash her camera. But now he wanted to leap across the space between them and shut her up forever.

The coldness in his eyes pushed her back against the couch. She'd seen some nasty looks from guys, but this was different. It made the knives he'd shot her after signing the girl's neck seem like butter knives. His newest volley were daggers of menace. She was glad the door was open. If he loaded his mouth with a couple of fangs, she could bolt.

She squashed her fear and tried a different tact. "Sorry

to be so harsh, but I think you're forgetting the big picture. I mean, last Thanksgiving you almost died, but you got a second chance. You're showing people that being a vampire doesn't have to be a bad thing. It can be a good thing."

The kindness in her voice softened his mood.

She continued. "You're showing people that you don't want to hurt anyone, you want to help them understand, to rescue them from their ignorance."

One of her words hit him with the shock of a late raindrop falling off an eave. "That's all I've ever wanted to do," he muttered. "To rescue people."

She smiled with relief. The Morning she knew was back. "And that's what you just did."

He answered with a rueful look. "Sure, but what kind of hero comes to the rescue *after* he set the fire."

She sat up, jolted by a connection. "Ohmigod. That's why you went to the firehouse. Before you were turned, you wanted to be a firefighter, didn't you?"

"No!" he blurted. "I didn't." The lie startled him, but he didn't regret it. The way she said it made it sound like such a childish dream, an embarrassment he wanted to hide.

The rising color in his cheeks was all she needed to catch him in his lie. "You could still be one."

"Even if I did," he said with a scowl, "you have to be eighteen."

"Are you nuts? With your skills, they'll rewrite the rules." She jumped up and began to pace. "Think about it. As a dolphin, you could be a rescue diver. As a bird, you could spot people on the roofs of burning buildings. As a cat, you could go up trees and talk down other cats!"

While Portia circled the room and continued her litany

of rescue animals, Morning was distracted by another sound. It began as a dim thud. At first he thought it was the thump of Birnam's chopper overhead. But the thumping didn't come from outside. It came from within. Inside his head. And it was more than a sound. It was a sensation. A dull throbbing in his mouth, under his upper lip. It reminded him of the tension he'd felt the night before which he'd written off as the ache of grinding his teeth. But this was different. It felt like his gums contained two tiny beating hearts. He had read about it, and heard about it. It was the first sign of *dentis eruptus*.

A riffle of fear shot through him. Not the kind that makes your hair stand on end. The kind that drains your strength. The kind that swells in your gut. The kind of fear that rises on a tide of pleasure.

The bass chords of his cell phone rang, yanking him back to the room.

Portia stopped, looked at him, and caught his tight smile.

Sliding his tongue across his throbbing gums, he spotted his cell phone on the side table. "That's probably my visitor."

She headed for the door. "Then I'll give you some privacy."

Watching her go, his eyes drifted over her slim figure. After she shut the door, he opened the phone. "Mr. Birnam—"

Birnam brusquely cut him off. "I got your message. I'm sorry you want to quit."

"I changed my mind."

"Obviously."

"No, I mean I *don't* want to quit. I want to keep going."

175

After a pause, Birnam's voice sounded relieved. "So you don't want to move to Borneo?"

"No."

"I'm glad to hear that. But I'm curious, what changed your mind?"

Morning fished for an excuse. "I think I was just exhausted from the double CD and flipped out. But after a couple of Lites I feel much better."

"And no one's twisting your arm?"

"Not at all. I mean, Portia just reminded me that I'm doing more good than harm."

Birnam let out a pensive grunt. "I see."

His tone made Morning regret bringing her up. "Don't worry, Mr. Birnam. Everything's cool."

"Good," Birnam said, sounding convinced. "Try to avoid the double CDs, and keep up the good work."

"Yes, sir."

"Do you need more Blood Lite?"

"No, I still have plenty."

"Excellent." Then Birnam added with a chuckle, "Wouldn't want you suddenly deciding to drink something else."

After hanging up, Morning wondered if Birnam had mind-reading powers and knew the real reasons he wanted to keep going. Portia had reignited his hope of becoming a firefighter. And, as dangerous as he knew the throb in his gums was, he wanted to feel it again.

25

Merder Sink

DeThanatos tightened the cord around the monk's robe he now wore, and moved down a street in L.A.'s warehouse district. As streetlights flickered on, he resisted the urge to stalk one of the workers scurrying from the sweatshops. He kept his eyes on the ragged parade of signs above small factories, discount stores, and bodegas. And he kept his mind on the new plan: Hire a hit man; mentor him through the three steps of vampire slaying; off the hit man for knowing too much; and show his fellow creatures of the night there was one vampire who had the fangs to enforce the law.

Shortly after sunset, DeThanatos had paid a visit to a local gang leader, who, with a little persuasion, had referred him to a hit man who had grown tired of whacking people with the same old lead delivery system and preferred unusual weapons. After the gang leader had coughed up the hit man's whereabouts, DeThanatos did the City of Angels a favor and sent him to the devil. For services rendered, DeThanatos collected his full fee: five quarts of people gravy.

The vampire disguised as a friar spotted what he was looking for: a bathroom supply store called Merder Sink. He entered and strode through a mushroom farm of dusty sinks. He stepped to the counter near the back.

Behind it sat a barrel-shaped man with long gray hair tied in a ponytail. He had a deep tan and tattoos covering his massive arms. Each tattoo depicted an instrument of death, from blowguns to guillotines. "Hello, Brother. What can I do for you?"

DeThanatos recited the line the gang leader had given him. "How do you pronounce Merder Sink?"

The man's eyebrows climbed his corrugated forehead. He flashed a smile, revealing a gold tooth. "There's only one way to pronounce it: Murders Inc."

DeThanatos uttered the next line. "If I order a custom-made sink, will you install it yourself?"

"Only if the customer is home to receive it," the man said with another grin, then offered his meaty hand. "The name's Golpear."

DeThanatos shook his hand. "Friar DeThanatos."

After Golpear escorted him to a back office, DeThanatos explained that he was an exorcist who had been given a task he couldn't complete himself. Although he was familiar with exorcising demons, he had no prior experience in slaying vampires. While he had learned the proper steps from ancient texts, he needed an associate with slaying experience to carry out the actual vampire slaying. He then named whom he was hoping to give a "custom-made sink."

Golpear's eyes lit up when he heard the name Morning McCobb. "And what kind of tool should I use to install this sink?" He watched as the monk reached under his robe and pulled out a three-foot wooden stake.

Golpear was impressed. "Now, that's a stake."

DeThanatos handed it over. "Right through the heart, pin him to the bed, and I'll be there to take you through the rest."

"The rest? Doesn't a stake do the trick?"

"Not quite," DeThanatos replied. "But don't worry, vampire slaying is as easy as one, two, three."

"So what's two and three?"

"You'll find out after one."

Golpear hefted the stake and studied its sharp point. "Okay. When's this installation gonna take place?"

"Tonight."

He shot the friar a dubious look. "Really? And how am I supposed to get into the Babylon Hotel on such short notice?"

"I have a plan."

It was after midnight when Golpear turned the hijacked bread truck into the Babylon's service entrance and parked it at the loading dock. He stepped into the back of the truck and made sure the wooden stake was wedged among the French baguettes in the large quiver of bread. He grabbed another bag of bread and carried the two bundles into the kitchen of the hotel's Hanging Garden Restaurant.

The plan was simple. Golpear was to enter the hotel in the guise of a delivery man. He would then make his way to the roof, where he would meet DeThanatos, who would help him rappel down to Morning's window. After he staked Morning to the bed, DeThanatos would join him with the necessary equipment to finish the vampire demolition.

As soon as Golpear entered the back of the kitchen, unforeseen circumstances intervened. The bread delivery man was immediately spotted by a panicked French chef. He thrust a finger at Golpear and shouted, *"Le pain! Le pain!"* A half-dozen kitchen workers rushed forward before Golpear could take evasive action or pull the stake from the quiver of baguettes.

"Give us the bread!" one of them shouted while the other workers tugged at the bags.

Golpear tried to hold on to the bag hiding the stake, but found himself in a tug-of-war with a trio of workers. "You have to sign for it first!" he shouted.

"No time to sign!" one yelled.

Another tried to explain. "Drunken Porta Potti sales group having food fight because no bread on cheese plates!"

"Give it!" the third screamed, kicking Golpear in the shins.

As Golpear cringed in pain, the bags were ripped from his arms. He watched helplessly as baguettes were spilled on a counter and set on by a half-dozen bread slicers. In the explosion of crumbs and flashing knives, he saw one slicer try to cut into the stake, and curse its hardness. Golpear started forward to reclaim it, but the worker pitched the "stale loaf" down a garbage chute.

Golpear nixed the idea of finding where the chute emptied and rescuing the stake from a night's worth of garbage. It wasn't the first time he'd been separated from his intended weapon on the way to a hit. Once, he'd had to procure a backup crossbow; another time he'd had to replace a vial of poison. Finding a backup wooden stake would be easy. And knowing a thing or two about the Babylon, he knew exactly where to find one.

Ten minutes later he was on the roof being helped into a climbing harness by DeThanatos. They were dimly lit by the landing lights on the helipad above them.

"You've got the stake?" DeThanatos asked.

Golpear patted his bulky jacket. "Good to go."

"When the rope goes slack, I'll know you're in," DeThanatos said. "After you've staked him, give the rope a tug, and I'll come down."

Golpear scanned the surrounding shadows. "Where's the rest of the equipment?"

"It's around," DeThanatos answered with a hint of irritation. "One step at a time."

"You're the boss." Golpear disappeared over the edge of the roof.

26

Mistakes Happen

Morning slept on his back with his mouth slightly open. His breath quietly sawed in and out.

The stillness framed in the window was broken by the dancing end of a rope. A moment later, Golpear reached over, opened the window wider, and pulled himself into the room. As he silently stepped toward the bed, the rope tether stretching behind him scraped on the frame.

Morning groaned and rolled toward the window.

Golpear froze.

Outside, a large bat landed silently on the awning and hung there, upside down. DeThanatos wanted to watch.

Morning's breathing resumed its steady rhythm.

Golpear wasn't going to make the same mistake twice. He stepped back to the window. As he turned, the bat dropped and disappeared in flight. Golpear guided ten feet of slack rope through the opening, then quietly made his way to the bed.

The bat landed on the awning again.

Golpear reached into his jacket and pulled out his alternative stake. It was much smaller than the original. It had colored rings painted on the top half. A croquet stake. He had stolen it from the Babylon's croquet court in the inner courtyard. To the best of his knowledge, no one had ever been whacked by a croquet stake. He even liked the name it might earn him: the Croquet Killer.

Morning rolled onto his back.

Golpear smiled with a glimmer of gold. His victim couldn't be more cooperative if he'd worn bull's-eye pajamas.

In the suite's dark sitting room, a robed figure shuffled toward Morning's bedroom door. Portia put her ear to the door and listened to see if he might be awake.

Inside the room, Golpear raised the stake over his head.

Seeing the skinny stake with its colored rings, the bat flared its upturned nostrils in anger. Its mouth opened with a fangy hiss.

Golpear turned toward the sound, but by the time his eyes fell on the awning, the bat was gone.

With her ear still pressed to the door, Portia heard a *thunk*. "Morning?" she whispered.

Morning writhed and thrashed on the bed. His hands clutched the croquet stake impaled in his chest. His mouth stretched open in a silent scream.

Golpear's delight over his perfect blow was cut short by the rope snapping taut on his climbing harness. He staggered backward, knocked over a chair, and was vacuumed out the window.

Portia whispered louder. "Morning, what are you doing in there? Playing horseshoes?" She waited. No answer. She grabbed the door handle and was shocked to feel it turn on its own. The door swung open, accompanied by a "Shhhh."

Morning stood in the doorway. The croquet stake protruded from his chest. The bloody sheet hanging from the stake looked like a disheveled toga from a production of *Julius Caesar.*

Portia opened her mouth to scream.

He threw a hand over her mouth and yanked her inside. "Don't scream. Promise not to scream," he rasped.

Wild-eyed, she nodded.

He removed his hand, shut the door, gathered the sheet, and moved back to the bed. "It's not as bad as it looks."

"Not as bad— You've been *staked*!"

"Sort of. It's more like a bad case of heartburn." He lay down on the bed. "Help me get it out."

"What?"

"It's not any different than tying a string between a baby tooth and a doorknob, and shutting the door."

She cringed. "I could never do that."

He propped himself up on his elbows. "Look, if you don't help me with this before my body heals around it, I'm going to spend eternity looking like I lost a game of extreme croquet."

Portia hesitated. It wasn't the blood, it was the weird objects-sticking-out-of-people part that turned her stomach. She clenched her jaw and moved to the bed.

Morning lay back and gripped the stake with his hands. "Grab on and we'll pull together, on three." She clutched the top half of the stake and clamped her eyes shut. "One, two, *three.*"

The stake came out with a squishy slurp.

Torn between wanting to upchuck and wanting to know, Portia took a peek. Luckily, her mind won the race to her mouth. "Shouldn't you be destroyed?"

He held up the bloody stake. "This is oak. Oak doesn't do the trick. It's gotta be the right type of wood."

Unable to take her eyes off the bloody stake, she fought off another wave of nausea with know-it-all bravado. "Right. Anybody who's read *Vampire Slaying for Dummies* knows that."

He tucked the stake out of sight. "Give me a hand."

"What?"

There was no time to explain the procedure he'd learned in Vampire First Aid. He grabbed her hand and held it over the wound in his chest.

She watched, transfixed, as the blood on the sheet receded and disappeared under their hands. She felt a strange heat as the hole in his chest healed. The tingling warmth ran up her arm and radiated through her body. The sensation was like nothing she'd ever felt. She'd known guys who'd made her weak in the knees, but this was something else. A quavering current that ran from head to toe like an underground river. A river she wanted to ride. A river she wanted to dive into and never come up from. Something yanked her out of the tumbling current—the sight of Morning's hand lifting her hand off his chest.

They both stared at the bloodless hole in his T-shirt. The only evidence of a wound was the pinkness of new flesh. Even Morning was impressed. He'd seen a video in health class, but never the real thing.

She spoke in a shaky whisper. "You really are immortal."

"Yeah, it's like our bodies have an invisible finger on

the reset button." His mouth twisted into a bittersweet smile. "Nothing ever changes."

She heard the regret in his voice.

He realized he was still holding her hand. To his amazement, his palm was cool and dry. He didn't want to let go. He found her eyes. "Can this be a secret?"

She wasn't sure which secret he meant. His immortality? Her secret ride on the underground river? Her fear that everything had shifted? That he was becoming more than the star of her movie? The only thing that hadn't shifted was her skill at covering up by cracking wise. "Cross my heart and hope to die, no one will ever know we held hands."

His palm flushed with heat. He pulled it away. "I mean the part about the stake. Nobody can know."

The request startled her. "That's crazy. This wasn't some whacko fan wanting an autograph. Someone wants to destroy you. You need bodyguards."

"No," he insisted. "Your mother can do all the fan security she wants, but I have to handle whatever slayers come at me."

"Why?"

"I can't explain. But you have to promise me, not even your mother knows about this." She still looked skeptical. "C'mon, Portia, you have to trust me on this. Promise me."

Before she could speak, the door swung open. Penny swept into the room. "Young lady, *what* are you doing in here?"

"Young lady" was always the opening shot in a knock-down-drag-out. The kind of knock-down-drag-out that ended with Portia getting grounded for a month. "The truth?" Portia asked, buying time for her brain to concoct an explanation.

"The truth," her mother demanded.

Under normal circumstances, Portia's hyperspeed synapses would have whipped up a credible story. But the multiple shocks of the staking, the unstaking, and Morning's bizarre request to keep it secret were still over-loading her circuits. She had to go with the unthinkable: the truth. "If you really want to know, I couldn't sleep."

Penny crossed her arms. "Okay, that eliminates the sleepwalking excuse. Go on."

"I couldn't sleep because when I was talking to Morning this afternoon, there was a moment when he looked at me like he hated me. Like he hated us. It kept bugging me and kept me awake. It bothered me so much I came to ask him about it."

Penny's eyes narrowed with doubt, and curiosity. "And what did he say?"

Up to this point, Portia had told the unvarnished truth. But since she had never gotten the chance to ask Morning the question that was bugging her, the answer didn't exist. She swallowed as her mother, and Morning, waited. If she was ever going to get more footage of him, if they were ever going to lock fingers again, she couldn't tell about the staking.

As she floundered for a credible answer, she remembered something Morning had said. *Nothing ever changes.* The way he said it, with a bitter edge, darted through her. She glanced down and caught his eyes fixed on her. They were more than eyes. They looked like pools she could dive into, beckoning waters pulling her back into the under-ground river. She didn't need to dive. The sensation that moved through her made her feel as if she were already there, submerged in the currents of his mind. She had never believed in mind reading. Until now. She felt like she was swimming with his deepest thoughts. And there, lying like a dark stone in clear water, was the answer to her mother's question: *Nothing ever changes.*

She cleared her throat and told the lie that felt like the truth. "When I asked him about his nasty look, he told me it wasn't hatred. It was envy."

The word plunged through Morning. *How did she know that?*

Penny tilted her head. "Envy of what?"

Portia remained locked on his eyes even though they'd grown cloudy. It didn't matter. She'd seen what she needed to see. She hoped she wouldn't hurt his feelings. "Envy of growing up," she said. "He said that when he looked at me like that, he was seeing me as an adult, all grown up." She broke away and turned to her mother. "He was mad at me for leaving him behind."

Although his insides churned, Morning refused to let one ripple of emotion escape.

Penny stared down at him. "Is that true?"

He covered the storm under his skin with a shrug. "Pretty much." Then he tried to push it deeper with a joke. "Immortality ain't what it's cracked up to be."

They laughed, breaking the tension.

He pulled the sheet up to his chin. "Now, can I get some sleep?"

Penny guided Portia to the door. "Absolutely. And maybe you should lock your door to protect yourself from prying mortals."

Portia turned back with a smile. "Good night, Morning." As the door swung shut, she let out a giddy laugh and repeated it. "Good night, Morning."

He closed his eyes and tried to still the two emotions

thrashing inside him: terror that she had unearthed a vampire's darkest secret—envy—and thrumming excitement over the memory of holding her hand. The coil of feelings spun through him, a tightening vortex that rushed to one place—his mouth—where all sensation poured into the twin throbs beneath his upper lip. The place where peril and pleasure melded into one.

His eyes shot open. He shook his head, casting off the sensation. The pulse disappeared, but not the truth impaling his mind. Portia was right. He had fallen in envy.

27

A Visit from the Boss

After DeThanatos extracted the Croquet Killer from Morning's room and hauled him to the roof like a yo-yo, the vampire barely stopped himself from tapping Golpear for five quarts and tossing the empty off the roof. Instead, he ordered him back to Merder Sink and told him to wait for further instructions. DeThanatos then fogged his way into the sitting room and went through Penny's briefcase until he found the information he needed.

An hour before sunrise, DeThanatos reappeared at Merder Sink driving a rental truck. He woke the sleeping hit man, instructed him to drive the truck to Las Vegas that afternoon, handed him a ticket to a concert at the Volcano, and told him that Morning would be introducing Lycanthrope, the most revered death metal band in the world.

"Are you going to be there?" Golpear asked.

"Of course," DeThanatos answered.

"Then why aren't you coming with me?"

DeThanatos spread his arms, displaying his robe. "I'm a friar. I have a day job. I'll fly out later."

When the sunshine flooding through the window woke Morning, he thought it might have been a dream. Then he felt the wooden stake resting against his leg.

He pulled it from under the sheet, jumped out of bed, and found his cell phone. He speed-dialed Birnam's number and got his voice mail. "Did you have a nice night, Mr. Birnam? Mine was pretty good until I got staked!"

After slapping the phone shut, he threw on a fresh T-shirt and jeans and went into the sitting room. Penny and Portia were gone. He found a note. They were having breakfast downstairs in the restaurant. The note instructed him to get ready to leave for Las Vegas.

As he showered, he wondered what he should do with the stake. Leave it? Hide it? Take it? He decided to keep it. It might make a funny gift for Portia someday. That is, if he could remember his basic bloodlust-management skills, keep his urges in check, and not jump her veins.

He packed and took his bag to the sitting room as Penny and Portia came through the door. He immediately went into envy-management mode, and practiced strategy number one: *Don't look at the object of envy; seeing is desiring.* Not sure if this included using peripheral vision, he saw just enough to catch Portia retreating to her room. Penny instructed him to go up to the helipad ahead of them. They had to finish packing and would be coming shortly.

When Morning stepped onto the helipad, he thought

the waiting helicopter looked familiar. As he approached the chopper's glass bubble, the sight of Birnam at the controls caught him by surprise. "That was fast."

Birnam greeted him with a warm smile. "I try to stay close, in case of an emergency."

"Like getting staked."

"Right." Birnam waved him into the copilot's seat. "Get in, we need to talk."

Duh, Morning mouthed as he stowed his backpack and drink case in the back. He climbed in, and Birnam began firing up the chopper. "What about Penny and Portia?"

"They're going by car," Birnam shouted over the rising whine of the rotors. He signaled for Morning to put on his headset.

He threw it on. "Where are we going?"

Birnam's voice crackled through the headset as the skids lifted off the helipad. "To Santa Monica Airport, and then you'll all fly to Vegas."

Morning secured his shoulder harness as Birnam tilted the stick. The chopper plowed forward. He didn't want to look as the helipad slid under them. As they flew over the building's edge, the ground went one direction, plunging to the street far below, and Morning's stomach went the other, delivering a heaving uppercut. He pushed his stomach back down while the chopper rose over Beverly Hills.

Birnam's voice came through his headset. "Obviously, this vampire slayer wannabe is a Lifer who doesn't know what he's doing. Otherwise, you wouldn't be here."

Morning couldn't believe how casual Birnam sounded, like all he'd gotten was a bad haircut. "I still ended up with a croquet stake in my chest!"

"A croquet stake?"

"Yeah!"

Birnam repressed a smile. "Wow, he really is an amateur."

"Amateur or not, what are you gonna do about it?"

Birnam pulled up a box from beside his seat and handed it to Morning. "In case this wannabe does his research and discovers the correct impaling wood, I brought you a present."

Morning opened the box and stared down at a white vest. It was made of a tightly woven material that looked like cotton candy pressed flat. "What is it?"

"A stake-proof vest. Our scientists have been working on it for some time."

He lifted it from the box. It was amazingly light.

"It's made from one of the strongest materials in the world," Birnam added. "Spider silk."

To Morning it looked about as sturdy as a place mat. "Spider silk is going to protect me from a stake?"

Birnam reached into his jacket, pulled out a switchblade, flicked it open, and tried to plunge it into his own chest. The knife tip only got through his shirt. Morning stared in amazement. To drive the point home that a stake-proof vest was the ultimate defense against any point being driven home, Birnam stabbed himself several more times. "Impenetrable," he said with a smile.

Morning held up the vest. "Will it stop a bullet?"

"Yes. But it's not as strong as Unus the Untouchable's force field in *X-Men*."

Morning was impressed by the demonstration, and by Birnam's knowledge of supervillains, but it didn't make him feel better. "Great, now I'm the first ambassador to Lifers *and* the crash-test dummy for stake-proof vests."

Birnam chuckled, then called in their landing to the Santa Monica tower. "I can't give you bodyguards, Morning, but I can help you defend yourself. Wear the vest whenever you don't have a CD planned."

"Why can't I wear it all the time?"

"It's not Epidex, it won't CD with you. I don't want you leaving it lying around for the taking. It's too early to start giving away our scientific secrets to Loners."

Morning shook his head with disdain. "Meaning, giving them me is enough for now."

Birnam's eyes darted between the instruments and the field as they began their descent. "Basically, yes."

The chopper landed near a private jet. The jet's nose was painted with a ferocious wolf head and the name of the infamous death metal band Lycanthrope. They had sent their jet to bring Morning to their concert that night in Las Vegas.

The rotors wound down and Morning and Birnam pulled off their headsets. As Morning stuffed the vest in his backpack, Birnam turned to him. "What you need to remember most is that surviving slayers and the pitfalls of instant fame isn't your ultimate test."

"Oh yeah, what is?"

"Portia."

Morning huffed with exasperation. "I told you everything's cool. I mean, she's making this documentary on me, and I just want to help her out."

Birnam's gaze never wavered. "Is that all you want?"

Morning flushed as he wondered if Birnam had bugged his room, or had snuck in as some tiny creature and seen them holding hands. "If you're so worried about it, why don't you have Penny send her home?"

"Sending away an object of craving doesn't eliminate the craving. It might even strengthen it."

"Whatever," Morning sulked. "There's nothing going on."

An understanding smile invaded Birnam's somber expression. "Spoken like a teenager."

"Really, Mr. Birnam. It's nothing."

"It's nothing you haven't been trained to control. Need I remind you why it's so important?" He didn't wait for an answer. "Whether Lifers accept us or not boils down to one test: How we treat their daughters. That's why Portia stays. To tempt you."

Morning went back to playing dumb. "Tempt me to do what?"

"To drink from the forbidden well."

He squirmed in his seat. He felt like he was having the dreaded sex talk with a parent. The one that's so gross because talking to them about sex makes you imagine *them* having sex. Despite the ick factor, he knew the topic had become unavoidable. "So what happens if I do, you know, get tempted?"

Birnam's eyes hardened. "You'll fall into drunken bloodlust, feed on Portia, and destroy all hope for people of mortality *ever* accepting us as people of peace."

Morning wanted to come back with a sarcastic *Oh, is that all?* But he kept his mouth shut. It wasn't like Birnam was making it up. Last night, the siren's whisper had called from the forbidden well. The voice had been Portia's.

"But nothing like that is going to happen," Birnam said, shifting to upbeat and patting him on the knee. "Because I picked the right vampire for the job."

A sound pulled Morning from his worries. He spotted a black limo coming across the tarmac.

Birnam saw it too and spoke quickly. "I want you to go ahead and tell Portia and Penny about the IVL and our hopes for Worldwide Out Day. But don't reveal locations, and absolutely nothing about the Mother Forest."

The request caught him by surprise. "Why now?"

"It's time to turn another page in the playbook." Birnam tossed him an encouraging smile. "Now go, before Portia gets here. I'm not ready for my close-up with Ms. Spielberg."

28

To Vegas

A rental truck rode a ribbon of highway through the Mojave Desert. Golpear was at the wheel. His eyes fixed on the sliver of shimmering mercury in the distance. In a few hours, Las Vegas would rise out of the mirage. This much he knew.

What he didn't know was what the truck was hauling. DeThanatos had told him it was the equipment he would need to finish Morning off after he had been impaled with the right stake, not a croquet post. Golpear hadn't seen the equipment. The back of the truck was locked and DeThanatos had the key.

Golpear was also unaware that he was more than a driver. He was a chauffeur. In the back, sleeping peacefully, was DeThanatos.

Before Portia followed her mother out of the limo and saw Morning for the first time since the night before, she took a moment. She raced through the strategy she had devised after she'd woken up to a thrilling, terrifying, and troubling fact. Her little after-staking handhold with Morning had nudged her swoon meter into the red zone. But it was going to be okay, because her morning-after-Morning plan rested on four solid legs.

(1) Forget about asking, *What would Christiane do?* Or even calling her and asking, "When you're on assignment, in the middle of the biggest story of your life, how do you handle falling for a guy?" Morning wasn't a guy-guy, he was a vampire-guy.

(2) Rewrite your guy credo. *Assume the worst* was still in play—more than ever—but the disastrous consequence of getting starry-eyed and slipping into *assume the best* had radically changed. Now it read: one minute you're young, vivacious, got a career on cruise control, then bam!—some vampire grabs your hand and yanks you into the underground river of ecstasy, and the next thing you know you bob to the surface as a bloodless corpse, some guy hauls you into a police boat with a pole, and they're all staring at you thinking the same thing. A young girl's tragic end always begins with the same choice: thong underwear.

(3) Play the dead hand. Not the literal dead hand. Play the dead hand of pretending nothing earthshaking has happened, and everything has defaulted to how it was before you dove into Morning's eyes and swam with the fishes of his deepest thoughts.

(4) The most important leg of your strategy. Hide behind your camera. No, that wasn't how you put it this morning in bed. Neither snow, nor rain, nor heat, nor

fang of vampire will stop this director from swift completion of her cinematic quest! Yes, that was it.

Fortunately, when Portia emerged from the limo, recording on her Handycam, Morning had already boarded the jet. "B roll," she muttered as she grabbed a shot of the wolf painted on the jet, and made sure that if he was looking out the window it looked like she knew what she was doing.

Events continued to cooperate with her new strategy after she boarded the jet. Before takeoff, she exchanged a noncommittal "Hey" with Morning. Then, after reaching cruising altitude, an amazing thing happened. He actually asked her to fire up her camera.

As instructed, Morning told Penny and Portia about the International Vampire League, and Birnam's dream of Leaguer vampires living peacefully and openly among Lifers. During his account he continued to follow standard bloodlust-management procedure, and focused his attention on Penny rather than Portia.

His revelations led mother and daughter to a few of their own. Penny now understood why Birnam was paying her so much money and giving her an unlimited expense account. Vampire Morning was just the test model for a much bigger rollout. Portia, having added another cinematic gem to what was becoming the documentary of the century, was convinced she could skip film school altogether and go straight to Hollywood. She was also thrilled to learn that her star was far more than a bumbling vampire who'd stumbled out of the woodwork. He was history in the making. He was what Cortés was to Mexico, what Christopher Columbus was to America. The insight even inspired a new film title. *Morning McCobb: The Jackie Robinson of the Vampire League.*

After Morning divulged the bullet points on the IVL and the Leaguer Way, Portia fought off the urge to hit him with a million questions, and retreated to the middle of the cabin. She wrapped herself in the audio cocoon of her iPod, and the satisfaction that her morning-after plan was working flawlessly.

While Penny was duly impressed by Birnam's dream of Worldwide Out Day, she had more immediate concerns. Like briefing Morning on his next appearance.

She didn't get far before Morning interrupted. "I don't get it. Why are we going from *The Night-Night Show,* with a gazillion viewers, to kicking off a death metal concert? It feels like a huge step backward."

Penny eyed him over her reading glasses. "That's what most people don't understand about creating a megastar. It's not about the size of the audience, it's about covering all the demographic bases."

"What's a demographic base?"

"A type of audience. I put you on *Wake Up America* to expose you to the nine-to-five niche and the senior set. I put you on *The Night-Night Show* for the thirty- and forty-somethings. You're opening for Lycanthrope, and appearing in the HBO film of the concert, for the under-twenty-fivers."

Morning ran a hand through his hair. "How many more of these things do I have to do?"

"That's up to Birnam. Right now, my job is to stretch your fifteen minutes of fame to twenty-four/seven until he tells me otherwise. And I'm sure he'd approve of you opening for Lycanthrope."

"Why?"

"It'll show the world that even when you're surrounded by a bunch of wild and crazy wolf-heads, you don't have a wild bone in your body. It's the playbook's major theme."

He shot her a curious look. "And what theme is that?"

"Four words: 'I'm not a monster.' "

He resisted the urge to tell her Birnam's take on the same theme. *It all gets down to how I treat your daughter.*

While Penny went over the details of his appearance, Morning yawned. She didn't take it personally. "Since you didn't get a full night's sleep, and you'll be introducing Lycanthrope pretty late, you should grab a nap."

As he headed for the couch at the back of the cabin, he had to pass Portia. Her head bobbed to the music on her iPod. It wasn't the same head he'd been avoiding a few minutes before. She'd gotten into the Lycanthrope swag bag, which was filled with all the stuff you needed to turn yourself into a wolf-head for the concert. She now wore three colored hair gels, two shades of mascara, orange and black lipstick, and was busy applying purple eye shadow with the help of a compact.

He chuckled at her Halloween-punk look. It was partially from relief. *It's easier to look at your object of craving when it's camouflaged.* He started to say something, but sensing Penny right behind him, he kept moving to the back of the cabin.

Penny stopped and frowned at her daughter's cosmetic chaos. "What are you doing?"

Portia talked loudly over her music. "It's a Lycanthrope concert, Mom. I have to find a look."

"What happened to the dispassionate observer, the neutral filmmaker?"

"Oh, she's still shooting tonight, but to blend in, I have to go as a wolf-head. You know, when in Rome."

Penny gave her a wary look. "Fine, as long as you don't hook up with any 'Romans.' "

Portia laughed and shouted over her iPod. "Gimme a break, Mom, you're the one who hooks up with the weirdos!"

Morning felt like she'd jumped up, turned around, and nailed him with a dart. It confirmed what he'd been thinking ever since she boarded the jet and was so aloof. He had misread last night. Their handhold, their eye-lock, was probably just something she did with guys. To toy with them.

The second the word popped out of her mouth, Portia wanted to jump up and take it back. She wanted to shout something clever, like *Present weirdos not included!* But she couldn't. Not if she was going to stick to her morning-after-mooning-over-Morning plan. Play the dead hand!

Morning stretched out on the couch and tried to look on the bright side. If what happened last night had been a one-way street, it was for the best. This way he wouldn't get another visit from the *dentis eruptus* fairy. This way he wouldn't have to go into major bloodlust-management mode. This way he wouldn't ruin Birnam's grand scheme by plunging headfirst into the forbidden well.

29

The Music Scene

After sunset, when Golpear stopped at a roadside diner on the edge of Las Vegas, DeThanatos slipped from the back of the truck, took the form of a Flyer, and headed into the city.

By the time the truck arrived at the concert stadium, the Volcano, DeThanatos had secured a parking permit in the restricted area near the stage. He'd also found time for a light snack. In vampire parlance, "a light smack."

Golpear edged the truck toward the restricted area through a steady stream of wolf-heads moving from tailgate parties in the parking lot and into the stadium. With wigs, elaborate makeup, and canine ears, every fan had their own werewolf look, from arctic foxes to saber-toothed wolves.

DeThanatos met the truck in front of the security gate. He now wore a set of black motorcycle leathers "borrowed" from a biker who had changed into a Chewbacca werewolf suit. DeThanatos climbed into the cab. A few moments later they parked the truck behind the stage, next to an ambulance.

DeThanatos reached under the passenger seat, pulled up an odd jumble of titanium and graphite, and put it on the seat between them. "Do you know how to use one of these?"

Golpear answered the insult to his expertise in weaponry by lifting the assemblage, unfolding it, and swiveling it into a sleek crossbow. "Where's the arrow?"

DeThanatos pulled up a smaller version of the stake he had given Golpear the night before. Despite the twisted grain of the wood, it looked like it would shoot straight and true.

Golpear took it with a smile. "Maybe this installation will be worth the drive after all."

DeThanatos scowled. "No improvising this time. Take your shot from the wolf pit at the front of the stage. Then get back here as soon as possible. After the EMTs put Morning in the ambulance and take off, we'll follow and finish the job on the way to the hospital."

"How do we finish the job?"

DeThanatos remained all business. "Church secret."

Golpear gave his athletic-looking client the once-over. "You sure don't look like a monk."

"And you don't look like a wolf-head. But you will when I'm done with you."

Lycanthrope's bodyguards surrounded Penny, Morning, and Portia and escorted them through the tunnel up to the stage. Penny wore a Lycanthrope hat, with its snarling wolf logo. Morning was dressed in blue jeans and a Lycanthrope

T-shirt. He wasn't wearing his stake-proof vest because he was about to perform another CD.

Behind them, Portia was filming a tunnel-to-stage shot. She wore black leather pants and a T-shirt with a mottled pattern of brown, black, and white. The pattern of her "coat" matched the wolf-head she was going for: an African wild dog. Her nose, cheeks, and eyes were blackened, and a black stripe ran up the middle of her yellowish white forehead. Her hair was gelled to the max and streaked with yellowish brown. The only thing that betrayed her sinister look was one of her dog ears. The ear flopped forward as she walked, lending her badass look a touch of goofy puppy.

They reached the wings of the stage as the last warm-up band, Iron Rage, screamed its death-growling, Cookie Monster vocals. The band was dressed in cavemen fur and armed with guitars resembling wooden clubs. They rode a strangulated whammy-bar bridge to their feedback-frenzied finale. Morning jammed his fingers in his ears against what sounded like a head-on clash between pods of armored whales.

As Iron Rage stormed off stage, they wielded their guitar-clubs against the light arrays, which showered the stage in fiery cascades of exploding lights and smoke. Forty thousand wolf-heads howled their approval from the craterlike stadium.

Penny turned to Morning and screamed over the reverb still shaking the speaker towers. "Don't you love the music scene?"

He managed a grimacing smile.

Having escorted the trio to the wings, the bodyguards disappeared back down the tunnel to fetch Lycanthrope.

"Ladies and gentlemen!" boomed a voice. The crowd

quieted to a droning roar. "Brothers and sisters of the wolf pack!"

Portia turned her camera to the man onstage, addressing the audience. Lycanthrope's manager was a towering black man with dreadlocks down to his waist. His face was covered with gray and black fur replicating a gray wolf. His name was Alpha Male.

He raised an arm and bellowed, "Who do ya wanna smell?"

The crowd hushed as their arms rose in unison.

Morning squinted at the fans jammed against the front of the stage in the wolf pit. They were all holding something. At first he didn't believe what he was seeing. They all held up a toy version of the Lycanthrope wolf. He watched as forty thousand toys were turned on their heads, and their squeeze-box innards emitted a collective roar. It sounded more like forty thousand groaning doors than a full-throated roar, but to the crowd it was the call of the wild. They answered with a bellowing *"Lycanthrope!"*

"Who do ya wanna stalk?" Alpha Male yelled back.

Having reset their toys, the wolf-heads flipped them again, emitting another pathetic roar.

"Lycanthrope!"

Morning laughed at the absurdity of it. Forty thousand werewolf-wannabes holding toys with squeaky roars.

"Who do ya wanna eat?" Alpha called out.

Fists and toys pumped the air. *"Lycanthrope!"*

"And I will serve 'em up," Alpha answered. "But tonight, we've got a little appetizer. A surprise guest to start the feast. Put your paws together for Morning McCobb!"

The crowd fell silent in disbelief.

Penny gave Morning a push. He stumbled into the light and found his stride.

The murmur of recognition started in the wolf pit, then rippled through the stadium. Before it reached the nose-bleed seats it was drowned out by thunderous applause.

At the back of the wolf pit, a burly man made up to look like a jackal squeezed past several wolf-heads as he pushed his way closer to the stage. Golpear only had one shot, and he wanted to be front and center when he pulled the trigger.

30

Audience Request

Morning joined Alpha Male center stage.

Alpha greeted him with a toothy grin. "Ever been to a Lycanthrope concert?"

Morning shook his head. "No."

"You haven't seen nothin' yet." He gestured to the cheering crowd. "And they haven't either." He dropped a hand on Morning's shoulder as the crowd quieted. "All right, Morning, the world's seen your Fog Prince, your Johnny Appleseed, and your Flipper. But if you wanna be down with Lycanthrope, you gotta check your face at the door and be a wolf-head."

The crowd took up a thundering chant. "Wolf! Wolf! Wolf!"

As the chant reverberated around him, Morning watched a cameraman rigged with a Steadicam move into position at the front of the stage. He glanced into the wings.

Penny threw him a thumbs-up. Portia continued to shoot.

The audience's chant pounded against his chest like a drumbeat. He raised his hands and asked for quiet so he could concentrate. The chant bellowed louder. *"Wolf! Wolf! Wolf!"*

Morning cringed at the sound. He opened his mouth in protest. A roar exploded from him like a sonic boom.

The bone-shaking explosion stunned the crowd, reducing them to a frieze of terror. They'd heard death-metal growls before, but never one like this. The only thing still moving was the blinking light on Portia's camera.

Morning's hand flew to his mouth, as if he'd released a ripping belch in the middle of church.

"Whoa," Alpha said, taking a step back. "Everything okay?"

"Yeah," Morning muttered. "I just need quiet so I can focus." He shut his eyes and plunged into the dark labyrinth.

The great herd of wolf-heads craned forward, waiting breathlessly. The cameraman in front of Morning pushed to a close-up.

Morning's T-shirt and jeans collapsed to the stage. A wiggling shape, led by a white tail, struggled out from under the shirt. A lanky Dalmatian popped into view and celebrated with a bark.

The crowd answered with tepid applause and murmuring disappointment.

At the back of the wolf pit, DeThanatos listened intently. His outrage over Morning's commandment-breaking shape-shift had given way to curiosity about the crowd's discontent. A frisky Dalmatian was not the fearsome wolf they'd hoped for. DeThanatos realized the crowd's displeasure was the perfect cover for Golpear's shot. He shouted over the fading applause. "You call that a wolf-head?"

"No!" someone bellowed. "We want a wolf!"

Onstage, the Dalmatian's tail drooped.

The crowd resumed their booming chant. *"Wolf! Wolf! Wolf!"*

In the wings, Portia swung her camera to get a shot of the agitated audience.

The Dalmatian's wet eyes swam with confusion.

Alpha leaned down. "C'mon, Morning. Be a wolf-head, not a puppy-head."

Golpear squeezed to the front of the wolf pit just below the stage. He reached under his long coat and began manipulating the crossbow to lock and load.

DeThanatos snatched the Lycanthrope toy from the fan next to him and hurled it at the stage.

The toy flew over the cameraman's head, bounced, and slid past the Dalmatian. The dog flinched. The cameraman kept shooting as toys pelted the stage, emitting their squeaky roars.

The Dalmatian cowered. Alpha scurried out of the way, scolding the crowd. "Hey! Wolf-heads don't turn on each other!"

The pack howled back, launching a new salvo of toys.

The Dalmatian tried to juke and dodge, but several toys bounced off him. One stung him on the nose. He yelped.

Portia didn't have to ask *What would Christiane do?* She ran onstage.

"Portia!" Penny yelled after her, but it was too late.

Moving and shooting, Portia scooped up a toy with her

free hand and fired it back at the audience. "Leave 'im alone!"

Pressed in the dark shadows at the front of the stage, Golpear lifted the crossbow from under his jacket. The Dalmatian was only thirty feet away.

Morning tried to yell at Portia to go back, but it came out as a strangled bark.

She grabbed another toy and rocketed it at the wolf pit. "Stop!"

The wolf pit answered with escalating fury, and whatever else they could throw.

As the barrage of bottles, cans, flasks, chains, and coins arced toward her, Portia ducked and thrust her camera in the air to get the shot. The camera went untouched, but not her head. An unopened can of beer nailed her with a sickening thud. Her camera clattered to the stage.

Golpear exhaled and slowly squeezed the trigger.

Seeing Portia drop to all fours fired the twin barrels of Morning's shadow-conscious and animal instincts. He crouched to leap—the stake-arrow knifed over his head and impaled a three-thousand-watt floodlight in a geyser of sparks.

No one noticed. They were riveted by what the Dalmatian had exploded into as it sailed through the air: a massive wolf not seen since the Ice Age.

A dire wolf.

The huge wolf, with thick legs and an enormous head, landed between Portia and the crowd. Its black lips snapped open, exposing a massive prow of daggered teeth. Its yellow eyes blazed with carnivorous rage.

The crowd recoiled, then, realizing that its request had been granted, detonated with a guttural roar.

Golpear threw the crossbow under the stage in disgust and cursed DeThanatos for not giving him a quiver of stakes. His target was now gigantic and only ten feet away.

The cameraman with the Steadicam rushed toward the wolf for a tighter shot. Big mistake. The wolf answered the threat. He lunged at the cameraman with a bone-chilling roar.

Morning felt the roar quake through his body and knew something had snapped. His shadow-conscious had no more control than a driver whipping around a corner and hitting black ice. Bestial instincts had taken the wheel.

For the cameraman, zooming in on what looked like the ripping jaws of a T. rex triggered his own instincts. He staggered backward. Bigger mistake. To a wolf, a retreating body meant prey.

The wolf lunged toward him.

The cameraman tripped and fell on his back. His Steadicam pointed uselessly upward.

The wolf sprang into the air with a slavering roar and landed between the man's splayed legs. The beast sank its teeth into the Steadicam and ripped it away like a loose button.

The man's terrified face contorted as he clutched his chest.

The wolf's head suddenly cocked, perplexed.

As Morning stared down at the man's twisted face, his dim conscious felt a tug of pity. The feeling gripped him, pulling him out of his wild spin. He shuddered as the full realization of what was happening sank in.

Behind him, Penny pulled Portia, still conscious, to her feet. "Are you okay?"

Portia barely heard as she touched the swelling knot on

her head and squinted at the bizarre events unfolding at the front of the stage. The huge wolf leaped off the cameraman. In midair it distorted and contracted into human form.

Morning dropped to the man's side and raced through the CPR steps from his EMT course. He bent close to the man's ear. "Can you hear me?" No answer. He checked the man's face for movement. His eyes were open but lifeless. He checked for breath. Still breathing. For a pulse. Faint. He ripped open the man's shirt.

Despite her mother's steadying arm, Portia felt woozy and sick. Not just from the blow to her head, but from the sight of the man sprawled on the stage and the knowledge that it was her fault. If she hadn't rushed out and provoked the crowd, none of this would have happened. The man's life wouldn't be hanging in the balance.

Every eye in the house remained fixed on Morning kneeling over the cameraman and pumping his chest. Every eye but the two most familiar with death. DeThanatos was riveted to Portia. This teenage girl, with her long legs and long locks, had triggered something in Morning that he thought Leaguers were no longer capable of: shape-shifting into a beast of terror, reacting with the cruel ferocity of a *true* vampire.

His lips snaked into a leer. This girl, the beauty who brought out Morning's beast, was the perfect weapon to use against him. Not only to destroy Morning McCobb, but to expose Luther Birnam for the fraud that he was and annihilate the Leaguer movement.

31

Dentis Eruptus

In a penthouse suite in Ducats, the largest hotel-casino in Las Vegas, Penny looked down through one of the corner windows at the dancing lights of the casino's pirate theme park. In Hangman's Square, police held back thousands of fans longing for a glance of Morning McCobb. Many scanned the hotel's lighted windows with binoculars, spyglasses, and telephoto lenses. Penny was on her cell phone, fielding requests from companies clamoring for Morning to be their spokesman. Or, as the CEO of a major auto company put it, "to go claw to claw with Tiger Woods."

On the other side of the suite, a large screen aired a shot of EMTs wheeling the cameraman on a gurney toward a waiting ambulance. Morning was walking beside it, giving the revived cameraman his undivided attention. A reporter added voice-over. "Earlier tonight, while introducing Lycanthrope, Morning McCobb's newest shape-shift went from hairy to heroic. After his wolf stunt gave a cameraman a heart attack, Morning helped resuscitate him. The man got a near-fatal scare, and Morning got a few million more fans."

"Change it," Morning moaned. Slumped in a chair and nursing his second Blood Lite, he was back in blue jeans and a sweatshirt. The double CD of the Dalmatian and the dire wolf had drained him of everything but his foul mood.

In another chair, Portia held an ice pack to the knot on her head. It wasn't the only thing that had taken a hit. Her camera had been broken when it dropped to the stage. Even worse, her plan of playing the dead hand with Morning had suffered a major setback. Every time she replayed the memory of him transforming into a ferocious wolf to protect her, her dead hand flushed with a little more life.

She lifted the TV remote and hit a button. The new channel carried the same story. "Tonight at the Volcano, it was Nosferatu to the rescue, and Morning's latest transformation: Undead American Hero."

Morning leaped out of his chair and punched the TV off. "I'm no hero! I almost killed a guy! Why don't they call me what I am? A freak!"

Portia stared up at him. "You're not a freak."

Penny joined them, shutting her phone. "If you were a freak, I don't think companies would be begging to put you in their commercials."

He scoffed. "Commercials for what?"

"Cars, soft drinks, you name it."

"What about dog food?" He snatched a can of nuts off the minibar and pretended to hawk it. "I not only feed my dogs Alpo, I go wild for it myself. Grrrrr!" He slammed the can down, scooped up a can of Coke, and slid into Dracula-speak. "I don't drink . . . Pepsi."

Portia might have laughed if she hadn't been shocked by his cynicism. It was so not him.

"Believe me," Penny assured him, "if Birnam thinks doing endorsements are part of the playbook, we'll have creative control."

"Control!" he blurted. "That's what I don't have. I totally lost it. The worst part of me took over."

Portia tried to lighten his mood. "But you saved me from stoning by squeaky toys."

"Exactly!" he shouted. "Everywhere I go I put people in danger. People get hurt!"

Penny jumped in. "You're not going to hurt anyone else."

He wheeled on her. "How do you know? Next time I give someone a heart attack we might not be so lucky! But you're right; I'm *not* hurting anyone else! No more appearances—no more animal acts—no more nothin'. I quit!"

Before they could react, a cell phone bleated. Penny checked her caller ID. "It's Birnam. I'll be right back." As she went into the bedroom she gave Portia an order. "Don't let him out of your sight."

Portia said nothing as Morning stalked to the window. He stared down at the theme park. He winced as the muffled screams and shouts of recognition rose from Hangman's Square. The cacophony grew louder, but he didn't move. "Look at them. I'm nothing but some bizarre animal in the zoo."

Portia got up and pulled the curtain across the window. "If you think about it, you're an entire zoo."

She didn't even get a smile.

A cell phone sounded a four-chord ring.

Morning spun around and glared at his phone on a nearby table.

"You want me to answer that?" she asked.

"No."

It sounded again. "It could be Mr. Birnam."

"No, he's on the phone with—" The instant he realized someone else might have his number he darted to the phone and snatched it up. "Who is this?" There was a short pause. "How did you get my number?"

Portia watched his expression change from surprise to disbelief, then finally bend around a frown.

"There's only one problem—I'll never be eighteen." Morning listened for a moment, then shrugged. "Yeah, sure, whatever." Then he snapped the phone shut.

"Who was that?" Portia asked.

"The firefighter I met in New York. Birnam gave him my number."

"Why?"

" 'Cause Birnam must have figured out how I feel about still being a firefighter, and it's his way of keeping the carrot in front of the donkey."

Portia blinked in confusion. "What carrot?"

"The fireman said if I still wanna be a firefighter he'd talk to the Fire Academy about waiving the minimum age requirement."

"That's great!"

"Yeah, really great," Morning said flatly. "They'd get two for one, a fireman and a Dalmatian." He turned away and gazed out the other window at the smog of neon encasing the city. As much as the fireman's offer had momentarily lifted his spirits, he didn't want to get his hopes up. If his buried dream of becoming a superhero was turning into a nightmare, there was no telling how his old hope of becoming a firefighter would backfire.

Portia searched for some comeback or quip that would pull him out of his sour mood. But nothing came. She stepped behind him and put her hands on his shoulders.

He flinched.

"Jeez, Morning, relax." She rubbed his corded muscles. "Didn't Sister Flora ever give you a massage?"

He didn't answer, or object to her kneading fingers. His mind told him to move away, but his muscles, taut as bridge cables, told him to stay. Just for a moment.

"You know," she said, feeling his shoulders relax. "I never got to thank you for coming to my rescue. It's the first time a guy's ever turned into a wolf for me."

"I hope it's the last," he muttered.

She kept rubbing. "Maybe sometimes losing control can be a good thing. Sometimes it's good to let your hair down."

"Even if it turns into fur?"

She laughed. "Morning made a funny. He must be feeling better."

"A little."

She massaged for a while without speaking. "I don't want you to quit," she finally said. "But if tonight was too scary, I don't blame you. It's your life."

"Exactly," he said. "And I want it back. I wanna go back to being a nobody."

"That's impossible. You're too famous."

"I could get a new identity, have my face reconstructed."

"No, I've seen you heal before. Whatever cosmetic surgery you got would just heal back to what you look like now."

"You're right." He sighed loudly, then added with a mocking tone, "Nothing ever changes."

"There's another reason you can't go back to being a nobody."

"What?"

She turned him around, stopped massaging, and left her hands on his shoulders. "There's a bunch of people who want you to be somebody. The fireman wants you to come back and be a firefighter. Birnam wants you to be the Jackie Robinson of the Vampire League." His chuckle made her smile. "I knew it was a good title. Which reminds me, I want you to be the star of a movie that has a happy ending." She felt his shoulders tense.

"Is that all you want?"

She didn't break from his wary eyes. "No. After you walk into the sunset, or whatever the last shot's gonna be, I'd like to keep seeing you just like this. Without my camera."

He felt the prickle of heat in his cheeks.

Watching his face redden, she tried to chase away his apprehension, and hers. "Is that Blood Lite in your cheeks, or are you happy to see me?"

He laughed and came back to her eyes.

The silence wound tighter.

As their eye-lock felt like it went on longer than a mission to Mars, Portia wondered how someone who knew so much about turning into animals knew so little about turning the right moment into a kiss. "Can I ask you a question?"

He nodded.

"Have you ever kissed a girl?"

His nervous smile tightened. "No."

"Has a girl ever kissed you?"

He shook his head and ignored the tingle under his lip.

"You know what one of those Greek philosophers had to say about moments like this?"

He fought off a grin. Leave it to her to think of Greek philosophers when all he could think of was the tightening in his gums. "What?" he mumbled.

" 'Is it our chief aim in life to avoid risks?' " She leaned in and kissed him gently on the lips.

The tension in his gums turned to an ache.

She pulled back. Her forehead wrinkled. "On a scale of one to ten?"

He murmured through his clenched jaw. "This is dangerous."

Her eyes twinkled with mischief. "I'll take that as a ten." She pushed in for another kiss, a more pressing one. She felt herself let go. The underground river swirled up, pulling her into the quavering darkness.

The ache in his gums pulsed to a throb. He groaned in discomfort and delight.

The sound brought her back to the surface. She broke from the kiss and wrapped him in a hug.

Freed from her lips but not from the pounding sensation, his mouth pushed open. Instead of two fangs, *all* his teeth were swelling. A new fear seized him. It was the worst form of *dentis eruptus*. The twentyfold fangs of *maximus dentis eruptus*.

As Portia pulled back for another kiss, he broke away and stumbled for the door. He slapped a hand over his mouth, now ballooning like a bag of microwave popcorn.

She was mystified. On the one-to-ten scale, they'd been pushing eleven. "What's wrong?"

He tried to answer, but his ivory-choked mouth only managed "Mmrrf-mmmrf!" He yanked open the door and fled.

32

friends & flamethrowers

While Morning and Portia were fumbling through their first kiss, DeThanatos was in Morning's suite on the other side of the same floor. He was naked and stood over two things on the bed: the Ducats bellhop uniform he had borrowed to make his way to the room, and Morning's open case of Blood Lite. DeThanatos held an electron accelerator, known in the food irradiation business as an X-Irray Gun. A small blast from an X-Irray Gun kills the microscopic things in food that can make you sick. A megablast destroys almost all of a food's nutritional value. The megablast he was giving the dozen cans still in the case was fatal to a normal human being. Not a worry to the guy holding down the X-Irray's trigger.

The backup plan to destroy Morning was simple. If he didn't get his daily dose of protein from Blood Lite, his gut would start looking for it elsewhere. If his craving for a blood boost mixed with an attraction to Portia, bloodlust would ensue. And if Morning tapped Portia for the full five quarts, which was common for young vampires who didn't know when to stop, his reputation as the IVL poster boy would be ruined. With his reputation in tatters, physical annihilation would follow at the hands of whoever got to him first: mortals, Leaguers, or Golpear. And best of all, Birnam's blasphemous fantasy of living openly among mortals would be down the drain. Or, in this case, down the vein.

Hearing someone running down the hall, DeThanatos shoved the X-Irray Gun and the Ducats uniform under the bed, and closed the case. Then he wafted into a mist and slid out the window.

A moment later, the door flew open. Morning jumped inside, shut the door, and collapsed against it. His teeth had retreated to normal, but a sharp pang twisted through his gums. Vampires had a name for it: blue gums.

A loud knock propelled him off the door. "Who is it?"

Portia answered. "I know you're freaked, but I think we should talk about it."

"No."

There was a pause.

"So what are you going to do, Morning? Crawl back under a rock and never see me again?"

"I don't know what I'm going to do, but I'm done being Birnam's guinea pig and your freak movie star. I'm done with the tour, and I'm done with you."

His declaration was met with silence. He let out a sigh of relief.

"Morning," Portia began calmly, "if that was meant to devastate me, make me burst into tears and go away, it didn't work. I'm tougher than that, and smarter. But I'm thinking about leaving anyway because it was such a lame attempt on your part. I mean, if you can read a guy's mind through a door, what does that say about the guy?"

"What does it say about the girl who's chasing the guy?" he fired back.

"Who said I'm chasing you?"

"Prove you're not by going away."

There was another pause. He wasn't sure if she'd left. "You still there?"

"Aha! You don't want me to go."

"Yes, I do," he groaned.

"I will, after I say goodbye. To your face. And I don't care how many teeth are sticking out of it."

"You saw that?"

"I caught a glimpse. But it's okay, I'm not mad at you. I used to have braces. I know what it feels like to have an alien invasion in your mouth."

He eye-rolled in surrender and opened the door. He didn't offer to let her in.

She flashed him a smile. "So, what happened in my room?"

"I thought you were just going to say goodbye."

"After we talk about the kiss."

He looked at the floor. "I'm sorry about that."

"Don't be. Did you wanna bite me?"

"No, no, I didn't!"

"So"—she searched for the right words—"is it just that when you kiss a girl and get excited, your teeth go ballistic?"

He shifted uneasily. "I guess so. I don't know, it's never happened before."

"Never?"

"Never."

Portia swelled with a heady mix of pride and fear. She was his first, but first what?

"There's nothing to worry about," he said, trying to re-assure himself as much as her. "I know how to handle it."

"Right. You run out of the room."

He wasn't amused. "Look, it won't happen again."

"The kiss or the run-out-of-the-room part?"

He grabbed the edge of the door, hoping she'd get the hint and leave. "Both, okay?"

"Good," she said. "That'll make it easier."

He studied her face for a clue. "Make what easier?"

She gave him a Mona Lisa smile. "I think"—she ex-tended her hand for a shake—"we should just be friends."

It was fine with him, especially if this was the last time he was going to see her. He wiped his palm on his jeans and shook her hand. "Okay, just friends."

She kept shaking past the squeeze-'n'-go timing of a guy's shake. "Your hand's awfully cold."

He pulled away and moved back into the room. "It means I haven't had enough."

She followed him into the room. "Enough what?"

He grabbed a Blood Lite from his case and popped it open. "Fuel to change into a Flyer and get out of here." He waved at the window. "It's not like I can walk out the door and catch a cab." He took a long drink.

"Where are you going?"

He swallowed. "I'll send you a postcard."

"Will you send me one too?" another voice asked.

They both spun, startled by the man in the doorway.

Birnam moved to Portia and greeted her with a nod. "I'm Luther Birnam, the man behind the kid who's taking the world by storm."

She didn't skip a beat. "I'm Portia Dredful, the girl be-hind the camera making a documentary that's going to take the Oscars by storm."

224

"How long have you been out there?" Morning demanded.

"Long enough," Birnam said with a playful cock of his head, then returned his attention to Portia. "At some point, I suppose you'll want to interview me."

"Absolutely. All I need is a new Handycam." She started past him toward the door. "There's an electronics shop downstairs."

He stopped her with a touch. "It'll have to wait. I think we've all had enough excitement for one night."

The blush that pushed into her cheeks from realizing how much he'd overheard was cut short when something dawned on her. "Wait a sec, weren't you just talking to my mom?"

"Yes, I was." He turned to Morning. "She was telling me how you felt about your big bad wolf."

Morning threw back another slug of Blood Lite. The wolf reminder deepened his resolve to escape as soon as possible.

"Right now," Birnam said to Portia, "I need to talk Morning out of jumping ship at this crucial moment in our voyage." She started to speak, but he cut her off. "Good night, Portia."

She nodded. "Right. Good night."

As she left, Morning threw himself in a chair and glared at the floor. "I'm through."

"Almost."

"No, I mean it. I can't do any more stupid shows."

"You don't have to."

He looked up. "What do you mean?"

Birnam sat in a chair facing him. "We're ready to launch the website."

"What website?"

Birnam grinned like a proud parent. "IVLeague.us. It's volume two of the playbook. You've shown the world what a Leaguer is as an individual. The website is going to show them who we are as a minority."

Morning felt a surge of hope. "That means I'm done."

"Not quite. I want you to launch it."

"Launch it?"

"It's not a public appearance. It's a little promo we want to shoot. You'll be passing the baton to the website. After that, you'll be free to do what you want. You won't be 'Birnam's guinea pig' anymore."

Morning bristled. "You heard everything."

"Not everything, but enough to know you passed a very important test. You looked into the forbidden well and didn't fall in."

"How do you know I won't fall in next time?"

"I don't. That's why I have something for you." Birnam reached in his jacket pocket, pulled out a cookie-shaped wafer of wood, and offered it.

Morning took it. He felt the warmth of the wood and saw the gnarled reddish grain. "Bristlecone pine."

"It's not only for good luck. It's a reminder of where you're from, and where you can go if you control your urges and stay on the Leaguer path."

Morning turned the smooth piece of wood in his fingers. The other side was painted with a blue Maltese cross outlined in gold. The points of the cross displayed four red letters:

$$
\begin{array}{ccc}
 & F & \\
N & & Y \\
 & D & \\
\end{array}
$$

He glanced up, confused. "You want me to be a fire-fighter?"

"Not just a firefighter, a *superhero* firefighter."

"Why?"

"It's part of the experiment." Birnam answered his puzzled look. "I told you before. You're the very first Leaguer allowed to resurrect the dreams that died when you became a vampire. You're in uncharted territory. And I'd bet all the blood in China that the closer you get to seizing those dreams, everything will intensify. Your passions, your selfishness, and the temptation to fortify your ambitions by tasting the aspiration that runs in mortal veins."

Morning threw up his hands. "But I'm already there! I popped a mouthful of fangs for Portia. Bottom line: my bloodlust-management skills suck!"

"No pun intended," Birnam added.

Morning ignored his cavalier tone. "And if it's like you say, it'll only get worse! Why can't I just disappear? Why can't you go on with your website and Worldwide Out Day without me?"

Birnam stared at him with stone-cold eyes. "Too late. The world knows too much about you, and so does Portia. Believe me, if I could replace you with someone else I would. But I can't. In the eyes of Lifers, you *are* the IVL. And our little experiment has reached critical mass." His mouth cracked toward a smile. "But don't feel bad, Morning." His lips parted, revealing the prongs of emerging fangs. "The thrill of the endgame is getting to me too."

While DeThanatos waited for Morning's anemia to bloom into self-destruction, he didn't give up on Golpear accomplishing a more traditional annihilation. A two-pronged offense comes naturally to vampires.

Later that night, fueled by a fresh feeding on a juicy Cirque du Soleil performer, DeThanatos used his skills to visit Penny's suite in Ducats. There, he ascertained where Morning would be shooting the commercial the next day. He then rendezvoused with Golpear, and they drove the truck to a production studio in the desert outside Las Vegas.

Before he disappeared into the back of the truck for the day, DeThanatos placated Golpear's frustration by giving him the second weapon in the three-step process of vampire slaying. He presented him with a flamethrower.

Golpear was thrilled. He had only used a flamethrower in his line of work once before. In Malibu, a homeowner had hired him to do a hit on a neighbor's hedge because it was blocking his view of the ocean. The prospect of hitting Morning with the one-two punch of a wooden stake and a flamethrower so excited Golpear he had to ask, "What's the third step? What's the coup de grâce on a vampire?"

Once again DeThanatos demurred and told him he would find out after Morning had been staked and baked.

Before sunrise, and before surreptitiously slipping into the back of the truck, DeThanatos gave Golpear one last order. "Even if you have the shot, do not stake him, or light up the flamethrower before sunset. After sunset, I'll return, we'll hunt him together, and then you'll learn the final step."

33

Going Up

The sun rose, illuminating the box-shaped production studio and an abandoned golf course stretching into the desert. An hour later, DeThanatos's order was tested.

A black limo arrived at the studio. As Morning and his entourage got out, Golpear fought off the urge to shish kebab and barbecue him on the spot. His restraint was aided by the dusting of white sugar on his shirt and lap from a breakfast of powdered donuts. His professional pride had suffered enough without his becoming known as the Powdered Sugar Slayer.

In the studio, the morning passed quickly with rehearsals, rewrites, camera walk-throughs, and finally a dozen attempts to shoot the ambitious spot Birnam and his creative team had conceived.

The final effect was going to be one continuous shot of Morning walking, climbing, running, and swinging up, down, around, and through a labyrinth of web pages on the IVLeague.us site, while he told the world about the International Vampire League. But the first step was to shoot Morning's part on what the production team called a green-screen set. The set resembled a giant, multilayered assemblage of playground equipment, painted in electric green, along with the floor and walls around it. This allowed them to shoot Morning's action against a green screen, which could then be dropped out, and replaced with the website he would seem to be traveling through.

To accomplish his part, Morning had the challenging task of hitting all his marks, saying all his lines at the right moment, and doing so in one continuous take. After lunch, and the twenty-third take, Birnam began to wonder if he had overestimated his protégé's acting ability. If he got his line right, he missed his mark, or when he swung on a rope, he sometimes missed the platform he was supposed to land on and disappeared behind it with a loud crash.

Morning was not only frustrated and embarrassed by his countless goofups, he felt weak and shaky. Since breakfast, he had downed three Blood Lites, but they'd done little to boost his flagging energy. He figured his body was still recovering from yesterday's two CDs and an outbreak of *maximus dentis eruptus.*

By midafternoon, they still didn't have the shot. If anything, it was getting worse. "Back to number one," the director ordered when Morning forgot his line after zipping down a slide.

Morning began climbing the long ladder to the top of the set. The tension in the studio was palpable. He wanted to nail the take more than anyone. This was his swan song, the last thing he had to do for Birnam, and for the cause. Then he would be free.

Birnam sat in a canvas chair under the towering camera crane that followed Morning during the shot. He watched his star climb with concern. He knew Morning's frustration and unhappiness stemmed from more than not getting the take, it was also part of the emotional escalation he had predicted. Birnam needed to keep that intensity focused on the positive. "Hey, Morning," he called. "I've got a good feeling about this one."

"You and nobody else," Morning muttered as he reached the starting platform. Despite his exhaustion, he did what he did at the beginning of every take. He reached in his pocket and touched the cookie of bristlecone pine for luck. But so far, the good-luck charm had been a dud.

The camera crane extended toward him like a giant grasshopper leg.

The floor director counted down, "In three, two . . ."

Morning flashed a friendly smile. "You know me, Morning McCobb." His mind went blank. The camera lens stared back at him, cold and gleaming. His vision blurred. The lens morphed into the eye of a great snake, hypnotizing him before it struck.

"Back to number one!" the director barked.

Morning snapped out of his hallucination. "I'm at number one!"

Birnam jumped in. "All right, everyone, let's take five."

Morning winced at the throb of a growing headache and made his way down the ladder. He glared at the floor as he trudged past Birnam, Penny, and Portia.

"Where are you going?" Birnam asked.

"To my dressing room for a drink," he said without stopping.

They anxiously watched him go.

"I'll go help him with his lines," Portia offered.

"Is that a good idea?" Penny asked.

"If it'll help us get a good take," Birnam said, "I'm all for it."

Portia tried to reassure her mother. "Don't worry, Mom, I've seen his fangs, and—"

"You what?" Penny exclaimed.

Portia continued in blasé fashion. "Yeah, and he'd choke to death before he nailed someone with 'em. Right, Mr. Birnam?"

"Absolutely," he replied, and shot Penny a charming smile. "We're lovers, not biters." As Portia started after Morning, Birnam continued his assurances. "In fact, after Worldwide Out Day we're hoping to found a sports team called the Nurse Sharks. Nurse sharks are the only sharks that don't bite." He knew he was overselling the point, but if Portia could help Morning out of his funk, it was worth the risk of Morning taking out his frustrations on her neck. Birnam had faith in his chosen one, faith in his cause, and he just needed one good take.

Portia headed to Morning's dressing room without her camera. Her new Handycam was already loaded with more than enough footage of the making of the spot. She had stopped shooting shortly after lunch, after Morning had snapped at her. She had approached him between takes and saw him pull something out of his pocket. She zoomed in and saw it was a piece of wood with a stubby blue cross on it. When she asked him about it, he jammed it in his pocket and snarled, "Don't ask." That was when she realized her camera was only making things worse and put it away. After that, she had watched him struggle through take after take. Her heart was breaking for him, but there was nothing she could do to help. Until now.

She knocked on the dressing room door. No answer. She slowly opened it. Morning sat in a straight-backed chair against the wall. He was slumped over, staring at his tennis shoes. She had noticed how drained he'd looked in the last few takes. Now he looked even paler. "Are you all right?"

He shrugged. "Been better."

"Can I come in?"

"Can't stop you."

She swiveled the big makeup chair in front of the mirror so that it faced him, and slid into it.

Without looking up from his cloud of fatigue, he was struck by an odd sensation. He could smell her. Not the deodorant she was wearing or her flowery shampoo. He could smell her skin. It was earthy and pungent. Like the odor first raindrops kick out of the dust.

"I thought I might help you with your lines."

His head snapped up. "I don't wanna run lines." He took in her startled expression as her scent flared his nostrils. More than an odor, it felt like twin vines curling into his head. They reached up, grabbed his throbbing headache, and pulled down. The throb descended to the roof of his mouth; the ache shifted from pain to pleasure. He felt his teeth pulse against his upper lip. This time it wasn't all of them. There were only two.

Portia stared at his wild expression and his puffy lip. She wanted to run but invisible straps seemed to hold her down. Her legs felt like lead.

He stood, his lips still concealing his fangs. His jaw ached to spring open. All he had to do was leap across the space and plunge into her. He would feed. One pint, two pints, that was all he needed. Then he'd have the strength to go back, get the take, be done with Birnam, and be who he wanted to be.

He started toward her, but a movement startled him. His eyes darted toward it—his reflection in the big mirror. But it wasn't right. The lanky boy in the mirror was wrapped in a fireman's bunker coat covered in blood.

Morning sucked in a sharp breath and bit his lip. The taste of his own blood seared his mouth like hot metal. His eyes dropped to Portia's petrified face.

He bolted from the room.

Portia shuddered with the realization of what he was running from. It was the second time he had rescued her. The first time, he had protected her from others. This time, he had protected her from himself.

She leaped out of the chair and ran after him.

Unfortunately, his heroic act of resistance had unraveled Portia's guy credo: *Assume the worst.* And thrown her on the path of broken hearts: *Assume the best.*

A banging door jerked Golpear awake. Turning toward the sound, he saw a skinny kid dash away from the building. The hit man shook off the cocoon of sleep and recognized the figure sprinting onto the overgrown golf course.

Golpear checked the horizon. The sun would set in an hour. He couldn't pass up the opportunity. He decided to leave a note for the friar. By the time he got it, Golpear would have Morning impaled, incinerated, and ready for step number three.

As he wrote the note, the exit door banged open again. He looked up. A tall girl with dark hair ran out of the building, stopped, and looked around. She seemed panicked.

Portia saw the truck across the street, and the man inside. She shouted, "Did you see someone run away from here?"

Golpear recognized her from the night before. She was the one who'd run onstage and spoiled his shot at the Dalmatian. She wasn't going to ruin his next one. "Yeah," he yelled, and pointed in the wrong direction. "He ran that way and disappeared in the brush." As she started down the road, his gold tooth flashed. "You're welcome."

34

Chemical Change

Morning ran until the studio was a box on the horizon. His lungs burned in the dry air. He collapsed on a weather-beaten bench. Behind him, a tumbleweed hedge clung to a rail fence.

He buried his face in his hands. His heaving chest tightened toward a sob. Fighting it off, he snatched the small disc of wood from his pocket. He swiped at his eyes and stared at the Maltese cross with its four letters: FDNY. He suddenly hated the sight of it. Ever since the fireman had called him and kick-started that dream again, everything had gone crazy. His first kiss had turned into a disaster. He couldn't shoot a stupid commercial. And he'd almost parked his fangs in Portia's neck.

He flung the wooden charm in the sandy dirt.

A metallic clank sounded behind him. He jumped up, spinning toward it.

On the other side of the tumbleweed hedge, a grinning

man with a gold tooth stared him down. He had some kind of tank on his back. He raised a crossbow. Morning saw the narrow stake loaded in the groove before it disappeared with a *pffft!*

The stake bounced off Morning's chest and stuck in the tumbleweed like an oversized knitting needle.

Golpear blinked in disbelief.

Morning was equally stunned. Then he remembered the spider-silk vest he had put on that morning under his shirt.

Golpear tossed the crossbow away with a leer. "Very clever, stake-proof vest. But you don't look fireproof." He lifted the fat muzzle of the flamethrower.

Terrified, Morning staggered backward.

The hit man pulled the trigger. *Whuummp!* Fire mushroomed from the weapon.

His target disappeared in a thrashing ball of flames.

After shouting Morning's name and finding no sign of him, Portia turned back to the studio. That was when she saw it. Over the old golf course black smoke billowed up. Orange tongues of fire snapped at the cloudless sky. She broke into a run.

By the time she got there, the fire had almost burned out. Tiny flames sputtered around the edges of a smoldering hole in a tumbleweed hedge. The blackened skeleton of a bench squatted nearby. Then she saw the smoking pile of ash in a circle of burnt ground. As she stepped toward it, something on the ground caught her eye. She picked it up. A small disc of wood. She turned it over and recognized the blue cross.

Her scream pierced the desert stillness. She fell to her

237

knees next to the circle of burnt ground. A sob racked her body. He was gone. She collapsed to her shins and stretched her arms over the hot earth. *He was gone.* Her grief spilled into the blackened sand as she hugged the ground where he had last stood.

When she opened her eyes again, she caught a movement beyond her veil of tears. She pushed herself up, wiped her eyes.

Birnam stood over her.

Her dirt-streaked face tightened with rage. "It's your fault!"

Birnam cocked his head. "My fault?"

"If you hadn't made him do the commercial, we wouldn't be here! He wouldn't have run away." She sobbed in a new spasm of anguish. "He wouldn't be—he wouldn't—"

"Be taking a powder?" Birnam offered.

Her fury propelled her to her feet. "It's not funny!"

"It's not over."

She stopped, unsure of his meaning.

"To destroy a vampire, you've got to *scatter* the ashes." He waved at the pile of ashes. "Morning's just a little dehydrated."

She stared at him. "You mean you can revive him?"

"Reconstitute," he corrected.

She looked at the ashes, trying to comprehend. "With water?"

"Thicker," he hinted.

Her eyes expanded like gum bubbles. "Blood?"

He nodded.

"How much?"

"How much doesn't matter. What matters is from whom."

She met his somber gaze. "What do you mean?"

"To bring a vampire back from the ash takes a rare and special kind of blood."

"Do I have it?"

"I don't know. Are you a virgin who's lost her heart to love?"

A tremor rolled through her body. "We're about to find out." She pushed the wooden FDNY charm into Birnam's hand. "Hold this."

She snatched a stick of greasewood off the ground and broke it in half. It splintered into twin daggers. She tossed one aside and opened her hand. She couldn't believe what she was about to do. She blocked out the thought. She couldn't hesitate. She gripped the wooden dagger and stabbed hard. She yelped, clutching the stinging pain in her palm. When she opened her hand again, blood welled from the wound.

She shoved it under Birnam's nose. "Now what?"

He gazed at the blood in her palm, blooming like a liquid rose. Its heady bouquet of mushroom and rust invaded his nostrils. It carried him back to his long-forgotten nights as a Loner. Nothing compared to the taste of human blood—the ambrosia of mortal ambition.

Portia's voice pierced his reverie. "C'mon, Mr. Birnam. If Morning can resist, so can you."

He shook off the ancient urge, and thanked her with a smile. "You're right. We all can." He took her hand and closed it around the wound. "Now, let's see what you're made of." He stretched her fist over the ash pile, and squeezed.

A trickle of blood rained down. It splattered in the ash, making a tiny crater.

He pulled her hand back.

They waited.

She took the wooden charm from him and held it in her good hand.

The first thing Portia noticed was a smell. But more than one. It rose from the ashes like a braid of scents. The dank bloom of a dirt floor—the sweet surprise of honeysuckle—the pungent sour of grapefruit.

She stared in awe as the ashes began to stir.

Birnam let out a relieved sigh, then turned to Portia. "With your blood in his veins, he will share your hopes, desires, and the beat of a heart surrendered to love."

The ashes suddenly swirled up in a dust devil.

She shielded her eyes. When she lowered her hand, Morning stood before her, wearing his Epidex. She wanted to leap forward and hug him, but something stopped her. His eyes were glassy, unfocused, lifeless.

"One other thing," Birnam said. "He won't remember this. Not for a while."

"What do you mean?"

"The memory of what happened to him out here will only come back to him as his DNA reasserts itself over your blood."

"How long will that take?"

"A couple of days, maybe longer."

"What about his 'heart surrendered to love?' " she asked with a single-digit air-quote. "Will his DNA erase that too?"

Birnam gave her a crafty smile. "That's up to the two of you. Now, slap him."

"Slap him?"

"Haven't you ever wanted to?"

Even though her insides thrummed with excitement, she eye-rolled *What a dumb question.* "Well, yeah. Of course."

"Then do it."

She gave Morning a stinging slap.

He came to with a start. Recognizing Portia, he broke into a jaunty grin. "Thanks, I needed that." He eyed the smear of dirt and tears on her cheek. "Whoa, looks like someone tried to make a mud pie on your face." Before she could respond, he saw the disc of wood in her hand. His face pinched with anger. "Where'd you get that?"

"I found it on—"

"It's mine." He snatched it from her and turned to Birnam. "C'mon, we got a shot to get." As he strutted off, he flipped the wooden charm in the air, caught it, and began running his lines with swaggering confidence. "You know me, Morning McCobb."

Birnam emitted a satisfied chuckle as he turned to Portia. "You have strong and willful blood."

She stared after Morning. "Is that what I'm like?"

He gave her a benign smile. "Not all the time." Then he started after Morning.

Portia wiped her dirty cheek and frowned. "I'll never give blood again."

In case someone suspected a connection between Morning's disappearance and the truck in front of the studio, Golpear drove down the road and parked behind an abandoned building. At sunset, he would go back to the studio, rendezvous with the friar, and tell him how he'd conveniently reduced Morning to a pile of ash; then they'd finish Morning off with step number three, whatever that was, after which he would collect his final payment and get back to L.A. by midnight.

In the meantime, the thrill of whacking his first vampire

with a flamethrower had burned up all his powdered donut calories and put him in the mood for a power nap.

He was still napping as the setting sun slathered the western sky with red icing.

Golpear woke with a start when DeThanatos poked him with the empty crossbow. "Where's the stake?"

"Good news," Golpear reported, pawing sleep from his eyes. "It got incinerated when I torched Morning on the golf course." He didn't see the point of mentioning that he'd skipped step one: Staking.

"I told you—"

"Hey, he's toast," Golpear interrupted. "Sometimes you gotta whack when you gotta whack."

DeThanatos didn't like being interrupted. But instead of biting Golpear, he bit his tongue. "Did you scatter the ashes?"

Golpear's eyes lit up. "So *that's* the third step!"

"Yes," DeThanatos growled. "Now explain this. Why is Morning in the studio right now, shooting a commercial?"

Golpear's mouth dropped. "You're kidding."

"Would you like to see for yourself?"

Golpear held up his hands in protest. "Okay, Brother, listen up and listen good. This isn't working for me, okay? I've whacked the kid twice, and I've only been paid half. I'm gonna need to see some more green before whack number three."

DeThanatos flashed a disingenuous smile. "How about we make it red and call it a night?"

Golpear's puzzled expression lasted a nanosecond before setting in the mask worn by so many of his victims. The mask always asked the same question. *Is that a weapon?*

The last thing he saw were two glistening fangs rushing toward him. Golpear's gold tooth glistened in return as he gasped for air and life.

A few seconds later, he drifted into the opposite of a power nap. The Big Blackout.

35

Flirtation

As much as Morning wanted to get the shot in one last take and be done with it, he faced new problems. His refreshing and reinvigorating break in the desert had him so pumped he flew through the obstacle course too fast for the camera to follow. And he was rushing his lines. It took several takes, along with adjustments on both sides of the camera, before the director, Birnam, and Morning reached a happy medium.

Climbing to the top of the set for what he was sure would be the perfect take, Morning spotted Portia talking to a stranger. He was a head taller than her, had longish blond hair, was built like a swimmer, and looked about nineteen. He was the hunk Morning knew he could never be. It sent a pang of jealousy knifing through him. But it was more than jealousy. Since fighting off the urge to feed on Portia in his dressing room, another feeling stirred in him. Possession. He had spared her. If anyone had a right to her, he did. He decided to deal with blondie-boy after he nailed the take.

DeThanatos had acquired his preppie look after visiting the studio's costume department. He had swapped his monk's robe for chinos, a crisp white shirt, and a tie. He had also procured a blond wig. Even though he had never come face to face with Birnam in the centuries they'd both haunted the earth, he didn't know if he had been spotted by whatever surveillance Birnam might have on Morning.

DeThanatos had convinced Portia he was doing a college internship at the studio, and had slipped onto the closed set to see the famous Morning McCobb. Portia had told him how difficult the shoot had been, but that Morning was on the verge of the perfect take. DeThanatos was more intrigued by the nasty looks Morning was shooting him as he climbed to the top of the set. They were looks DeThanatos hoped to fashion into a weapon: Jealousy. Mortals called it the green-eyed monster. For vampires it was more like the white-fanged monster. In either case, jealousy could make you do things you'd regret later.

DeThanatos decided it was time to go for the jugular. Figuratively, of course. "To be honest," he said to Portia with a casual smile, "Mr. McCobb doesn't interest me as much as you."

She answered his flirtation with a dubious look. Just because the guy was older, and hot, didn't mean she couldn't see right through him. A cocky guy was a cocky guy. And it was only a matter of time before he took his first swing at getting to first base. "Oh, really? What's so interesting about me?"

DeThanatos coolly backpedaled. "Not you personally, what you're doing."

She'd seen that move before too: step from the batter's box of intention to the batter's box of indifference. This guy was smooth; he was a switch-hitter. "What do you think I'm doing?"

He glanced at her Handycam, which she had fired back up after Morning had turned into the full-of-himself actor. "If I had to guess," he said with a lazy shrug, "I'd say you're making the movie of the making of Morning McCobb."

His clairvoyance impressed her. "How did you know that?"

"From the camera, of course, but the real giveaway is in your eyes."

"Really." Despite his leap back into the batter's box of blatant intention, her curiosity kept her in the game. "What do my eyes give away?"

He glanced up at Morning glowering down at them, then back to her. To fan the flames, he studied Portia for a long moment before speaking.

She felt uneasy under the heat of his gray eyes, but she refused to look away.

He broke into a teasing smile. "Your eyes have the look of those women who go to Africa and devote their lives to studying lions or gorillas." He looked back up at Morning. "Or some other wild animal."

She laughed.

DeThanatos laughed too, for Morning's benefit.

"You're right," she said, watching Morning accelerate his climb toward the platform. "I'm fascinated by my subject."

"But there's more than burning curiosity," he added, resuming a serious tone. "There's also a hunger in your eyes."

"Are you saying I'm a vampire?"

"Of a sort. You're a psychic vampire. You feed on people's stories."

Portia stared at him, not sure if he meant it as an insult or a compliment. Most guys she could talk circles around. This one was different. But she wasn't sure how.

"Hey," he added with a casual shrug, "it takes one to know one."

"Oh, you're a psychic vampire too?"

"Yes and no. In truth, I'm just a plain old people person."

She scoffed at the funny sound of it. " 'A people person.' If you want to bring it to the twenty-first century, maybe you should try 'a peep's peep.' "

He shook his head. "No, I prefer a people person."

His stubbornness impressed her. Even if he was a guy on the make, at least he wasn't twisting into a pretzel to please her. "How many times a day do people tell you you're weird?"

He grinned. "None." It was the most honest thing he'd said yet. "But I'll admit, I'm old-fashioned. I mean, if I change my ways to impress you, you might think I want something."

Her insides jumped as his clairvoyance struck twice. This guy was more than a switch-hitter, he had a corked bat. She started to speak but was interrupted by Morning's shout.

"Let's do it!" Back on the platform, Morning was ready to go. This time he didn't touch the wooden disc for good luck. He didn't need it. Watching Portia flirt with the tall stranger had charged him with all the motivation he needed. He was going to blow both of them away with his performance.

As the director shouted orders, DeThanatos walked away.

It caught Portia by surprise. "Aren't you going to watch the shot?"

He kept moving toward the exit. "No. I like to see things when they're all wrapped up, neat and tidy." He tossed her a friendly smile, and sauntered out of the soundstage.

She shook her head. "Preppies. They can be so twisted." Her words contradicted the squishy feeling in her stomach. She hoped to see him again. Brushing the thought aside, she raised her camera and zoomed up to Morning at the top of the set.

The take was perfect. After Morning uttered his last line, the studio burst into cheers and applause. His only disappointment was that the blond invader had disappeared.

During all the backslapping and congratulations from Birnam, the director, Penny, and the crew, Morning looked for Portia. He spotted her at the row of tables where dinner had been served earlier. She was picking at a salad. After the celebration died down he walked over. Trying to look unaffected by his triumph, he pulled out his cell phone, turned it back on, and pocketed it as he joined her. "Glad it's over? Or do you think I can do better?"

She flashed a smile. "No, that was incredible!"

"You sure?" he asked with a sneer. "I could do another take if you'd like more hang time with blondie-boy."

Her face fell. "Blondie-boy?"

"Yeah. Who was that guy?"

She pulled back, trying to figure him. For someone

whose circulatory system was supposed to be churning with her hopes, desires, and the beat of a heart surrendered to love, he had a rude way of showing it. "I didn't get his name. Besides, I thought we decided to be friends."

"Right," he said, then air-quoted with his index fingers. " 'Friends.' "

She gawked, waiting for him to realize what he'd just done. He was oblivious. Birnam was right. He had no clue what had happened in the desert. She just wished his heart were as obedient as his fingers.

Morning's cell phone bleeped, signaling a message.

Portia was glad for the excuse to get away. "Hey, that's probably from Tiger Woods, crowning you the new king of commercials." She turned and walked off. She also wanted to go outside and grab a shot of the spot where he had been reduced to ashes and reborn as the blood brother she wasn't sure she wanted.

Watching her go, he flipped open his phone and got his voice mail. There was a message from the fireman. He listened with irritation as the old man explained that he was running into resistance from the fire department's brass. While they loved the idea of having Morning join the FDNY, waiving the minimum age requirement for one sixteen-year-old might lead to a flood of lawsuits by other sixteen-year-olds wanting equal treatment. As the fireman promised to keep working on it, Morning saw Birnam coming toward him. He shut the phone and stuffed it in his pocket.

Birnam joined him at the food table. For a long moment they watched the crew break the set apart like a giant green iceberg. Birnam ended the silence. "I know I said this was the last thing you had to do. But before you go back to

New York, would you like to see the final product? We'll be debuting it in Leaguer Mountain tomorrow night. It would be great if you were there."

Before the shoot, Morning had planned to don a disguise, catch a flight back to New York, hide out at St. Giles, and start studying for the entrance exam to the Fire Academy. But there was no point in studying for an exam they might never let him take. "Who's going to be there?"

"Thousands of Leaguers," Birnam said. "And your graduating class."

Morning flashed back to the cheer the crew had given him minutes before. It was a cheer his class had denied him. The runt of the litter would be returning as a conquering hero. "Okay," he said. "I'll go."

Birnam nodded with pleasure. "Good. That way we can all thank you for leading us out of the *selva obscura,* to the very edge of the dark wood."

After Birnam walked away, a wave of bone-deep exhaustion engulfed Morning. He sagged with fatigue as a scent slithered into his consciousness. The smell pulled him to the source.

A platter on the table held a decimated roast beef. The hunk of tattered meat sat in a puddle of greasy blood. He pushed the meat aside, lifted the platter, and drank. Even polluted with fat, it was the best thing he'd tasted in a long time.

36

To the Mountain

After returning to Ducats, Morning tumbled into the abyss of sleep. He wouldn't climb back out until the next afternoon.

Portia had a fitful night of sleep, followed by a morning at the hotel pool where she continued her mental tossing and turning. She was mystified by the changes in Morning since reviving him with her blood. If her hopes and desires were supposed to be running in his veins, why were they coming out so twisted? Where was the heart that Birnam said would be surrendered to love? If Morning was supposed to be a reflection of her personality, at least for a couple of days, why had he become conceited, jealous, and hard-edged? Was that who *she* was? Or was that who she'd be if she were a guy?

But the biggest change she noticed was in his eyes. She used to take pleasure in catching his averted glances. Now she found herself avoiding eyes that were harsh and accusatory, like she had done something wrong.

The more his personality change gnawed at her, the more the dreadful truth emerged. The fun, good-natured vampire next door she thought she was falling for had become like so many other guys: predictable, egocentric pillars of testosterone. Once upon a time, he had shape-shifted into a fog, a tree, a dolphin, a pigeon, a puppy, and a wolf. Now he had transformed into just another jerk.

Fortunately, Portia was back to *Assume the worst.*

Unfortunately, Morning wasn't the only one running through her mind. Another guy kept popping into view: the stranger she'd met in the studio. While Morning slogged through her mental labyrinth like a spent marathoner, the stranger flashed like a sprinter. And there was no doubt which one made her heart beat faster.

But Portia knew herself well enough to know where the intriguing stranger fit in the astrology of guys. He was the eye candy, the talk taffy, that made a girl feel good when there were troubles with guy number one. It didn't make him guy number two. He was more like cough syrup. Good to get you through a troubled night, but not something you wanted to swig every day.

Besides, she kept reminding herself, there were far more important things to obsess about than Morning and yesterday's crush. She had to come up with a new film title. After Morning almost lost it in his dressing room, and then got so cocksure and abusive after the blood transfusion, the whole Jackie Robinson–sainthood thing didn't fly. It was more like *Dr. Jekyll and Mr. Hyde.* Several new titles came to mind. *A Tale of Two Mornings. Morning McCobb: Creature of the Lite or Creature of the Night?* Or if she wanted to go with an autobiographical slant, *How I Juiced the Jackie Robinson of the Vampire League into Barry Bonds.*

While Morning slept, and Portia vacillated between guy angst and title brainstorming, Penny had a long breakfast meeting with Birnam. After telling her that Morning's role as the first Leaguer ambassador was almost over, Birnam congratulated Penny on a job well done and gave her a fat bonus. Then he filled her in on the next volume of the IVL playbook. Lastly, they went over the talking points she needed to cover when she met the media mob still gathered outside Ducats Hotel and Casino.

In the last twenty-four hours, the news dealers who supplied celebrity junkies with their daily dose of gossip had grown anxious without a new headline on Morning. To fill the void a rumor had been started: Morning had been destroyed by a vampire slayer. Penny's job, as Birnam made clear, was to assure the public that Morning was safe and sound, and would be making an important announcement that evening during a commercial break on America's hottest new TV show, *Based on an Urban Legend*.

After Penny held the news conference, and ducked a barrage of questions, Birnam offered her a full-time position with the IVL as they continued their march toward Worldwide Out Day. She appreciated his lucrative offer, and told him that handling the first outed vampire had been the experience of a lifetime.

"However," she said candidly, "while I can handle being around one or two vampires, being surrounded by them every day would push my comfort zone."

"How about giving it a try for one night?" Birnam asked. He continued off her puzzled look. "Tonight, when we air the commercial for IVLeague.us, and launch the website, we're throwing a huge party. You and Portia should be there."

She arched an eyebrow. "And where is there?"

He grinned. "You don't want to know. But I'll fly you and Portia to the party, then back to Vegas tonight."

Late that afternoon, Birnam piloted his helicopter toward a crimson sun sinking in the White Mountains of California. Morning sat in the copilot's seat. Penny and Portia sat behind them. They both wore blindfolds.

Portia was dying to sneak a peek to see what they were flying over, but she suppressed the urge. It wasn't because she had promised her mother not to cheat, it was because she had asked herself, *What would Christiane do?* The answer was obvious. If by not peeking you earned trust points with the president of the IVL, and became the first Lifer to see the secret school where Leaguer vampires were trained, you didn't peek or even open your eyes under the blindfold.

Not cheating benefited her in one other way. She didn't have to stare at the back of Morning's head and try to imagine what he was thinking. The irony didn't escape her. After turning him into a blood twin, his mind had become unreadable, a foggy mirror. But there was reason for hope. A day had passed since he had gone from ash to a-hole. Maybe his DNA would start reasserting itself and he'd go back to being the old Morning.

Her stomach lurched as the helicopter made a sharp descent. After the chopper landed, Birnam told them to remove their blindfolds.

Portia and Penny found themselves on the dusty street of a ghost town, in the deep shadow of a mountain. Half of the rickety buildings clung to the rocky mountainside. The most unusual sight was the greenish glow of solar lights puncturing the dusk.

As they exited the chopper, Birnam told Morning to grab their guests' garment bag and asked the ladies to follow him.

Morning grumbled as he hauled the bag out of the back. He didn't like being reduced to a bellhop, and he didn't understand why someone wasn't there to meet them. The oversight heightened the agitated mood he'd been in since waking up that afternoon. He didn't know if it was the jangles that sometimes came from too much sleep, or some kind of hangover from roast-beef blood, but he felt like nails ran through his veins. Following the trio, he carried the bag into a dilapidated hotel jutting from the mountainside.

The hotel lobby was carpeted with wall-to-wall dust. It softened the thud of their footsteps. The only light came from a flickering chandelier that looked more like a giant firefly caught in a ceiling of cobwebs.

"Welcome to Leaguer Mountain," Birnam announced.

From the second they entered, Portia sensed her mother's rising hackles. She tried to defuse them. "Hey, if you've seen one party house, you've seen 'em all."

Birnam's easy laughter filled the room. It even got a chuckle from Morning. Portia gave him a relieved look. So there was *one* good thing about having a blood double: he was a sucker for your jokes.

Birnam raised a remote and hit a button. The hotel desk, and the wall behind it, swung open, revealing a modern lobby, brightly lit and sparkling with polished stone. "The Leaguer Mountain Guesthouse," he announced.

Penny's doubts melted away—at least the ones about Birnam's sense of style.

Birnam led them into the lobby.

Morning noticed that the guest room doors seemed to

lead deeper into the mountain. But he couldn't remember anything inside the mountain that could have been the back of the guesthouse. "How long has this been here?"

"A few years." Birnam pulled a key card from his pocket. "I've been planning the interface between Leaguers and Lifers for some time."

As Birnam handed Penny the key card, Portia asked the question she'd been sitting on since they'd taken off. "Can I bring my Handycam to the launch party?"

"Absolutely," Birnam replied. "On one condition."

"What?"

"I keep all the footage until after Worldwide Out Day."

"How long will that be?" Portia asked.

"If all goes well, in a month or two."

She nodded happily. "Deal."

Morning handed Portia the garment bag, along with his take on Birnam's condition. "We can't have you outing any Leaguers before Worldwide Out Day. Until the big day is a slam dunk, this experiment only has one guinea pig," he said, doing a one-digit air-quote on "guinea pig." "And that's me."

Birnam tried to soften the testy remark. "It's a crude way of putting it, but that's about right." Then he gave his guests a welcoming smile. "Someone will come and fetch you at eight."

As Birnam and Morning left, Portia realized she hadn't gotten any close-up footage of his personality change from sweet kid to schmuck-stick. She added it to her shot list for the night.

Birnam and Morning made their way through the ghost town's saloon, entered Leaguer Mountain through the rock door at the back of the stage, and moved along the tunnel toward the Academy.

"Is coming back here putting you in a bad mood?" Birnam asked.

"I don't know," Morning answered as he searched for why he felt so on edge. "Maybe it's like you said, it's uncharted territory, and everything's getting more intense."

Birnam was tempted to tell him that being caught in the riptide of Portia's blood and his own DNA trying to reassert itself might have something to do with it. But the night was too big to risk sabotaging it by undercutting Morning's confidence with the knowledge that he was running on Portia fuel.

Morning finally got to the question that had been bugging him since they boarded the chopper in Vegas. "Why did you invite them?"

"They've both made a huge contribution to your success."

"And they got paid for it."

Birnam answered his truculence with a patient smile. "Portia hasn't made a dime."

"She's getting to shoot a film that's going to make her famous."

"Isn't there enough room in the spotlight for both of you?"

"I'm not jealous of her, if that's what you mean."

"You're certain of that?"

Morning's chest tightened. He wondered if Birnam had been eavesdropping outside the dressing room when he'd almost attacked Portia. "Look, Mr. Birnam, it's like you said. I hovered over the well, I've bitten the bloodlust bullet, and I'm over it. I'm over her."

They entered the courtyard in front of the Academy's main building. Birnam stopped and placed his hands on Morning's shoulders. "I believe you. I also believe in the feelings I still hear in your voice. You want to know why I invited them? They're still part of your test—our test."

Morning stepped back, breaking from his hands. "I'm done with tests. I passed 'em to earn my diploma, and I passed 'em with Portia. I'm here to enjoy the night."

"Yes, and revel in the fact that you're this close"— Birnam held up his thumb and index finger—"to becoming the first vampire to turn back the clock and pursue his Lifer dreams. Keep that in mind as you enjoy the night."

Birnam started away, then turned around. "Oh, I almost forgot. We left your room like it was. You'll find a tuxedo. Wear it. I'll see you at the party."

37

Reunions

Birnam was right. His room hadn't been touched. Even his tattered copy of *Watchmen* still lay on the bed where he'd tossed it. The only thing that was out of place was Morning's sense of time. He'd been away less than a week, but it felt like months.

Morning stood in front of the mirror on the back of his door. He had never worn a tuxedo before. He was thankful for the instructions that came with it. Otherwise he never would have been able to figure out where to put all the studs, or to wear the cummerbund with the pleats facing up, not down.

He was dazzled by how it changed him. The jacket's padded shoulders made him bigger. The shoes' thick heels made him taller. The tux made him handsome in a way he'd never thought possible. The outfit's bold lines and crisp pleats seemed to carry into his face. His jaw was squarer. His cheekbones were higher. His nose seemed longer and stronger. It was an outfit for a superhero.

He smiled at a thought. If they refused to admit him to the Fire Academy, and let his superhero costume be a firefighter's turnout gear, then a tux would be his second choice.

The sound of voices outside his room yanked him away from the mirror. The party was beginning.

He moved to the dresser to collect his wooden charm. He scooped it up and started to slip it in his pocket. He stopped, turned it over, and stared at the blue Maltese cross with FDNY. Then he remembered the one time in the studio when he hadn't touched the wood for good luck. It had been before he nailed the perfect take. Maybe the charm wasn't so lucky after all. Maybe it was even bad luck. He tossed the wooden disc toward the bed. It skipped off the cover of *Watchmen* and landed on the bedspread.

When he stepped out of his room, an explosion of sound knocked him back on his heels. It blasted up from the thousands of Leaguers crowding the parade ground.

Birnam rose from below the edge of the walkway. Wearing a black tuxedo, he rode in the pod of a giant cherry picker. "Your chariot awaits you!" he shouted over the cheers as the pod drew level to the walkway. He swung the small door open.

Morning stepped in and Birnam began maneuvering the pod down toward the sea of adulation. The roar melded into a thundering chant for Morning. As he beamed and waved, he scanned the throng for familiar faces. He picked out several classmates, and found the lens of Portia's camera pointing up at him.

For the next hour he was mobbed by Leaguers and signed autographs until his hand cramped. He kept seeing Portia's camera thrust above the pushing crowd like the head of an electronic ostrich.

He finally caught a break from the crush when a band began blasting a song from the stage floating on Leaguer Lake. Birnam also pulled Leaguers away as he began a Q&A session in the grandstand and addressed the rumors going around about Worldwide Out Day being in the near future. He dodged the most direct questions. He wanted the airing of Morning's commercial and the simultaneous launch of IVLeague.us to be a complete surprise. The only hint was the huge screen that had been hung from the graduation platform.

Morning retreated to the row of quaffeteria stations set up on the edge of the parade ground. Reaching the Vegan Veins stand, he perked up at the sight of his old friend, Dolly.

She gave him a knuckle tap, congratulated him for his transformation from class klutz to the school's most famous graduate, and slid a Blood Lite across the counter. "The usual."

"That's another thing that's changed," he said, sliding the drink back. "I'm a recovering vegan." The phrase popped out of his mouth. He knew he'd heard it somewhere before but he couldn't place who had said it.

Dolly's ears pulled back like a curious cat's. "A recovering vegan?"

Hearing it again triggered the details. Portia had said it the first time they'd met. "Yeah, for some reason I've lost my taste for soy blood substitutes. I've gone animal."

"Well, if I had to deal with Lifers all day," Dolly said with a sardonic smile, "I'd need something stronger too."

"Hey, Morning," someone shouted.

He turned toward the voice. Rachel Capilarus, in a tight red dress, moved toward him. Watching her approach, he remembered she didn't just walk, she conquered space, and harvested hearts with every step.

261

When she vanquished the space directly in front of him, Morning's pleased expression wasn't lost on Dolly. "Okay, I'll let you two catch up." She disappeared behind the drink station.

Rachel gave him a wry smile. "Are you so famous you don't remember me?"

"No one forgets Rachel Capilarus," he said, then made a big show of looking around. "Except maybe her date."

She threw her head back with a throaty laugh.

He didn't miss the chance to check out the roof of her mouth. It was more alluring than ever.

"The truth is," she explained, "I'm dateless."

"C'mon, you're kidding."

"Nope. I'm the gorgeous cheerleader whose reign ends the day after graduation."

"But you had Dieter Auerbach wrapped around your little finger. Isn't he here?"

"Couldn't make it," she answered. "So he said. But I think he was jealous."

"Of who?"

"You, of course. For being so right."

"How was I right?"

"You predicted the future."

"I did?"

"Yep. You told him you were going to turn into a super-hero named Moth-Fire who gets his power from drinking fire and flies around the world saving Leaguers like us."

As she spoke, a vision suddenly blinded Morning. A ball of fire rushed at him. It was so real he felt the searing heat on his face. He jumped back. Then the fire was gone, replaced by Rachel's face. Her forehead was wrinkled with concern.

262

"Are you okay?" she asked.

"Yeah, fine." He shook off the lingering vision. "Believe me, I haven't turned into Moth-Fire."

"What's in a name?" she quipped. "If the rumors are true, you'll be known as the superhero who led us out of the woods."

Her words infused him with pride. Then the intoxicating effect of her praise was cut short by another vision. This one was no hallucination. A Handycam pushed toward them.

"Moth-Fire?" Portia echoed from behind her camera. "Great name for you, Morning."

He quickly took in Portia's white dress and her shiny dark hair falling in long curls over her bare shoulders. He also noticed that her high heels made her much taller. Whatever boost he had gotten from his shoes, she had doubled. He tried to chase her away with a glare. "Can't I have a moment to myself?"

Portia swung the camera to Rachel. "Hmm, you have a funny definition of 'myself.'"

Rachel gave the camera a friendly wave. "Hi, I'm Rachel Capilarus, an old friend of Morning's."

"Portia Dredful," Portia said, continuing to shoot, "a new friend of Morning's."

Rachel flashed her radiant smile for the camera. "Well, since rumor is that tonight's all about putting the old behind us and bringing in the new, he's all yours." She started away.

"Rachel," Morning protested, "wait."

She tossed a wave and moved toward the lake as the band started a new song. "Catch me later, Moth-Fire, for a dance."

When Portia swung her camera to get Morning's reaction, he pushed his hand over the lens. "What else are you gonna do to ruin my big night?"

She yanked the camera away, turned it off, and jammed her free hand on her hip. "You know what, Morning? You wouldn't be having a big night if it weren't for me."

He shot back a derisive laugh. "Talk about having it backward. If it weren't for me, you and your mother would be back in New York hanging out with alien-abducted Elvises and two-headed wrestlers."

His words stung, even though she knew it was exactly the kind of thing *she* would say. She wanted to lash out with the truth of what she'd done for him. But she didn't want to be thanked. She didn't want him thinking he owed her. She didn't want a mercy friendship. She tried to strip the anger from her voice. "Morning, ever since I visited you in the dressing room yesterday, you've been pissed at me. What did I do that was so wrong?"

His eyes bored into her. "You don't have to do anything. You just have to be you." He turned and hurried away before the throb in his gums got worse.

Portia refused to let the tightness in her throat creep any higher. *What's the point of crying,* she told herself, *when it wasn't just him insulting me, it was part of me, in him, insulting myself!* It made her want to jump up and scream, *Is there an exorcist in the house?* If she could exorcise the inner Portia out of him, she *might* get through the night.

She yanked a compact from her camera bag and checked her makeup. When she lowered the mirror, her eyes fell on a tall figure at the edge of the crowd listening to Birnam. He was a young man with wavy black hair. Something about him seemed familiar.

As she started forward for a closer look, he turned his head. The shock of recognition stopped her. It was the guy from the studio, the twisted preppie. But what was he doing here? And why did he look different?

Seeing her, DeThanatos grinned and moved closer.

Watching him glide across the ground in his tuxedo, she focused on the easier of her questions. What was different about him? As he reached her she grabbed the answer. "Yesterday you were a blond."

"True," he acknowledged. "My internship takes me to all the departments in the studio, and yesterday was hair and makeup. I did the wig myself. Not bad if it fooled you."

Her eyes widened as her first question couldn't be answered any other way. "But if you're here, that means you're a, a . . ."

DeThanatos nodded. "Yes, a Leaguer. But you fooled me as well. I had no idea you were one—"

"I'm not!" Portia blurted. "My mother and I are guests." She smiled with pride. "And the first mortals to visit Leaguer Mountain."

"I see," he said with a wry smile. Then he spread his hands in an elegant gesture. "Welcome to our closet."

"I'd hardly call it a closet."

"It is unless you're Morning McCobb. We're all in the closet until Worldwide Out Day." He leaned closer and lowered his voice. "Did you hear the rumor about the big day?"

"No, what is it?"

He glanced around to make sure no one was close. "Out Day isn't going down exactly like Birnam is selling it."

His conspiratorial tone piqued her interest. She wanted to raise her camera and start shooting, but it would probably shut him up. Without lifting the camera, she pressed the record button. At least she could get some audio. "Really?"

He waited until someone passed by. "There's a hidden agenda that's got nothing to do with kinder gentler vampires."

"What do you mean?"

DeThanatos paused again to let a laughing couple pass. "I can't talk about it here. Too many good ears in the room."

Portia brimmed with excitement. "Where can you talk about it?"

"Outside the mountain, during the broadcast of Morning's spot."

Her excitement skidded to suspicion. She thought only four people knew what was about to be aired on national television: Birnam, Morning, Penny, and herself. "How do you know about that?"

"Another rumor."

Then she remembered what he'd said about Morning's commercial in the studio. "Wait a minute, you said you wanted to see it when it was 'all wrapped up, neat and tidy.' "

"And I will," he explained. "It'll be on YouTube before midnight." He gave her a flirtatious wink. "If you want to know the real truth behind Leaguers, meet me outside during the commercial."

She had to make a decision. To trust her instincts and not go, or throw caution to the wind. *What would Christiane do?* The answer came the instant she realized the story of Morning McCobb wasn't a groundbreaking documentary anymore. It was a scoop. She might even uncover a conspiracy. "How do I get outside?"

"Same way you came in."

"We were blindfolded when we came inside," she explained.

His eyes darted toward the nearby jam of people.

She followed his look and saw a commotion in the crowd, like someone was trying to push through.

He spoke quickly. "At the front of the school, across the courtyard, there's a tunnel. Follow it to the red button, press it, and you'll be outside. See you then. Gotta fly." He hurried away toward the Academy building.

Two burly Leaguers burst through the crowd and raced after the young man. Portia tried to follow them, but heels aren't running shoes. She saw him dash and dodge through bystanders. Then his tux flattened and collapsed to the ground as a bird soared upward and disappeared in the glare of lights. When she looked back down, the two men chasing him were gone. So was the empty tuxedo.

It all happened so fast that if it hadn't been for the shocked faces of the Leaguers who witnessed it, she might have thought she imagined it. The only Leaguer she'd ever seen shape-shift, until now, was Morning. She thought it was forbidden. Obviously, the twisted preppie had his own set of rules.

She was only certain of one thing: when the time came, she was going outside. Like the Greek guy said, "Is it our chief aim in life to avoid risks?"

38

Surprise Guests

Morning plunged into the crowd enjoying the music blasting from the stage on the lake. He wanted to find Rachel and ask her to dance. But between Leaguers shaking his hand and classmates trying to make up for months of harassment in a moment of sucking up, he was still fifty yards from the dancing throng.

When he finally reached the edge of the mosh pit, he surveyed the gyrating dancers. He spotted a woman in a red dress. Her raven-black hair whipped up and down as she danced. He wasn't sure it was Rachel, and he couldn't tell if she was dancing with someone or by herself. Above the pounding music, he heard her shout with joy. A pair of dancers blocked his view.

When he found her again, he stared in horror. She was still writhing and tossing her hair, but she was engulfed in flames, an undulating column of fire. He covered his eyes and moaned. He looked again.

The fiery dancer was gone. So was the woman in the red dress.

He turned and pushed his way back through the crowd. He had to find Birnam. He wanted to know what was happening to him. Either someone had slipped him a drug, or he was going crazy, or drinking roast-beef blood had some major side effects.

He shut out people calling his name and pushed on. He felt a tap on his back. He ignored it and squeezed through several more gaps. Ten feet later, he felt the tap again, more insistent this time. "Leave me alone," he snarled.

An old voice answered. "When the pigeons take back the Williams Bird Bridge."

He spun around and came face to face with Sister Flora. He blinked and tried to shake away the sight. It had to be another hallucination. But she was still there. She grabbed his arm and pulled him into the shadow of a light tower.

"Sister, what are you doing here?"

Her crepe paper skin folded into a smile. "Can't a nun get down and party?"

He could barely form the words. "You're a Leaguer?"

"One of the first."

He still didn't believe it. "But I thought you were locked up in St. Giles praying for my soul. And when I CDed in front of you, you fainted!"

"Just keeping up appearances."

He shook his head at the craziness of it. "But why a nun?"

"Being a nun is a huge advantage."

"How?"

"I don't have to relocate every few years. A nun can look the same age for a decade or two and nobody notices."

Morning laughed and gathered her in a hug.

"And the longer I stay in one place," she said, patting his back, "the longer I can look after my boys." When they drew apart, she gave him a mischievous wink. "Who do you think found you after you were turned and got you into Leaguer Academy?"

"You?"

She nodded. "A few days after Thanksgiving, I went to the house in Staten Island to check on you, and I discovered what had happened. I called the Leaguer Rescue Squad. They swept in, took you out, and removed all evidence you'd ever been there."

"So I wouldn't be a suspect in the double murder."

"It's the least I could do, Morning. It was my fault you were there on Thanksgiving. Otherwise, you'd still be a Lifer, with Lifer dreams."

He gave her a knowing smile. "Yeah, but if Birnam's plan works out, we can all go back to our Lifer dreams." His head cocked at a sudden thought. "Wait a sec. I always thought being a nun *was* your Lifer dream. But since you're a Leaguer, it can't be. Before you were turned, what was your dream?"

"Oh, it's been so long I can't remember," she said with a dismissive laugh. "If I can keep looking after my boys, that'll be fine with me." She held him with her piercing eyes. "And nothing would make me happier than to see you become a firefighter. Or have you forgotten that?"

He squirmed under a gaze he'd seen many times. She knew more than she was telling. "What makes you say that?"

She reached into her sweater pocket and pulled out his wooden charm with the cross on it. "You left this in your room."

"Why did you go to my room?" he demanded.

She dismissed his umbrage with a smile. "That's what sisters do when they're looking after their boys." She pushed the charm toward him. "Take it."

He hesitated. "Why?"

"Because until you're eighteen, I'm your mother protector."

He laughed. "But I'll never be"—he air-quoted with double fingers—"eighteen."

"Exactly." Her eyes twinkled as she slipped the charm into the breast pocket of his tux. "There. Keep your dreams close, and you'll never lose them."

He didn't resist. There was no saying no to Sister.

"Now," she said, turning toward the wriggling mass of dancers. "I'm going to go find some old vampire to dance with."

As he watched her go, the band finished a song and the crowd roared their approval.

The lead singer's voice boomed over the mike. "We've got time for one more song, and then the real show begins. Oh, and the headmaster wanted me to make an announcement." The singer dropped into his best impression of the Academy's headmaster. "Morning McCobb, please report to the base of the graduation platform. Morning McCobb to the platform."

The crowd *oohed* in mock trepidation, and the band kicked into the first licks of another tune.

Waiting for him at the base of the platform, Birnam greeted Morning with a proud smile. "Ready for your swan song?"

"The sooner the better," Morning told him. "I thought Penny was joining us."

271

"She is." He nodded toward the spiral stairs. "I sent her ahead." He started up the stairs that wound up the tower behind the huge movie screen.

Morning followed. "I just ran into Sister Flora. Are there any more surprises I should know about before the night's over?"

"Yes," Birnam replied.

"What?"

"I want you to keep an eye on Portia."

"That's not a surprise."

Birnam stopped and turned back to Morning. "Security discovered we have a party crasher. A Loner."

"How do you know it's a Loner?"

"He CDed to escape being captured." Birnam pulled a picture from his pocket, a still from a security camera. He showed it to Morning. "That's him."

Morning recognized the handsome face. "It's blondie-boy."

"Blondie-boy?"

"He was in the studio yesterday, talking to Portia."

Birnam's face hardened. "Then he's definitely stalking her." He resumed climbing. "Why he's interested in Portia, I'm not sure. But I doubt it's for the obvious reason. He could feed on any Lifer. And what he's up to I'm not sure of either. He's spying on us, or he's got something up his sleeve."

Morning scowled. "You mean like destroying me in front of thousands of Leaguers. That would send a nice message."

Birnam kept climbing. "If he wanted to destroy you, he would have done it days ago. The important thing is for tonight to go without a hitch. That's why I want you to keep an eye on Portia."

"I can't keep an eye on her from the top of the platform. Do you want me up on the platform or down babysitting her?"

They had almost reached the top. Birnam stopped and turned back to him. "If you're not up here for the commercial's airing and the site launch, it would raise suspicion. As soon as it's over, find her and don't leave her side."

It was the last thing Morning wanted to do, but he reminded himself it was his final duty. After tonight, he was free. He gave Birnam a mock salute. "Yes, sir. Anything else I need to know about?"

Birnam answered Morning's insolence with a question. "No. Do you have anything to tell me?"

"Yeah, I keep seeing fire."

Birnam nodded. "That's a good sign."

His tossed-off response caught Morning by surprise.

"Your DNA is reasserting itself."

"What are you talking about?" Morning asked.

Birnam glanced at his watch. "You'll figure it out before the night's out." Before Morning could object, Birnam turned and bounded up the last few steps. "C'mon. It's almost time."

They joined Penny on the platform. She stood next to a large flat-screen TV. The crowd greeted the sight of Birnam and Morning with a booming cheer that echoed inside the mountain.

Morning scanned the crowd. Portia was easy to find. She had a Handycam glued to her face. Not only had Birnam made her the official chronicler of the event, she was the only one allowed to have a camera.

Birnam stepped to the edge of the platform, quieted the crowd, and let his voice thunder through the mountain. "In the end is beginning. In the beginning is end."

The words from every Leaguer commencement sparked a deafening ovation.

When the noise subsided, he continued. "Several days ago, one Leaguer ended his life of dark secrecy, stepped out of the *selva obscura,* and began his journey as the first outed vampire." He thrust out an arm. "Morning McCobb!"

The mountain erupted in another celebration.

Morning stepped forward. As he waved to a splash of red in the crowd he hoped was Rachel, the cheering ovation shook the air. He stepped back and relocated Portia.

Birnam quieted the throng. "Tonight, we're about to take another step toward Worldwide Out Day. Tonight, we launch the website that introduces us to the world— IVLeague.us!"

During the roar that followed, an avalanche of white balloons cascaded from above. Perfectly timed, the great cloud of balloons drifted past the huge movie screen flickering to life. On the screen, the last shot in a segment of *Based on an Urban Legend* faded out.

The crowd fell silent except for the steady pong of balloons being batted away from obscured eyes.

Morning squinted through the bobbing sea of balloons. He'd momentarily lost sight of Portia.

A commercial popped onto the screen. It began with a tight shot of an old-fashioned keyhole. A huge eyeball suddenly appeared in the keyhole.

The audience laughed with surprise.

Morning's voice began over the darting eyeball. "Hey, I see you out there wantin' to peep on my peeps. So,"—his hand squeezed through the keyhole with a balloon-squeaking sound effect, seemed to grab the viewers, and pull them through the keyhole—"c'mon in." Now Morning stood in front of the IVLeague.us home page. "You know me, Morning McCobb. You're in my crib now. Okay, make it website. Our website. IVLeague.us. C'mon, I'll show you around." The camera followed as he dove through an element on the website to another page.

The only one not watching the commercial was its star. Morning squinted through the darkness at the spot in the crowd where Portia had been a moment before. She was gone. It didn't make sense. This was a historic moment in the Leaguer cause and she wasn't filming it. It wasn't right. It wasn't Portia.

Then he saw a flash of white at the back of the crowd. At first he thought it was just another balloon. But it was moving too fast and willfully. It was a girl in a white dress. She was headed along the side of the school toward the courtyard, and the tunnel beyond.

His insides lurched with panic. Where was she going? If it was to the tunnel, how did she know about it? She and her mother had been blindfolded when they were brought inside. Someone must have told her. Blondie-boy's smirking face swam into view.

Morning slipped off the platform and dashed down the spiral staircase.

39

The White-fanged Monster

As Portia ran down the tunnel in her bare feet, her heart raced. Not so much from running but from the exhilaration of what waited outside. She was meeting a vampire with a dark secret about Leaguers. The fact that he was hot, and packed more sexiness in one strand of his dark hair than Morning had in his whole genome, only added to the thrill. By the time she reached the door with the red button, her fevered imagination was writing copy for the next generation of journalist-wannabes. *What would Portia do?*

She pressed the button and jumped back as the stone jerked into motion and began opening. She recognized the sound of the heavy metal hinges creaking and groaning. It was the same sound she'd heard when she and her mother had been escorted inside.

She stepped through the opening and onto the stage of the saloon. Like the old hotel, the saloon was dimly lit by weak solar lights hidden in cobweb-draped chandeliers.

The moonlight slanting through the broken front window and the doorway joined the effort to push back the looming shadows. Half a swinging door in the entryway cast a long shadow across the floor.

She reached into her camera bag and screwed a low-light lens on her Handycam. "Hello," she called.

The only answer was the ringing clunk of the stone door shutting behind her. She looked over her shoulder. There was no red button on her side. But this was no time to worry about how to get back in. She had a scoop to get.

She moved down the stairs at the front of the stage and stood under one of the chandeliers. "Hello." She felt a puff of air stir the hair lying on her shoulders. She swatted at it, thinking it was some kind of flying creature. Her hand collided with something solid. She gasped and jumped away.

DeThanatos stood behind her. He now wore a tattered buckskin jacket. Its leather fringe had a bad case of mange. His ripped jeans looked like they'd been stonewashed by a rockslide.

"You scared me."

He flashed his charming smile. "So soon?"

His perfect white teeth made her feel like a moth drawn to the flame. She cleared her throat. "What happened to your tuxedo?"

He raised his graceful hands to indicate their surroundings. "When in Rome."

"Okay, you're in cowboy Rome," she acknowledged, "but you're also in Leaguer Rome." She pointed at the V of bare, muscular chest exposed by his jacket. "So where's your Epidex?"

"I don't like Epidex. I'm all natural."

She let out a nervous laugh. "If you're so natural, why wear any clothes at all?"

"For your benefit."

"For my benefit?"

He smiled again and undid the jacket's top button. "Would you like this interview with a vampire to be PG-13 or NC-17?"

"Okay, okay," she jumped in, waving him to stop. "I didn't come out here to play strip poker."

His eyes never left her. "Are you sure?"

"Yes," she said a little too firmly. "I'm sure." She watched his eyes slowly travel down her body. They felt like two fingers tracing down her front.

His gaze settled on the camera hanging from her hand. "Then why haven't you started filming?"

"Good point." She brought the camera up so forcefully she almost clocked herself. She laughed away her clumsiness and fumbled the flip-out screen open. "So, what's your name?"

DeThanatos hesitated. He didn't like giving his name to Lifers. But if his fellow Loners were to know who led Morning McCobb to bloodlust and destroyed the Leaguer cause, a little publicity was necessary. "My name is DeThanatos."

She framed a shot and hit the record button. "What kind of name is DeThanatos?"

His gray eyes fixed on her lens. "A very old one."

"So, Mr. DeThanatos, you wanted to tell me about the hidden agenda of Worldwide Out Day."

"Yes." He glanced toward the stage. "But it would be much better if someone else showed you the truth."

The clunk of the stone door spun her around. "Damn."

The door was opening again. When she turned back, DeThanatos was gone. She whispered into the shadows. "Where are you?"

The only sound was the groaning door.

She slapped the flip-out screen shut and turned her camera off.

Morning squeezed through the door and ran to the front of the stage. "What are you doing out here?"

Portia shrugged. "I wanted some fresh air."

"How did you know the way out?"

"A little bird told me."

He jumped off the stage. His feet thudded on the floor and kicked up a cloud of dust. "You're lying!"

She turned away, smiling at the realization that her answer about a bird had some truth to it. Then she did lie. "I peeked under my blindfold, okay?"

"What kind of filmmaker comes outside during the biggest event of the night?"

"A dizzy filmmaker. I felt sick. I told you, I needed some air."

He stepped closer. "You're dizzy all right—dizzy for a guy."

She met his accusing eyes. "So what," she said defiantly. "He won't be the first Leaguer I'm into. I can handle it."

"He's not a Leaguer. He's a Loner."

A chill skittered down her neck. Then she realized what he was up to. "Now *you're* lying."

"We don't know who he is, but he's *not* a Leaguer. And he'd think nothing of draining you like a six-ounce Coke."

"I don't believe you."

He threw up his hands. "Why would I lie to you about something like that?"

"Because you're jealous!" she spit back. "If he wanted to chug me, he would have done it by now!"

Her revelation put him on his heels. He tried to probe the darkest corners of the saloon. "He's here, isn't he?" His eyes shot to the floor. Footprints cut through the carpet of dust and disappeared behind the bar. He whispered sharply, "We gotta go inside, *now*."

She crossed her arms and didn't bother to lower her voice. "I'm not done with my interview. He was about to tell me some dark truth about Worldwide Out Day. He said you could tell me too. If you tell me, I'll go inside."

Morning stared in bewilderment. "There's no dark truth. Don't you get it? He made it up to get you out here!"

Before she could accuse him of lying again, they heard a skitter near the door.

The tail of a retreating rodent was all Morning glimpsed before it vanished outside. They both jumped as something hissed above them. He glanced up and saw the rain of dust coming through the chandelier. The dust sprinklers had been activated.

"Your interview's over," he said. "Blondie-boy just left the building."

She stuffed her camera in her bag to protect it from the showering dust. "How do you know?"

"Motion detectors. Leaguers coming in and out of the mountain cover their tracks."

She moved through the billowing dust, banged through the one swinging door in the entranceway, and called out. "DeThanatos!"

Morning followed her onto the boardwalk in front of the saloon. "We have to go back inside." He grabbed her arm.

She jerked it away. "You go." She shook the dust off her like an angry dog and called again. "DeThanatos!"

Across the moonlit street, standing in the inky shadow of a doorway, DeThanatos watched, and waited.

Morning fought the urge to grab Portia and haul her inside. He could be stronger than her, much stronger. But for some reason the Loner hadn't struck. He still had time to reason with her. "Is that his name?"

"Yeah, that's as far as I got before you butted in."

"Do you have any idea what you're doing?"

She spun on him with flashing eyes. "Do I have any idea what *I'm* doing? Oh, that's funny! You're the one that doesn't have a clue what you're doing 'cause you're not *you* anymore!"

He blinked away the dust in his eyes. "What's that mean?"

"You're half me!"

His head tilted with confusion. "Huh?"

She dropped into an old chair on the boardwalk and dumped her camera bag beside it. She didn't want to tell him, but now it was out. "Didn't you wonder why you ran into the desert, then came back as a cocky actor and the supercool spokesman they're watching in there now? Didn't you wonder why you started air-quoting with single fingers? What do you think happened out there?"

He heard her words but couldn't see her. Another vision had invaded his mind. A matrix of smoldering ash, in the shape of a body. It seemed to be held up by nothing but fiery stitches. Then the threads of flame frayed into smoke, and the matrix collapsed on itself. His voice rasped as dry as the vision. "Fire and ash."

"That's right! And whose blood do you think revived you?"

Portia's dusty face loomed back into view. "Yours?"

She popped up from the chair. "Yeah, *my* blood!" She

ignored his stupefied expression and paced. "And then Birnam fed me a crock about how, with my blood in you, your veins would run with my hopes and desires. But here's the kicker. He told me we'd share the beat of a heart surrendered to love. Talk about BS!" She stopped in front of him. "But Birnam got it half right. Your heart surrendered, all right." She poked him in the chest with each word. "To selfishness, resentment, and envy!"

The last word struck like a knife. He wanted her to pull it out, take it back. "No," he whispered. "Why would I envy you?"

"Because I've got something you don't." She threw an arm toward the moon shadows. "You're not jealous of some guy. You're jealous of me—of my future! I bet you're jealous of *anyone* who's gonna get past sixteen!"

His knees buckled. He dropped in the chair with a plea. "Please don't say that."

But something had broken in her. A dam of anger and hurt that could only be mended by washing him away in the flood. "It's true! The curtain's coming down on your dream and you can't stand that it's rising on mine. My dream! Of making a great film, of telling the incredible story of Leaguers."

Morning sagged. His chin fell to his chest.

She stood over him, not letting up. "You had your day. You caught your big moment. And tomorrow you're going back to New York to maybe become a firefighter, or maybe not. But your ride to the top is over." She thumbed her chest. "My ride is only beginning!"

A tear dropped from Morning's hidden face, flickered in the moonlight, and splattered in the dust.

She felt a pang of sympathy for him but choked it back.

Now they were even. Both their hearts had surrendered to heartbreak.

She turned her back on him and looked down the street of dust and moon shadow. Her rage was spent, folded into the current of a greater river: her future. Her insides quaked with the thrill of tomorrow.

"Morning," she finally said quietly, "I never meant to ruin your big night. If I have, I'm sorry. But right now, I want you to go away before you ruin mine."

He lifted his head. His tears had dried in pale tracks on his cheeks. The only thing that caught the moonlight were his shining eyes, and the glistening daggers of two perfect fangs.

40

Bloodlust

Across the street, DeThanatos's face lifted into a smile as he watched Morning silently rise from the chair. Then he watched the vampire leap for Portia. His first attempt to sink his fangs missed, and the screaming and the struggle began.

DeThanatos shook his head with a low chuckle. The first swill and kill was always a clumsy affair. It took dozens of victims before a vampire perfected the three Ps: "pounce, pierce, and pacify."

Morning was still working on his pounce. The two figures, locked in a dance of flailing arms and kicking legs, stumbled into the street. They spun, tripped, hit the ground, and broke apart in a cloud of dust. Portia yanked up her dress, jumped to her feet, and tried to run. Morning leaped after her, grabbed her arm, and pulled her toward him. She slammed her free arm against his chest, trying to fight off his embrace.

DeThanatos heard the rip of fabric and saw the flap of cloth drop like a lolling tongue from Morning's jacket. Something ejected from it, as if the fabric tongue had spit out an unwanted candy. Then the object was lost in the shuffle of feet.

Morning shoved Portia against a hitching rail, caught her swatting arms, and pinned her against the crosspiece. She leaned back, trying to shift her weight and knee him in the crotch. But he was too quick. He plunged his fangs into her neck.

Her scream parted DeThanatos's lips, revealing his fangs. They dug into his lower lip, drawing beads of blood. DeThanatos never liked to watch. But seeing Morning drink the poison that would kill the Leaguer cause was worth the exception.

For Morning, it was more than drinking. More than pulling a warm liquid in and swallowing. It was swimming through a slipstream of sensation. There was the touch of fluid velvet caressing his lips, mouth, and throat. There was the sound of her blood coursing into him like a swollen river, and the double thud of her heart concussing like unseen fireworks.

Of all the sensations, nothing compared to the taste. It was spiced with euphoric flavors—chocolate, berries, cinnamon, caramel. They exploded on his tongue and swirled through his head. But the strongest flavor was one he'd long forgotten. It detonated in his mouth and shot tremors through his body. There was no describing it, only its effect. It shook his bones with excitement. It flooded him with hope. It pitched him into the confluence where blood and dream become one. It was the ultimate reward of bloodlust. A plunge into the river of delirious youth.

As he cavorted in the forbidden well and swilled the essence of mortal beings, an image intruded. Portia's face loomed in front of him. In his mind, he turned away, but wherever he turned her image waited, fixing him with dark eyes. Then there was a flash of white; he felt her stinging slap on his cheek. It was so real his eyes flew open and he yanked his fangs out of her neck.

He immediately realized it was just a vision, another memory returning from the desert. Portia's real face was right in front of him. Her eyes were unfocused, limpid, her skin pale and iridescent in the moonlight. He skimmed down the white road of her neck and found the double wound. All he wanted was to leap back into the river, to plunge his cooling fangs back into the hot lava still coursing through her.

She moaned. Her foot jerked like a dreaming dog's. It kicked something in the dust. The object slid into Morning's view. He thought nothing of it, and bent toward her neck.

But as his fangs sought her wound, the object caught his eye again. He froze. It looked familiar. He tilted his head quizzically. Then came the slap of recognition. The wafer of wood—the Maltese cross—the good-luck charm Sister had found in his room and tucked in his pocket.

He tried to look away and dive back into the wound. But the cross stared up at him like a four-pronged eye: a silent accuser.

Then everything slowed. A drop of blood fell away from his lips. He watched it tumble down. It hit the wafer of wood, leaving a crimson splatter on the blue cross.

The jarring combination paralyzed him. His memory was not so easily stilled. Images loomed into view. The cover of *Watchmen*: the arrow of blood on the eye of a smile button. The first panel: the yellow smile button, the sign of the first murdered masked hero—the Comedian.

He blinked in shock. The smile button was gone, replaced by the blood-spattered cross in the dust.

He struggled to clear his mind, but a new wave of images crashed through him: firefighters crawling over the jagged ruins at Ground Zero—the North Tower collapsing in a devouring gray spider of dust—the ashen web of his body crumbling in the desert—the flash of a vampire's fangs coming at him—the old fireman beckoning him to the fire table—Portia's fist squeezing out a stream of blood—the blood plunging toward a pile of ash—blood spilling over the Maltese cross.

With eyes shut tight, he violently shook his head, trying to free himself from the chaos. He yearned to open his eyes and discover everything had been a nightmare. He opened them and saw the spackle of blood across Portia's neck. And the wound. It was no nightmare. He had succumbed. Her eyes were more limpid and lifeless than before. He held a finger to her neck. She had a pulse. Faint, but she was still alive.

He scooped her up, carried her back to the boardwalk. He set her down in the chair and dashed inside. He had to find Birnam.

Across the street, DeThanatos watched the flapping saloon door with burning disdain. Then his gray eyes shifted to Portia. "I hate leftovers."

41

Negotiation

Having set off the sprinklers again, Morning dashed through the fog of dust. As he jumped onto the stage, he heard the stone door opening.

A moment later, Birnam came out and saw the blood and dust caked on Morning's mouth. Penny emerged behind him. Seeing Morning, she gasped and pushed past him.

He tried to stop her. "Please, don't—"

"Let her go," Birnam ordered.

Morning released her arm. Penny rushed down to the saloon floor. As she frantically searched for her daughter in the swirling haze, Birnam raised an arm and stretched his fingers toward her. She jerked to a stop next to a table, her arms fell to her sides. Her eyes stared blankly ahead.

Morning gaped in amazement.

Birnam lowered his arm. "Close her eyes so they don't fill with dust." Morning sleeve-wiped his mouth, moved down to Penny, and did as he was told. Birnam walked to the edge of the stage. "Some Leaguers retain the old powers," he explained. Morning felt his condemning eyes. "And some Leaguers can't restrain the old desires."

"I know," he blurted, "but she's still alive! We have to save her!"

"Where is she?"

He rushed toward the door. Birnam followed.

Morning escaped the cloud of dust billowing onto the boardwalk. He stared at the chair. Empty. "She's gone!"

Birnam scanned the street. The bright moon hung high in the sky. "Why did you two leave the mountain?"

"I followed her," Morning tried to explain, unable to hide the panic in his voice. "She was planning to meet the Loner. His name is DeThanatos."

Birnam stiffened, then let out a sigh of resignation. "Ikor DeThanatos. I should have known."

"You know him?"

As Birnam stared into the middle distance, his face pinched with concern. "We've never met. He's the only Loner who refused to sign the peace agreement at the end of World War V."

"I don't care what he did or didn't sign. He's got Portia!"

"Yes." Birnam nodded. "Which means she's still alive."

Morning sucked in air and hope. "Really?"

"Loners are predictable that way. Empties get left where they lie. Unfinished vessels get saved for later."

A pickup truck followed a two-lane highway snaking through low mountains.

DeThanatos steered the pickup he'd stolen from one of the partygoers who had returned to Leaguer Mountain. He still wore his ragged cowboy gear. Portia, pale as ash and held up by a seat belt, jostled in the passenger seat.

Her eyes fluttered open. She tried to turn her head, but she didn't have the strength. Her neck throbbed from the wound, now surrounded by an ugly bruise. In her semiconscious state, all she could make out was the pool of headlights and the road sliding through it. Her mouth was parched, her lips felt cracked. "Where am I?" she rasped.

"In a safe place."

She recognized the young man's voice. "What happened?"

"Morning tried to kill you."

The memory flooded back. She exhaled sharply. She felt like someone had punched her in the chest.

DeThanatos gave her a moment to recover. "That's the secret I wanted to tell you. In the end, Leaguers are no different than Loners. But Morning did a pretty good job of proving that."

More of the night came back to her. "And you're a Loner."

"Yes, I don't live a lie."

"Are you going to kill me?"

He chuckled. "No, I'm trying to protect you."

"From whom?"

"From Morning, Birnam, and any Leaguer who wants to cover up Morning's little deviation from the grand plan."

Portia winced with pain and confusion. "Why would they want me dead?"

"You just became the proof that the great Morning McCobb isn't who he says he is. That the Leaguer Way is a farce. And that a 'harmless vampire' is the most creative lie since 'wardrobe malfunction.' "

After Morning's attack she couldn't disagree. And DeThanatos was protecting her. At least for now. "Where are we going?"

"To a sacred place. To a place that if they send Morning or anyone else after you, we can destroy them."

She braced herself against the pain and turned her face enough to see him. "You want me to kill Morning?"

"You may not have a choice." He lifted a bottle off the seat, used his mouth to break the seal on the top, and put it in her hand. "Drink it. It'll help you regain your strength."

In the dim glow of the cab she recognized the label of an energy drink. She couldn't get the lid off fast enough.

Morning ran down the moonlit street. He shut his eyes and blocked out all sensation as he laser-focused on a great horned owl.

He felt a sharp jerk and almost fell backward as a force yanked him to a stop. He spun around. Birnam stood in the middle of the street, twenty yards away, one arm raised. As Birnam lowered his arm, Morning struggled to move but couldn't budge. He felt like he was wedged in a fissure of invisible stone. His eyes blinked. At least he wasn't as immobile as Penny. He still had vision and voice. "Let me go!"

Birnam ambled toward him. "No."

"He's going to kill her!"

"You should have thought of that before you left her outside for the taking." Birnam stopped in front of him.

"Please," Morning pleaded. "I have to try and save her."

"I'm afraid not. It's a trap to destroy you."

"I don't care about me!"

"I do." Birnam's brows slid upward. "And you've already fallen for one trap by coming outside."

"You told me to keep an eye on Portia!" he protested. "That's why I followed her!"

"Yes." Birnam's voice was calm, matter of fact. "You also followed your jealousy. That's what DeThanatos wanted. Then he stood by and watched you surrender to the trilogy of bloodlust: envy, vengeance, and a long drink from the forbidden well."

Morning stared fiercely back. "You sound like you knew this would happen."

"I had my worries."

"Then why weren't you watching me? You could have stopped it!"

Birnam nodded. "Yes, I could have. But I was watching the launch of IVLeague.us." A smile prowled across his lips. "The commercial was brilliant. Within five minutes the website got millions of hits."

"I don't give a rip about your stupid website!"

Birnam's smile vanished. "And I can't watch every Leaguer all the time. Especially after Worldwide Out Day."

Morning stared in stunned disbelief. "You can't go through with it, not after what happened."

"Just because you failed doesn't mean everyone else will."

"But you said I was the guinea pig, I was going into uncharted territory!" His voice cracked with emotion. "I just showed you where the path out of the dark wood leads. Right back into it!"

Birnam's eyes were as cold and hard as diamonds.

"Nothing will stop our march out of the *selva obscura*. Not even a little stumble by our first ambassador."

"A stumble? I almost killed her!" Morning raged.

"Okay," Birnam conceded. "Let's call it a colossal blunder."

Morning tried to thrust an arm toward the saloon, but it remained welded to his side. "You can't hide it from Penny!"

"Yes, I can."

"How? By having a Leaguer Rescue Squad make her disappear like they did with me at the house where the couple got murdered?"

"The old powers are more subtle than that."

Morning erupted in a scornful laugh. "Oh, so you'll kiss her like Superman kissed Lois Lane, and she'll forget she ever had a daughter, or had anything to do with me?"

"You're getting warmer."

Morning seethed with revulsion. He wanted to spit in Birnam's face. He wasn't the war hero from the Leaguer history books, or the great reformer he pretended to be. He was a dictator who would squash anyone who got in his way. "And what about me?" he demanded.

Birnam held him with a sardonic smile. "I don't plan on kissing you, if that's what you mean."

The crevasse of stone Morning felt trapped in squeezed tighter. "You can't risk your vampire poster boy turning Worldwide Out Day into Worldwide Truth Day, so you have to destroy me. Isn't that right?" Birnam's icy stare was the only answer he needed. Then a crazy thought came to him. His destruction was worth something; he could barter with it. "Fine," he declared. "After what I've done, I deserve whatever end you're planning. But if you're so sure

DeThanatos will destroy me, then let him do the job. Let me try and save her."

Birnam's head pulled back, like a startled turtle's. "Intriguing idea. But what if you survive?"

"Then I won't blow the whistle. I'll pretend I'm still the bloodlust virgin everyone wants me to be." He didn't blink or break from Birnam's intense gaze. "For you and your cause it's a win-win. I die and become the Leaguers' first martyr, or I live and you get your poster boy back."

Birnam stepped back and raised an arm.

Morning shut his eyes and braced for whatever was coming.

Flicking his fingers, Birnam released the binding thrall.

As the invisible shackles fell away, Morning's lungs filled with air.

"You'll find DeThanatos in the Mother Forest," Birnam said.

"Why there?"

"It's the Loners' favorite picnic ground. And the best place for a vampire to die."

Morning gazed at Birnam for a last second. He wanted to thank him and curse him. But there was no time for either. He turned and raced down the dusty street.

A moment later, Birnam watched Morning's tuxedo drop to the ground. A great horned owl rose toward the moon.

When Birnam stepped back onto the boardwalk, he felt older than his seven hundred and eighty-three years. Emancipating the world from its fear of vampires was a grueling mission. Especially when it required brushing a few things under the rug.

Inside, he joined Penny, still standing next to a table

like a dust-covered statue. He pulled out a handkerchief and cleaned off two chairs. Pushing one behind her, he thralled her into it, then slid her to the table. He sat in the other chair and gently brushed the dust off her face. He answered her blank expression with a bittersweet smile. "When the children spread their wings and leave the nest, all we can do is wait, and hope for their return."

He swept a sleeve across the table, pulled out a deck of cards, and began a game of solitaire.

THE LEGEND OF THE
MOTHER FOREST

We share our creation legend as an act of goodwill, and as the wind of tongues have shaped it over the eons.

Like yours, our earliest ancestors were more ape than human. And like the many early hominids shouldering their way toward modern man, our forebearers lived in trees. Not the trees of Africa, Asia, or Europe. Our Mother Forest was in the western part of North America. The trees provided our forefathers with protection from dangerous creatures, pointed sticks to hunt with, and nuts and bark to eat.

But then came the Great Dryness. The forests were shriveled by heat, ravaged by fire, and overrun by scrubland and desert. All the clans of tree people fought bloody wars to determine who would live in the dwindling forests, and who would be forced into the open, dangerous scrubland. During the long conflict, our clan became known as the Old Ones because the trees of our Mother Forest grew so withered and gnarled. The Old Ones defended our sacred forest against all enemies, and began a practice that no one had ever seen before. While the other clans and creatures drank the blood and ate the flesh of their conquered enemies, the Old Ones only drank the blood, leaving the drained body on the battlefield to strike fear in their enemies' hearts.

NEXT PAGE

In time, the Old Ones grew so powerful they were the only human clan left in the land. But the Great Dryness continued. With fewer creatures to satisfy their bloodthirst, the Old Ones ate more and more of the bark of their ancient trees. The bark began to give them strange powers: the ability to change into creatures of the hunt—the Runner, the Climber, the Flyer, the Swimmer. Stranger still, each generation of Old Ones lived longer and longer. They called the sacred trees that endowed them with their powers, saber-toothed pines. But as the clan grew in number and the Great Dryness worsened, they faced the choice of starvation, or feeding on each other.

A Grand Council was called. It was decided that the entire clan would leave the Mother Forest to find richer lands. Some went south and became the sorcerers and high priests of human sacrifice in Aztec civilization. Some went west into the sea and became the blood-drinking langsuir of Malaysia. A few went north and became the ekimmu of Inuit legend. Many traveled east into the rising sun, crossed another sea as Flyers and Swimmers, and arrived in the fertile crescent of Mesopotamia, where the Assyrians called them utukku.

Even though the Old Ones descended from the trees, abandoned their Mother Forest, and scattered over the globe, in the end, all Old Ones, all vampires, return to their native ground.

When a vampire is slain, he shape-shifts into the seed of a saber-toothed pine, and the wind bears him back to the Mother Forest. The seed is our spirit: our Eighth and Final Form. And the seed grows into the cradle and gravestone of our race—the saber-toothed pine.

42

Back into the Selva Obscura

Flying over the scrub desert, Morning was stunned by the invigorating power surging through his body and wings. Equally astounding was the clarity and scope of his shadow-conscious. He now understood why Loners craved human blood. It exploded through your body like rocket fuel, and turbocharged whatever brain you were packing with enough consciousness to enjoy the ride.

His sharp eyes spotted the sentries of the Mother Forest: the first bristlecone pines scattered on a rocky hillside. The moonlight striking their twisting limbs of bald wood turned them into pale flames frozen in the cool desert night.

Soaring over the hilltop, Morning watched the pines grow in number. While the crown of a bristlecone pine often resembled the writhing tentacles of a monster beseeching the heavens, the tree's midriff was a thicket of bottlebrush branches with dark green needles.

The great horned owl skimmed up a mountainside over the gathering forest. Shooting over the ridgeline, Morning looked down into a valley dotted with burly pines. With their multiple trunk stems, some of the biggest bristlecones were twenty feet wide at the ground, double that at the waist. Their fiery crowns of bald wood rose as high as fifty feet.

He had reached the heart of the Mother Forest. He circled and scoured the ground with eyes a hundred times more powerful than human vision at night. He spotted the telltale sign of Portia's white dress. He thrilled at the sight of her sitting on a bare branch in the middle of a tree. She was alive. But he was surprised by which tree she occupied. It was the largest and most ancient tree in the forest: the Matriarch.

He dove down silently, his ears tuned to the slightest sound of DeThanatos approaching in whatever form he might have chosen to welcome him to his trap.

The owl landed silently on a high branch above Portia. Morning closed his large yellow eyes and focused inward. A second later, he CDed back into human form. Under his new weight, the branch creaked.

Portia turned toward the sound, and gasped at the sight of Morning standing on a branch high above her.

"Don't be scared," he whispered.

"He told me you'd come."

Her voice sounded weak, but he was thankful that her pallid skin had pinked up a bit. "Where is he?"

"I don't know, but he gave me this." She held up a sturdy spear of bristlecone pine. "I pulled a stake out of you once. I can just as easily stick one in."

"I'm not here to hurt you."

"Yeah, right."

He heard the sound of great wings pushing against the air. "I don't blame you for not believing me. But I'll prove it."

"How?"

The beating wings grew louder. "Twice you've given me blood. This time, I'll use its power for the right reason."

He ducked just as a four-foot beak, armed with jagged teeth, snapped over his head with a resounding crack.

Portia screamed at the monstrous creature that flew over. She'd never seen anything like it. No human ever had. The Quetzalcoatlus had been extinct for sixty-five million years. That is, until DeThanatos pulled it from oblivion as his first weapon of choice.

Morning watched the pterosaur, with its forty-foot wingspan, wheel in the sky for another pass at his head. He wasn't sure how many CDs he or DeThanatos could do before needing to feed again. But he knew he must pick his creatures wisely and swiftly. He also knew the odds were against him. It was his first battle, against a warrior who had killed countless Leaguers in the war.

In the moonlight, he studied the pterosaur's flight as it began another dive toward him. He noticed that its wings weren't feathered. They were made of thick membranes, like a bat's. He shut his eyes and focused on the first arrow in his quiver.

As the pterosaur's decapitating beak scissored open, Morning imploded into a peregrine falcon, dipped under the snapping beak, and shot through the branches.

Portia twisted back and forth, trying to track both creatures, but the falcon disappeared. She could only watch the Quetzalcoatlus wheel again and look for its prey.

The falcon was now fifteen hundred feet above the forest. Portia was a speck of white in the Matriarch. The pterosaur looked no bigger than a circling buzzard. Morning began his dive.

In a few seconds, he was hurtling downward. If his memory of the superhero Falcon was right, he was already diving at one hundred miles per hour and would soon reach one hundred seventy. His wings made tiny adjustments to follow the pterosaur's flight as it loomed larger and larger.

The falcon punched through his enemy's wing like a missile. The creature lurched and rolled in the air. It struggled to compensate for its ripped wing, but it dropped steeply, crashed to the ground, and rolled in a cloud of dust.

When the dust settled, a four-legged beast stood in its place. The huge saber-toothed cat shook the pain from his foreleg and unhinged his massive jaws in a thunderous roar.

Morning countered with his next transformation. A giant grizzly bear lumbered out from behind a tree. He reared up to his full ten feet and answered the cat's roar.

The saber-tooth spun toward the sound and charged. The bear swatted him away. The cat rolled, jumped to his feet, and fixed his yellow-green eyes on the bear. He emitted a low growl and charged again.

As the saber-tooth crouched to leap, the bear raised his massive paw to strike again. But DeThanatos faked the leap, shot behind the bear, sprang off the tree trunk, and pounced on the bear's back. The cat sank his great fangs into one shoulder.

Morning bellowed in pain, dropped to all fours, and tried to shake the cat off. He only succeeded in shaking the fangs out of his shoulder. As DeThanatos lifted his head to strike again, the bear reared up and staggered backward, crushing the saber-tooth against the trunk of the pine. When the bear leaped forward, the cat fell to the ground, howling in pain.

Morning turned and raised his paw to rip open the cat's belly. But when his paw came down, the writhing saber-tooth shriveled into a rattlesnake.

Morning checked his blow enough to miss the strike, catch the ground, and blind the snake in a cloud of dust. He shuffled backward. A bear was no match for the speed of a snake. He wasn't sure anything was. Then another memory fired in his shadow-conscious. A film clip the Mallozzi twins had once shown him on the Internet. A clip of an animal doing battle with—and killing—a huge rattlesnake.

The rattler cleared his eyes and glared through the dissipating dust. Ten feet away was a cougar.

Morning felt the heat of his shoulder healing. Recovering from wounds sapped energy. They were even on that score: a broken wing, a bloodied shoulder. But he wasn't sure how many more wounds he could heal or creatures he could CD into. There was no time to think. The rattler was coming at him.

The cougar waited for the strike. The snake reared its head and shot forward. Morning watched it like it was in slow motion. He leaped clear of the gaping, pearly mouth. The snake recoiled and struck again. The cougar leaped in the air, saw the opening to strike back, and batted the snake's fat body.

The snake slithered to the side, out of reach—then shot forward again. Morning pounced and landed another blow. This time his claws were extended.

The rattler landed in the dust with blood oozing from its diamondback. Trying to seize the advantage, Morning went on the offensive. He feigned another blow to the snake's right. When it struck, its fangs pierced nothing but air. Morning jabbed with his left paw, hitting the body and drawing blood again. Morning vaulted out of range and felt a renewed surge of power and adrenaline. In his shadow-conscious, it felt like a laugh.

But as the rattler flickered its tongue, DeThanatos seemed to be enjoying a laugh of his own. The snake rattled its tail and was gone. A smaller, deadlier tail had taken its place. The sickle tail of a yellow scorpion. It packed a venom that could stop a human heart within minutes. It couldn't kill a vampire, but it would immobilize one long enough to complete step one in vampire slaying: a good staking with bristlecone pine.

The twelve-eyed scorpion eyed the cougar and waited for the next swat. It would be the cougar's last.

Morning paced back and forth, never taking his eyes off the scorpion. He knew he needed another weapon. A weapon of protection. Then he remembered another super-hero. He laser-focused on an animal with a very different sting.

The scorpion saw a flash of movement and cocked his tail for the sting. But nothing struck. His dozen eyes fixed on the dark, bristling body of a porcupine.

Morning knew this newest CD was risky. After all, the costumed villain Porcupine had died when he fell on his suit of quills and took one through the heart. Falling on his own quills wouldn't prove fatal to Morning, but it would slow him up enough to give DeThanatos the opening he needed.

He shook off the defeatist thought and charged before DeThanatos made a countermove. Because he was a porcupine, it was more of a scuttle than a charge. Just before reaching the scorpion, he spun and batted DeThanatos with the pincushion of his tail. But these pins were pointed out, not in.

When the scorpion righted himself, a half-dozen quills pierced its exoskeleton like spears. One protruded from an eye. His tail was still armed with a deadly stinger, but the searing pain, and the prospect of being run through by a quill, tossed the scorpion on DeThanatos's pile of discarded weapons.

By the time the porcupine turned to size up his opponent for another volley of needles, the scorpion was gone. Hovering in its place was a dense patch of fog.

The transformation froze Morning. He never imagined DeThanatos would be so foolish as to CD into the Drifter, much less its most vulnerable form.

The porcupine spun, vanished, and rose up in a dust devil. The whirlwind plowed forward to scatter the fog and spread DeThanatos so thin he could never come together again.

The fog darted away and sped through the trees. The dust devil raced after.

43

Under the Matriarch

Having heard the roars, screeches, and grunts of the combat go silent, Portia stood on her branch and strained to hear or see. She still clutched the crude spear DeThanatos had given her. The ominous quiet was more terrifying than the noise of battle.

Then she saw the swirling column of fog rush into the tree, followed by a roiling ball of dust. The dust devil was still rattling the tree's needles when something landed on the branch beside her.

She shrieked at the sight of the ape-man next to her. Her spear clattered through the branches below.

DeThanatos had taken the form of one of the first hominids to descend from the trees of Africa and walk erect over the spreading grasslands. *Australopithecus.*

The initial fright his furry, chimplike face gave her shifted to curiosity. He seemed to possess the same gray eyes as DeThanatos. And he was hardly a threat. His breath came in sharp gasps. He looked weak as he wavered un-steadily on the branch. His eyes slid toward her.

The sound of rustling branches pulled her gaze down. There was no telling what might be coming up to get her. Then she felt a hand on her back. She lost her balance and began to fall. She glimpsed an apelike hand. She grabbed for it, but it jerked away. She screamed as she plunged downward.

Seeing the ground rushing toward her, she flailed her arms, trying to grab anything to break her fall. Then she felt something clutch her middle, squeezing so tight it knocked the wind out of her. She spun and bobbed to a sudden stop. Her face hovered a foot above the ground. Something had caught her. She looked down to see what. The thick body of a python coiled around her ribs. She opened her mouth to scream, but her lungs were squeezed shut. A moment later, air rushed into them as the huge snake loosened its grip and dropped her.

Up in the tree, the python's neck coiled around a branch, and it stared down at Portia, now safely on the ground.

The branch shook as the ape-man landed on it. Before Morning could react, he felt the rib-breaking blow deliv-ered by the club in DeThanatos's hand. The python hissed in pain, gave up its grip on the branch, and fell.

Portia rolled out of the way a second before the writhing snake thudded to the ground. She stared in awe and terror as it slithered back into Morning. Sheathed in his Epidex, he clutched his chest and moaned.

DeThanatos dropped from above, landing with his feet straddling Morning. He was back to human form, and naked as night. He dropped to his knees, grabbed Morning's arms, and slammed them to the ground.

Morning grimaced as his broken ribs knitted together. He tried to gather his strength. He was running out of rocket fuel.

DeThanatos's eyes searched the ground and spotted the spear Portia had dropped. "Get it!" he shouted at her. "Stake him!"

She crawled to the long stake, gripped it, stood, and hesitated. *Why had Morning caught her if he had come to kill her? Why had she lost her balance?*

DeThanatos leaned away to give her a clear shot at Morning's chest. "Do it!"

Morning tapped his marrow for a last burst of strength, and flipped DeThanatos off him. They rolled and wrestled until they slammed into the trunk of the Matriarch. Morning was on top. He pressed DeThanatos's arms to the ground, pinned them under his knees, and struggled to break a shard of wood off the trunk. DeThanatos's lack of resistance was strange. Morning figured he was either too weak or knocked out. The shard of wood broke away. He was startled to find DeThanatos smiling up at him. He raised the dagger of wood. A pain shot through his gut, buckling his chest.

DeThanatos let out a weak laugh. "Have you wondered why I didn't destroy you days ago?"

Morning tried to gather his strength and plunge the dagger, but his intent was met with another bolt of pain.

DeThanatos's voice mocked him. "Why did I have to hire someone else to slay you?"

The answer froze Morning's blood. He stared down at DeThanatos. "You—you're my maker."

DeThanatos's maniacal grin widened. "Yes, my boy, we're blood kin. If I destroy you, I destroy myself. The same for you. Destroy your maker, destroy yourself." His eyes seemed to charge with new life. "Mortals call it a lose-lose."

Morning shook his head as he felt the joyous surge of revenge. "No, it's a win-win. If I destroy you, Portia lives. And I'm free of the vampire curse."

DeThanatos's smile vanished.

Morning lifted his dagger of wood as the vampire thrashed under him. Morning held him tight. Pain seared though his gut, trying to prevent the blow that would kill them both. He fought it, determined to drive the stake through his maker's heart.

His wrist suddenly exploded in pain. The dagger flew from his hand. Turning toward the source of the blow, a gnarled spear of wood plunged past his face and impaled DeThanatos. Portia gripped the other end.

Morning leaped off the twisting, screaming vampire as she drove the stake deeper. DeThanatos began to smolder. Flames ignited and skittered over his body. Then he burst into a fireball.

The two of them jumped back from the intense heat and belching black smoke. They stared as the vampire disintegrated into a layer of ash. They heard the rattle of pine needles in the tree. And they watched a gust of wind scatter his ashes.

After it was done, Portia spoke first. Her voice was shaken and confused. "Birnam told me it took three steps to destroy a vampire. Why did he go all at once?"

Morning looked at her with an exhausted smile. "That's how it happens when the stake is delivered by the hand of a virgin who's lost her heart to love."

She blushed.

He was glad to see her cheeks flush with blood.

As dawn drained the eastern sky of night, they walked out of the Mother Forest.

When they started down the hillside of scattered pines guarding the edge of the forest, the sky darkened again. They turned and watched a wall of dust swallow the rising sun.

"Dust storm," Morning warned.

They broke into a run, toward the highway at the bottom of the hill.

Back in the grove, under the Matriarch, a lingering bead of ash rose up, swirled into a purple seedpod, and was borne away on the dusty wind.

When the storm overtook them, Morning and Portia took cover behind the last bristlecone pine. They pressed against the tree's trunk as dust pelted the windward side. But they couldn't completely escape the swirling dust and stinging sand.

"Ouch!" Portia cried as something pricked her shoulder. In the blinding dust, she couldn't see what had drawn blood.

It fell to the ground. It was the purple seedpod with its sharp bristle: a tiny dart, now tipped with blood. The blood sucked inside the pod.

44

In the End Is Beginning

In the next few days, a lot of things came out in the wash.

Actually, it took three washings for Penny to get all the dust out of her hair, and three conditionings to restore its luster. It took longer for her to recover from the horrific reality of Morning planting his ivories in her baby girl. The healing process was helped by Portia repeatedly telling her the story of how Morning had redeemed himself by saving her from DeThanatos.

The fact that Birnam never got around to practicing a little old-school memory-deleting on Penny and Portia was part of the deal Morning struck with the president of the IVL. Morning held up his part of the bargain, and vowed to keep his "stumble" with Portia a secret. He persuaded Penny and Portia to do the same on the condition that, a few years hence, after Leaguers had been fully integrated into Lifer society, Portia would be given the rights to tell the real story of the night the IVL website was launched, including the moment when Morning almost sunk the Leaguer cause by sinking his fangs. Birnam agreed to all of this with one proviso: Morning had to retake the Academy's bloodlust-management course as a precaution against any future backsliding.

In the meantime, IVLeague.us continued to get millions of hits, and Birnam turned a Leaguer Academy building into headquarters for organizing Worldwide Out Day. He set the date, and posted it on the website for Leaguers and Lifers alike: October 1. He thought it was good date for all Leaguers to step out of the *selva obscura* of their secrecy for two reasons: (1) It stood apart from other holidays, which would help pave the way to Worldwide Out Day eventually becoming the first vampire holiday, and (2) It gave any kid who was thinking of dressing up as a black-caped, blood-sucking fiend for Halloween time to realize how politically incorrect his costume was and find another.

Back in New York, Morning visited the old fireman, and they both went to the Fire Academy Appeals Board to plead his case for admission to the Academy despite being underage. They argued that technically, yes, Morning would be the youngest fireman in the department. But in a century, when the fire department brass were long gone, he would be the "oldest" firefighter ever. Given their creative math, and the fact that Morning did come with special skills, he was allowed to take the written test for admittance to the Fire Academy, with one stipulation. He had to finish high school first.

Where he would go to high school was briefly an issue when thousands of families across the country offered to become Morning's new foster parents and adopt him. However, since he wanted to stay in New York, he decided

311

to reside in the only place that had ever been home: St. Giles Group Home for Boys. Sister Flora embraced the idea, as long as Morning understood that being sixteen forever meant she would be his mother protector for just as long. He agreed to her tough bargain with an eye roll and returned to St. Giles.

This meant that he returned to the same high school he had disappeared from the previous fall. The principal welcomed him back but laid down one rule: one shape-shift and he was out.

After resuming school, Morning's worries about being teased or bullied for being the freaky vampire kid were dispelled by two new friends and bodyguards: the Mallozzi twins. For them, the message tattooed across their biceps, DONT X R PATH, now applied to the most rad kid in the class.

Unfortunately, Morning's popularity with the twins only lasted a few days. After failing to get Morning to turn them into vampires so they would possess powers that would make them master criminals, they quit being his bodyguards and went back to harassing him. But not as much as before. The Mallozzi twins were malicious, but they weren't morons.

As for Portia, she plunged into postproduction on her documentary, *Morning McCobb: The Jackie Robinson of the Vampire League*. But now, because of the deal with Birnam, it was a two-part film. She was already brainstorming titles for part two. None of them were very good, but she wasn't worried. She had time to come up with something better than *Morning McCobb: Fangs for the Memories*. As for the first film, she had an open invitation to debut it at Sundance, and her mother had been talking to Christiane Amanpour about narrating it.

But before both Portia and Morning could get back to chasing their dreams at full speed, they had to figure out how they felt about each other.

Their first attempt to sort out their tangled relationship occurred after school one day. They met at the Jackson Hole restaurant on Third Avenue. Portia picked the place because it had the biggest, juiciest cheeseburgers in Manhattan. Fat, juicy cheeseburgers were the best cure for the lingering anemia she still suffered from after Morning's ass-over-teakettle fall into the forbidden well. Morning brought along his own after-school snack. Since his DNA had completely reasserted itself over Portia's first transfusion, his drink of choice had returned to his old standby, Blood Lite, which he ordered on a monthly basis from IVLeague.us.

After eating, drinking, and catching up on all that had happened since coming back to New York, they took a cab to Delancey Street and walked out onto the Williamsburg Bridge.

45

Yeah, Right—When the Pigeons . . .

When they stopped in the middle of the walkway, they looked down the East River toward the expanse of water sparkling in the late-day sun. The lady of the harbor, with her torch, rose up like the figurehead of America's vast ship.

Morning held up a hand. "You have to wave to her."

Portia gave him an amused glance. "Is this another one of your rituals?"

"Absolutely. Can't you see her thought bubble? 'Welcome home.' "

She waved at Ms. Liberty, then looked down at the river. "While we're doing rituals, do you see any paper boats coming down from Poughkeepsie?"

He smiled. "Tons of 'em."

"Me too," she said, playing along. "But I'm not sure what's written on 'em."

"That's the cool part. They're blank."

"How can that be?"

He looked up and watched her hair ruffling in the wind.

"Because they're all the messages we haven't written yet. You know, a fleet of notes, e-mails, text messages."

She held back a smile. "You mean to anyone?"

"No." He eye-rolled. "To each other."

She let her smile out. "I guess that means you still like me."

He shrugged. "Hey, how can you not like a girl who revives you with her own blood, then saves you by staking the badass vampire in the end?"

She sagged in mock dejection. "And I thought you liked me for who I am."

He laughed and found her eyes.

She broke away from his gaze. Ever since they had walked out of the Mother Forest, they'd been ignoring the elephant that had walked out with them. It had loomed over every word and gesture during their burger and Blood Lite at Jackson Hole. It was time to look their pachyderm in the paradox. She took a breath and began. "Okay, I figure we have two choices."

He feigned ignorance. "About what?"

She whacked him on the arm. "About us, ninny."

"Oh, right," he said nonchalantly, trying to belie the twisting sensation in his stomach.

She plunged on. "First of all, we've known each other for less than two weeks."

"Yeah, it's been kinda fast."

"And taking it fast ended up with you trying to drink me like a six-ounce Coke."

He gave her a sheepish look. "Are you gonna hold that against me forever?"

"No, as long as you leave it in your try-everything-once folder. What I'm saying is that maybe we should try taking it slow."

He nodded happily, seeing the light at the end of this

claustrophobic tunnel. "Sounds good to me." Then he remembered that she had mentioned two choices. His curiosity got the better of his instinct to drop the subject. "What's our other choice?"

Portia raised an eyebrow. "We decide right here and now that we're star-crossed lovers, declare this Star-Crossed Lover's Leap, and jump."

He chuckled with relief. She was back to her wisecracking self. "I have two problems with that. One, I'd survive, and two"—he looked over the rail—"you keep forgetting it's a long jump from here." She glanced at the two lanes of traffic between them and the far edge of the bridge. "We'd be more like tire-crossed lovers."

She laughed. "Morning made a funny. Maybe you still have a little of my blood hanging out in your funny bone."

"I hope not. If I still had a pint or two of you in me, I'd probably wanna tap into a burger like the one you just ate and get some real blood."

She turned to him. "There's only one way to find out."

He swallowed. "Find out what?"

"What you really want."

He took in her inviting eyes. The twister inside him wound tighter. "I thought we were going to go slow."

"We can't go *too* slow."

He stalled in confusion. "What do you mean?"

She faced the big bad elephant head-on. "In a couple of years, you're going to look like a kid to me."

He pulled away and watched the water roll under the bridge.

She turned and did the same.

Rivers could be slowed down, even stopped. Time couldn't.

316

He turned back to her. "And a few years after that, you'll look like somebody's mother."

"So what do we do?"

"I've been thinking about it," he said.

Her eyes brightened. "You have?"

"Yeah. Maybe we'll have a year or two before it falls apart. Until then, I think we should just suck it up and enjoy it. Enjoy us."

"But how?"

He pushed closer, lowered his eyelids on the world, and pressed into the twin pillows of her lips. She darted her tongue in search of fangs. Nothing. Just the sweet exploration of a first kiss. That is, a first kiss without *dentis eruptus,* or the envy that provoked it.

They pulled away, still wrapped in the danger and delirium.

"How did it feel?" she asked.

He couldn't stop grinning. "I feel like I'm the one who's been bitten. And it's giving me a fever."

Her eyes danced. "And the fever's mutating you into another form."

"Right. I'm shape-shifting. But what's the form?"

She didn't need to dive into his eyes and swim with his thoughts to find the answer. "Superhero."

Her prescience startled him. "Right. How did you know that?"

She gave a little shrug. " 'Cause that's how I feel too. Maybe that's what love does. It makes you feel like you can leap tall buildings in a single bound. Makes you feel like anything is possible."

He gazed at her for a long time, trying to memorize every detail of her face. He leaned in for another kiss. But a flurry of motion caught his eye. He glanced over her shoulder. At first, it didn't compute. Then he realized what it was. "Look," he breathed, turning Portia around.

The sight shocked her. The tower on the Delancey Street side of the bridge was quivering. Like it was made of bubbling gray iron. Then she recognized what swarmed over the bridge.

Birds.

Not just any birds.

Pigeons.

Glossary

BLOOD CHILD: A human that a vampire transforms into another vampire.

BLOOD LITE: An artificial blood substitute derived from soybeans. The most popular drink of squeamish or vegan vampires.

BLOODLUST: A vampire's darkest desire, driven by thirst and envy, to drink human blood. Slang: sink 'n' drink, drill 'n' swill, trap 'n' sap, chomp 'n' chug.

CELL DIFFERENTIATION (CD): Also known, by non-Leaguer vampires and Lifers, as shape-shifting.

DENTIS ERUPTUS: The swelling of teeth into fangs. Once known as *dentis erectus,* but changed to *dentis eruptus* to prevent arousing the interest of those who see sex in everything.

EPIDEX: The underarmor developed by Leaguer scientists so this story can eventually be made into a movie rated PG-13.

FORBIDDEN WELL: The human reservoir of blood, five quarts per adult human.

INTERNATIONAL VAMPIRE LEAGUE (IVL): A secret organization of vampires hoping to come out and be recognized as just another minority with special needs.

IVLEAGUE.US: The website of the IVL.

KNIGHT OF THE FIRE TABLE: A firefighter in touch with the deepest traditions of firefighting.

LEAGUER: A vampire who has conquered the craving for human blood and lives on a diet of animal or artificial blood substitutes. A graduate of the Leaguer Academy.

LIFER: A mortal, or age-challenged, human being.

LONER: A vampire who practices the old ways, and insists that being a bloodsucking fiend is part of his or her ethnic heritage.

MALTESE CROSS: The emblem of firefighters throughout the world.

MOTHER FOREST: The cradle and graveyard of the vampire race. The scattered forests of bristlecone pines in the western United States.

OLD ONES: The ancient race that evolved into vampires.

PASSING THE DEUCE: The double-fanged bite of a vampire that, via blood exchange, turns his or her victim into a vampire.

SANGFU: A blood f___-up. A vampire who was created by accident. An unwanted vampire.

SANGV: A blood virgin. A vampire who has never drunk human blood.

SELVA OBSCURA: In Italian, dark wood. (First used in Dante's *Divine Comedy*.) The netherworld of bloodlust and old ways a Loner vampire must escape from to become a Leaguer.

SEVENTH FORM: The seventh of eight vampire Forms, also called the Leaguer Form. The first Six Forms are: Drifter, Hider, Swimmer, Climber, Runner, Flyer. The Eighth Form is a vampire's return, upon death, to the seed of a bristlecone pine.

SHADOW-CONSCIOUS: The minimal human consciousness a vampire retains while taking one of the Six Forms.

SOLAR PHOBIA: A vampire's irrational fear of sunlight.

SOLAR PHOBIA FIXER (SPF): The only "sunscreen" a vampire ever needs.

THRALL: A vampire's power to physically control another sentient being. The effects vary from partial paralysis to catatonia. Banned by Leaguers for being unnecessarily manipulative and antisocial behavior.

TURNING: The act of changing a mortal into a vampire.

WATCHMEN: The classic graphic novel by Alan Moore and Dave Gibbons, which has a far darker ending than this story.

WORLDWIDE OUT DAY: The day all Leaguers plan to make themselves known to the mortal public. Presently slated for October 1.

ZERO: The odds of anything going exactly as planned. For example, Worldwide Out Day.

Acknowledgments

First, a big thanks to all politically correct producers in children's television who, over the years, have saved me from ignorantly offending minorities I was unaware of. Without their righteous guidance, I never would have realized that a tolerant, multicultural society should also include our bloodsucking brothers and sisters.

No tale about shape-shifters would be complete without doing some story-shifting. To my youthful readers, Ryan Brandt, Kevin DuBrow, and Kendall Meehl, thank you for sinking your eyes into early versions and sharing your wonderful ideas. I owe a monstrous debt of gratitude to my cohort and taskmaster Gerri Brioso, who understands that friendship includes telling me what sucks and what doesn't, and refusing to let me write female characters she doesn't like.

The novel's final transformation would have been a very different species if it weren't for the amazing story-shaping skills of my editors at Delacorte Press—Michelle Poploff, Joe Cooper, and Amalia Ellison—and my agent, Sara Crowe. Each hovered over the story and wielded their magic wands brilliantly. I have the bruises to prove it. I wouldn't have it any other way.

About the Author

BRIAN MEEHL is enjoying his third "shape-shift." After a career of wiggling puppets on *Sesame Street* and in Jim Henson films, he became an Emmy Award–winning writer for children's shows such as *Between the Lions* and *Magic School Bus*. He has now convinced himself that he is the author of two YA novels. When he recovers from this delusion, he will start thinking about his next incarnation.

In the meantime, he lives in Connecticut with his family of three females on a farm full of furry animals, and is working on a third novel. So he thinks.